For the girls who feel lost in a wood
stumbling, tripping, running
to the light in the trees ahead

Tender

Tender

Lauren Du Plessis

Influx Press
London

Published by Influx Press
www.influxpress.com
@InfluxPress

Published by Influx Press, London, UK, 2025
© Lauren Du Plessis, 2025

This edition 2025
Printed and bound in the UK by CPI Group (UK) Ltd, Croydon CR0 4YY
Paperback ISBN: 9781914391606
Ebook ISBN: 9781914391613

Cover design: Luke Bird
Text design: Laura Jones-Rivera
Editor: Gary Budden
Copy-editor: Dan Coxon
Proofreader: Fleur Tizard

Seed

I

Nell sits in a plastic chair at the service station, turning the pomegranate half over in her hands. Dried blood dots the rind, where she cut herself preparing it at five o'clock in the morning. The two deep reds are almost indistinguishable.

Behind her, bodies churn around fast-food counters, bubbling with the stress of getting to their summer holiday lets at check-in time, or home to check the fish didn't die while they were away. The sounds are sharp and painful – her senses must be heightened in the heat. She looks back to the pomegranate. After packing her lunch so carefully, she brought this along. She could have chosen a nice, clean apple. Who takes a pomegranate on a road trip? But the thought of it rotting in the bowl for over six weeks was worse than the thought of bringing it as a snack, so here it is. Nell pulls a tissue from the dispenser and smudges off the blood, then folds the tissue back into a square. Better.

There's a shriek from the automatic doors. A family stumbles through, wiping their brows and fanning themselves with magazines. One of the children is bawling angry gibberish, its face almost as red as the jewel seed Nell pops into her mouth.

Lauren Du Plessis

The tang pinches her tongue. As a kid she believed that if she swallowed a seed it would bed and sprout in her tummy, creep up her throat like ivy. As an adult she knows that her body will only ever be good for growing bacteria, and perhaps babies. Not that she feels a particular attraction to the idea at the moment. Orchids are loud in hue, but they don't scream. Sedge is sharp, but it doesn't grate on her mind. Nell cannot imagine her social media profiles reading: *Botanist, mother.*

The kid's face clots with mucus and tears. Its cries fill Nell's ears, even her vision. The world is pulsating and red. The mother tries talking, squatting down next to it, hugging it, shouting at it, her expressions unfolding from each other like nesting dolls. *It,* Nell thinks – she can't even assign it a human pronoun in her mind.

Nell's finger slips, squelches. Her rose-pink acrylics are sinking into the pulp between the seeds. She picks the flesh from under each perfect plastic oval, then stands. Her neighbour left a tray strewn with tissues and cardboard packaging, so she empties it into a nearby bin. Then she grabs another tissue, cleaning herself and the table until it really looks like nobody was ever there.

There is only half an hour left of the drive, which is a relief when her air conditioning barely works. Just half an hour, and she'll be standing in a field, staring down the trenches. She doesn't know how large or deep they are yet, so all she has in her mind is a twist of bone and branch, soil and flower.

As she passes the family, heading back to the car park, the kid and Nell flinch at the exact same moment as the mother's hand makes contact with its backside. Its screams stop. Nell's left glute burns in sympathy on the walk away.

4

Tender

*

Nell spritzes her wrists with jasmine and rose, picks the last of the pomegranate from her acrylics, and makes the right-hand turn back onto the M5. It has been a long time since she drove into Somerset, and she already feels strange, like a small, soft wildflower blown by an unexpectedly strong wind.

A few minutes before the junction turn-off, an incoming call pops up over her sat nav app. Nell checks the cars around her, which she tells herself is for road safety, and not to stall until her sister rings off.

"So you're here," Liz says when Nell inevitably answers. If they don't talk now, they will have to later.

Nell heightens the register of her voice, tries to find her usual singing tone. "Liz! Mum told you. I'm driving, can't talk long."

"In my direction, *two weeks* before Charlie's birthday. As always, I'm the last to know."

"You're always the last to ask," Nell says quietly. The words feel mean even as she says them, but it's too late now. She grits her teeth.

Liz's voice cools. "Try raising two kids, and see how much time you have to chase adult siblings."

The pile of reference books in the passenger seat shifts as she changes lanes, and Nell extends her left arm to keep it from falling. Potential responses to Liz tangle through her mind: that this dig could define her career, that she was asked for by name, or that Liz has never once visited her in Milton Keynes.

"Go on then, what are you doing back in our neck of the woods?"

5

She isn't here for the woods, Nell wants to say, but the wetlands. Flat, open fields languishing for miles, only interrupted by spatters of houses or the ripple of a small hill. The acid soak of a coastal plain. Good for preserving bodies.

"A dig. The burial that came up near Shapwick, after the winter floods. With the bodies wrapped in flowers. It was on TV."

"What happened to your old job?" Liz's tone changes for her daughter. "No no, darling, not now."

Nell hasn't told anyone about the redundancy. Somewhere in her brain is a kernel of relief, the relief of never again having to sort the rocks torn up by city developers. But the shame is riper, fleshier. She got comfortable labelling things until her knuckles felt like they were coming through her skin, but she was not good enough to keep on. If this dig hadn't miraculously shown up, she'd have nothing.

The book at the top of the pile slides and thuds into the footwell. While Liz struggles against her daughter Charlie's tantrum, Nell stares at the passenger seat. Then, without warning, her finger gravitates to the middle of the remaining books. She touches the one she wrote a chapter for, *The Secret Life of Wildflowers*, and pushes until the whole pile comes down. Covers splay, pages bend, the impact vibrating through the car. It feels horrible and satisfying at once, to make a mess but also have the mess over with. Nobody will see, anyway. She returns both hands to the wheel and focuses on the road.

Liz and Charlie bicker. "Angel, what did we say about waiting until I'm done on the phone? I'm trying to convince

Tender

your Auntie Elinor to come to your birthday party. *Elinor*. You might as well not *exist* to Charlie and Genie. It's so sad."

Nell rolls down the window to let in blustering warm air.

"Elinor. God, why is everyone I talk to a brick wall?"

"I'm listening. Of course I'll come." Nell doesn't know if she will, but it's easier to lie than to send Liz into one of her panics.

"That's it! Time to go to your room for some quiet thinking, Charlie!"

They say something like a goodbye. The engine hums through Nell's sit bones and nausea wreaths in her stomach.

They lived near Glastonbury as kids – the house Liz still lives in – but rarely explored the countryside around them. If they did, their parents would lead, instructing the girls to fit each small foot into their larger boot marks. The ground around their parents' footsteps was a thick sludge, hungry to slip them up. That was how their mother talked. *Be careful, don't touch that, god, why would you do that?* It got worse after a hospital stay when Nell was eight and Liz four, because, of course, when one was sick they were both sick. As children they were like two versions of the same girl. Now, every time they talk, Liz has drifted a little further away.

Sweat seeps down the back of Nell's neck. It's been a while since she thought about the roots that grew her. No, that's not the right analogy: stamen would be more accurate. But stamens don't enmesh. They breathe their offspring away. Such a gentle approach must exist somewhere, even if it's hard for her to imagine. But surely such parenting would craft creatures without edges – creatures that ooze and trample? She was trained to smile, step lightly, never to trample in the presence of others. For all she'd do differently from her parents, at least she knows where her edges are.

She veers onto the slip past the Huntspill River and turns onto a narrow country lane. The fields are like shattered bottle glass, trees and hedges lining uneven meadows. The concrete underneath her is smooth, recently resurfaced, and the heat shuddering off it distorts her vision whenever the car slows. Deeper beneath: carbon-rich earth. The sort that comes apart in your fingers, gets under your nails and marks your nail beds like crescent moons of ink. She can't decide if refreshing her acrylics last week was a great idea (they would conceal any trapped dirt) or a terrible one (dirt means bacteria, bacteria could mean a nasty surprise if she couldn't get them redone for six weeks). But she had already made the appointment when she got the email inviting her to the dig. Her nail appointments were the last thing in her life that felt regular.

Right now, the soft earth probably starts a few centimetres down. Several fields are grazed yellow on top by the long summer. Desperate pollen billows through the open window.

With five minutes to go, she rehearses her self-introduction and small talk. Her cheek muscles tense with repeated smiles. She'll explain that she's volunteering for the dig ahead of the lab work in the city (true) because her latest research contract just ended so why not (lie).

She researched them ahead of time: the supervisors Ingrid and Bill, the other botanist named Gunner, several student assistants; and, of course, two dead bodies. There will be photos, articles, and eventually papers, with their

Tender

names adorning the top. Maybe that's why she feels more aware of herself than usual. The nausea worsens.

She keeps herself together while passing through the tiny, red-roofed village. After a crop of birch trees, the farmhouse appears at the end of a long driveway. Brown vines splice through every crevice, as if slowly pulling the white brick house and the clump of outbuildings into the earth. A pool of bright flowers spews from the foundations.

Nell parks near four other cars and gets out. Distant voices tell her that something is happening around the back, and silverish smoke wisps up between two outbuildings. But right now, she's fixated on the pool of magenta. Meadow thistles, effusive heads sat on the ends of elongated stems. If she believed in anything like fate, perhaps she'd read it as a sign. Her last-minute invitation from Ingrid Marston – a bone specialist and friend of her old plant science professor – had mentioned only that they needed a wildflower expert to consult on lab work. One archaeobotanist was already attending the dig site. But Nell pushed until she secured a second slot. She's here because of plants like these, the unnoticed. It had always bothered her how quick people are to dismiss plants that grow in unwanted places, however exquisite or colourful.

The ground moves underfoot as she approaches. After so long crossing the concrete underpasses around her flat, she'd forgotten how the ground can feel alive. Grass crawling with insects, water squeezing like blood through root systems. The thistles are beautiful, far more beautiful than something called *weed* ought to be. She tries to take a photo for her Instagram, but her phone won't pick up the vivid hues like her eyes do.

A raucous female laugh tugs her back to reality. Nell jumps up, blood thudding into her head. She wobbles. But the nausea doesn't stop.

There is wrongness, and then there is pain. Her chest surges, stomach wringing itself inside out. She vomits. Pomegranate splatters the grass, flecking onto the white brick of the house's side wall.

"Oh god."

This cannot be her first impression. She scrambles to cover her body's betrayal, kicking at the dirt. The thistles seem willing to collude, bending and concealing. Curses bubble on her lips but she tucks her dark hair neatly behind her ears and wipes her mouth, before a woman emerges around the corner.

"Elinor, welcome! The rising star! I've read all your papers, you know." The woman, who is clearly the source of the earlier laugh, holds a hand to her heart. "Ingrid, trench supervisor." Nell sifts quickly through her mental research log. Ingrid has Facebook and Instagram, both of which consist mostly of sunsets and crime novels. She has worked on bog bodies across Europe. She crosses her arms, bitten nails exposed, but resplendent and thoroughly-brushed grey hair tumbles over her blouse. Her face is pale pink, sun-spotted, perhaps a little dry.

Nell prepares the calmest smile she can manage. "I've read all your work, too!"

That's a slight twist of the truth. Rheumatology feels so far removed from botany that Nell couldn't get her head around much of Ingrid's writing, which was dense with jargon and seemed to hold no space for pandering to laymen.

Tender

Ingrid gestures for Nell to follow and rounds the corner again. Nell hastily rearranges the flowers to conceal any last chunks of food, and does as she's told. Faces: an onslaught of them. Nell holds her smile. The first to approach and shake her hand is the site director, Bill, who introduces himself as just that and nothing more. For him, a roll back of the shoulders and a businesslike handshake is all she needs. The movement of his tartan blazer releases an overbearing oak musk.

"Can we see the trenches?" Nell asks Ingrid as they tour the group.

"No, it's far too dry. They have to stay covered. So, how was your journey?" Ingrid asks. Nell gets out half an answer before she continues. "You were MSc Environmental Archaeology at UCL, weren't you? I've heard great things..."

A camera flickers, presumably for the local council or Historic England. They pass the four research assistants, all of whom wave or nod, rather than shaking hands. Still, everyone seems settled. As Nell casts her eyes around the smiling faces, she can imagine herself fitting in nicely here. This is the kind of job promised to her since university: a close-knit team of passionate academics, days on site and nights clinking glasses and looking over notes. Perhaps she would even make time to sketch while she was here, adding floral details to her notebooks as she did before graduating. All that worry for nothing.

"Is the other botanist here?" Nell asks, keen to speak with her counterpart about what might be hiding beneath the tarp.

Ingrid drums her fingers rhythmically on the wood of a nearby table. "He'll join us tomorrow. I don't know, some kind of personal issue. But here's Beth, without whom none of this would be possible!"

She abandons Nell at the edge of a barbecue grill and strikes up a conversation with someone else.

Beth is flipping burgers. She's tall, with broad shoulders and an hourglass shape accentuated by a knotted apron. Randomly-placed grips pin back unruly ash-brown hair, sun-seared freckles mark her right cheek. She glances up, gesturing at one patty with a spatula. Her expression is unreadable, with no hint of guidance on how to act around her.

"Hi Elinor, you want this one? It's medium-well."

"You're the farmer who discovered the bodies," Nell says, and digs her nails into her hands for the clumsy phrasing.

"You make it sound like a whodunnit," Beth grins, closing the top lip of a bap. "You want this? Choose quick or I'll eat it."

The patty bubbles at the edges, but the centre blushes a soft pink. "Actually, I prefer well-done meat. Sorry."

"This one?" Beth leans over to skewer another.

"No, more."

"May as well set the damned thing on fire." She bangs the side of the grill, jangling cutlery. "It'll be rock hard."

They wait for ashy wisps to start curling off a patty near the edge, then Beth assembles Nell's blackened burger.

She lifts it to her nose, letting the scent hit the back of the cavity in her head, tingle her brain. Then she takes a bite. Charcoal, smoke. The meat crumbles in her mouth and crawls down her throat. She wipes her mouth and tries to smile, rather than cough. Beth laughs.

Tender

*

The sun begins its slow summer descent around six in the evening. When everyone has eaten, Nell offers to help Beth tidy. It was a generous meal, and she feels almost guilty to have eaten it, when surely the team is already intruding on Beth's life. They crinkle tin foil into tight balls, and wipe grease from the crusting metal.

"So, a botanist," Beth says. She sounds reserved, as if she'd rather not talk but assumes she must. "We probably have a lot in common."

"What do you mean?"

"You study plants and I, well, live them."

Nell finds herself repeating back, "Live them?"

"I mean my life is controlled by the weather, and the soil. And I mean this year I'm pretty much fucked."

"Oh, the heatwave."

"That'd be the one."

"I hope we're not getting in your way." Nell's skin bristles. She hates being in the way.

"Well, I have had to give up a field for you lot. But I get it. This place is weird, always spitting up bits of bone and pots."

"Have you found anything before?"

"Not me. My dad found an axe once. You know, one of those smooth flint ones. Apparently, they used to stick them in the marsh as offerings. Superstitious bunch, weren't they? Although I guess I'm one to talk."

She catches herself then, as if she's said too much. Nell waits; despite all the exciting talk of the evening, this is the most interesting thing she's heard so far. Superstition is rather alien to her. But Beth falls silent and begins carrying plates inside. There are the marks again, a patch of freckles and scars beside her ear, which is leafy in shape. A tight inflorescence, pink-tinged and curling into the centre.

Nell asks Beth about the farm as they sweep the patio. Beth's sentences are clipped now. *I inherited it*, and *local lads help out*, and *it's not the kind of place you get lonely*. Nell doesn't feel as if she's learned anything more about the farm or its owner as Beth turns from her and steps through a pair of partly rotten French doors.

Nell sighs. She is the only one left outside, lit in evening gold. She looks out over the fields. The surface is parched, cracks spider-webbing from her feet and out into the straw-like grass. This immediate field is empty, while carpets of salad crops, vegetables and bulbs sprawl beyond, edged by a distant line of trees and the proud bloat of sunset.

She squats at the edge of the paving and finds another meadow thistle there. She remembers the scientific name, *Cirsium dissectum*. From the Greek, *kirsos*, meaning 'swelling vein'. She fingers its long, slim stem. Then she pulls it free, twirling it back and forth between her thumb and middle finger. She stops when the urge to put it in her mouth becomes overwhelming.

It's an intrusive thought, the sort that comes when you're holding something made of glass, and your brain invites you to drop it with perverse glee. Usually she can bat the thoughts away, but this one catches on her nerves and won't let go. Under a microscope, or even a hand lens, many plants have hidden barbs and teeth, and this feels just like that.

Almost every part of a thistle is edible, once you've cut the prickles away. Root, stem, leaf, flower, seed. The stems can be sugar-dipped or stir-fried. In her first year at

Tender

university Nell lived in halls, and at the end of her corridor there was a girl who asked people to call her Cosmos. Cosmos had loud sex at three in the morning at least once a week, and always wore long sleeves and skirts as if hiding her body, but she was perfectly friendly to Nell. Once, while Nell waited for her curls to set ahead of the Summer Ball, she found Cosmos in the shared kitchen making cocktails with herbs and edible flowers. *It's got to be either petals or roots,* she explained, charring some to release their aromas, *then you get a fresh but sweet flavour.* Nell declined to try any, but returned to her room and scrolled through recipe blogs until it was time to shake out her hair and pin it into a dignified but 'effortless' up-do. Cosmos dropped out in second year, and they didn't keep in touch.

She gazes at the flower for a while, before replacing it on the ground to rot and be reclaimed. Pain takes root in her chest. She glances around to check she's alone, then reaches underneath the cotton of her top, to where her sternum flared before the vomiting incident. But when her forefinger reaches the line of her diaphragm, it catches on something.

A red spot. Nell rings around its tiny circumference. She reaches her other hand to it and jabs a nail in each side until pain stabs at the base of her brain. Her eyes water. But the spot doesn't burst.

Another intrusive thought: there's something lodged in her skin. She shakes herself as if it makes any difference, then steps back towards the house, rubbing her chest. Even crushed with heat, the earth here is so alive she feels watched.

Lauren Du Plessis

*

At the other end of the village is the guest house, its ground floor a kitchen and shop combined, with a large cool box and two shelves against the back wall where visitors can buy bread, eggs and other essentials. Nell jumps when the elderly owner taps her shoulder in the doorway and introduces himself as Gordon.

Gordon, she learns on the way up warped stairs, was raised in Glastonbury, moved to the States for a flashy computer science job in the eighties, and came back after his first wife left him. Fell in love with the countryside again, fell in love with a woman again, and now keeps the B'n'B from sinking into the bog.

"I always knew I'd come back. The fens stay with you."

"So I bet you're excited to see what we end up with?" she smiles.

Gordon pauses at the opening to a dark corridor. "Nothing special to find the past coming up round here, love. Your room is on the left, that other botanist will be in the one opposite."

He shows Nell in and leaves. One single bed, set on an iron frame with curling, botanical details on the posts. It's hot, even with the window pushed up and the lace curtains floating lazily in the breeze. The floorboards creak so loudly that even moving her bags across them makes her cringe. The corners and windowsill are stained with mildew, tamed and reborn over and over.

She unpacks slowly, trying not to disturb whoever is staying in the room below. Her first aid kit, her clothes, then her books with their newly cracked spines and dents;

what had possessed her to push them over? She orders them on a shelf by spine height, and adds three sprays of jasmine and rose as finishing touches.

It's only when she lies on the bed that the smell of wetness under her perfume curdles in her nose. She splays her fingers and presses into the duvet. How can it be damp in this heat? She sits up, traces over the walls, where the wallpaper bubbles. The sill is moist too; she grabs a hand lens and peers closer. Tiny droplets. Almost imperceptible.

The place must be saturated with marsh water. She'll be lucky if she doesn't develop a breathing issue after six weeks living in here. But maybe, in some strange way, the damp is what preserves it. Like the objects they'll be excavating, or the Sweet Track. The six-thousand-year-old causeway, used by Neolithic peoples to cross the fen, probably runs right beneath their feet around here. She read that local conservationists regularly pump the rotting wood with water to keep it from vanishing.

As the sun sets, Nell tries to forget the subtle ooze of the guest house by reading over the health and safety documents. She flicks through the papers, curling her legs into the lightweight sheets and blanket. But however she sits, they cling to her uncomfortably. She tries to work out if the sheets are sticking to her, or she to them. It's like the hairs of her skin have hardened. Or her goosebumps have turned to barbs. Nell kicks the sheets off and tries to settle into the warm air.

But her skin is on fire. Perhaps it's an allergic reaction. She sits, stands, creeps around the room, wincing at every yelp from the floorboards. But underneath this, she hears a hum. Low, sustained. Like something in the walls has grown too big, stretching every beam, coiling and moaning into the mortar. After a few minutes of burning and sticking her fingers in her ears, she goes to the bathroom at the end of the hall.

The door is so warped that the latch doesn't fit into its corresponding lock. She kicks a heavy doorstop into place. The mirror is dingy, spotted brown in the corners, so it's hard to tell if her skin looks rashed. But the bump is there, the one she felt earlier. And it has grown. She strips off her tee and holds her breath.

Red, minuscule broken capillaries light the pea-sized shape in the middle of her torso. The skin on top, usually the pale hue of birch wood with moss olive undertones, is so thin as to be almost translucent, her pulse almost visible in it. And when she touches her finger lightly to its alien surface, she feels something protruding from it. She leans closer. Hairs? But they can't be hair, because they are bruise-purple.

Nell stumbles against the wall, pulling her T-shirt back on and trying to crush the bump with the heel of her hand. Sweat and panic. Her brain draws up paranoid lists of parasitic infection and cancer symptoms. There's a loud voice in her head telling her to drive to the nearest hospital right now.

"Calm down," she tells herself firmly. "It's not an emergency. It's a bump. If it sticks around, you'll find a GP and get it treated." She takes a few breaths and pulls her phone from her back pocket.

She barely used it all evening, so a few Instagram likes and a message from Liz wait for her on the lock screen. She dismisses them at first, instead opening the internet.

Tender

The first potential explanation is that it's a skin reaction. The pollen count is high, which can make any body sensitive and quick to react. The air is strange here, no doubt full of mould. There are a hundred things she could be allergic to, but a cooling cream and some antihistamines should sort it out – both of which she has in the first aid kit.

On the other hand, it could be an infection. She ought to clean it too.

Back in her room, she douses the lump with alcohol gel, then a cream, and covers it with a large plaster. Finally, she swallows a tab of loratadine. All bases covered. Whatever this new appendage is, it should soon be gone, absorbed back into her normal, familiar body.

The voices of her colleagues reach her ears from downstairs. Another of Ingrid's belly laughs. She really should go and see them. It would take her mind off this thing. Nell quickly checks her notifications in the doorway. One by one she adds the amateurish thistle photos to her Instagram story, applying filters to draw the colours out. Her feed has a scheme: blush to dusty pink, with lilac and brown to add drama and shadow. She is the curator of her very own museum of the self.

Then, there is the message from Liz. Since Nell left home, they've spoken only a few times each year, and now she hears from her sister twice in twelve hours? She thumbs it open, other hand waiting eagerly on the doorknob to take her to the others, and to distraction.

Sorry to message late. And I'm sorry about earlier, it's just hard when you only have one pair of hands! Please come to Charlie's 5th bday, I'll send you all the details nearer the time. I want to give you some stuff, we've been clearing out the attic and there are some boxes which I think are yours.

Then Liz sends another message, and Nell has barely finished reading it when it vanishes.

Do you remember being in hospital?

A few seconds pass. Nell stares at the deleted message notification. Liz was small at the time, it's not surprising that she'd forget. But it's also odd for her to bring it up, when they haven't talked about anything personal in years.

Nell replies quickly. *Of course! Wouldn't miss the party!*

Then she opens her door and walks down the corridor, trying to push aside the off-kilter feeling of being back on the Somerset Levels. She pictures the pomegranate and the meadow thistle shrivelling into husks, then dust, and tries to brush them firmly from her mind, focusing instead on the friendly chatter seeping from beneath the kitchen door.

II

Nell rolls the hems of her pink cargo trousers, and crouches to tuck her fingers under the trench's tarp covering. The horizon is already a lustrous blue – the hot blue of distant stars, which she learned about from a university boyfriend who studied Physics. He taught her that blue light carries the most energy. She had told him her favourite flowers were cornflowers, because they looked like petite, volatile blue stars. She had thought that was a fitting answer.

She relishes the cool trapped air as they peel back the tarp. The sun hasn't risen far, so the soil still bears an inky darkness even near the surface. As they work, she recalls the invitation email, which mentioned how mornings would be spent excavating, while afternoons were for sorting until the feverish weather broke. She had received the email at home in Milton Keynes, while screaming into a pillow so her neighbours wouldn't hear. She had been saved that day. From the embarrassment of going to live in her parents' spare room in Clevedon, from bankruptcy, from having to cancel her nail appointment the next day. She'd already chosen the colour and the finish.

Ingrid recounts the story from her clipboard as they uncover the first trench. "The field was fallow last year, to refresh it for the next crop. Then, of course, it flooded."

It had been all over the news. Two rivers reaching over their banks with watery fingers, creeping higher and higher until the wetland lakes became little seas, houses floating on the surface.

"Beth found the first bone fragment in February. Now, on a three-hundred-year-old farm that's nothing to write home about. But it was a human metacarpal bone, as you all know. The police did their bit, and the coroner designated the site as a source of potential treasure. You read the articles."

Ingrid had shared a photo in her invitation email, too. The narrow, roseate bone that looked out of place on a white examination table.

Ingrid continues as they pull the rest of the tarp away, exposing the first trench at a metre and a half deep, and the second at thirty centimetres.

"Bill and my first team dug the test grids and found significant samples of preserved biomass as well as bone fragments. The ground scan revealed deep artificial chambers and two sets of human remains – so we are assuming this to be a grave, perhaps for someone important. We ordered in the peat cutters, and here we are now. You four, sampling, please."

Ingrid points in the direction of the assistants, who step into the shallower trench. They pick up their sample pots and communal trowels, and Nell watches them creep around, each footstep causing only the slightest sound. She wants to tell them not to be so worried – the peat cutter chopped a hand off, which has been delivered to the lab

Tender

ahead of everything else, and later they'll agitate and sieve everything. They couldn't do much worse. But she remembers first-dig jitters, the way it feels like the earth has sprouted through your legs and ensnared your nervous system. *Don't touch me,* it seems to say, *I'm precious.*

Ingrid continues. "Where is the other botanist, Nell?" As if Nell could have any idea why he hasn't shown. "Whatever, it can't be helped. Let's start in area one marked here. The first complete body shouldn't be too far below us."

Once Nell crouches into the cushiony mud, she can no longer see the farm. It is navy blue above, brown-black below. It's a nice moment, tranquil, until she reaches into her bag and the world oscillates. She feels herself rock.

"What's the matter?" Ingrid asks.

Nell pulls her metal flask from her backpack to take a sip of water. She draws in air, rubs her chest. The bump is still there, but it's too soon to say anything about it. The timing isn't right, the moment too important to be undermined by something personal. Nell chooses the most innocuous words she can think of.

"Do I have something in my eye?"

Ingrid squints, and shakes her head. "Not that I can see. Shall we get started?"

Nell unzips her backpack and pulls out her tools, which have pink handles to blend into her Instagram. Beneath them are her bug repellent, sun cream, antibacterial gel, a mini first aid kit, water bottle, logbook, Sharpies, gloves, packaged snacks, a lighter, and even a pocket knife at the bottom, although she's never had to use it. The bag's zip encircles all of these items, revealing their pleasing arrangement whenever she opens it.

"You're a girl after my own heart," Ingrid says.

It's been a long time since Nell has sunk gloved fingers into the cottage-cheese softness of fen earth. Since childhood. Everything she excavated at university or for the city developers was through clay or chalk. She parts the soil as gently as if it was silk. The soil reddens. Slow, then all at once, like a spreading bloodstain.

"I think there's something here," she says.

"Let me see." Ingrid clacks her trowel against Nell's, so she backs off. The clumping soil comes away easily, until Ingrid's trowel hits something. She switches to a brush. Then a small, tawny-brown dome erupts like a crowning baby.

"Body number one." Ingrid's voice rises to a bellow. "Bill: here, now!"

She stands, and stabs north arrows into the ground for photos. The others arrive and climb down, clumping around the skull like leaves caught in a drain. The air grows warm and wet, coagulating in Nell's lungs.

As far as Nell has thought until now, the ground is a substrate, a thing which roots grow through. It holds nutrients and provides structure so that plants can thrive in it. But of course, the ground is also full of bodies – meat and bone and biomolecules. Where else would those nutrients come from if not the past, settling in layers, packed tight by the feet of the present?

And now, here's a body. It hardly resembles a living thing. It has become ground-like, planted so deep like a seed.

As Ingrid clears the dirt around the skull, her hand slips over the area where its face should be.

Tender

"How odd," she says, dusting granules until the explanation becomes clear. There is no face. It's obvious, even to Nell's untrained eye, that they are looking at the back of the skeleton's head.

"Are they buried face-down?" Nell whispers.

Ingrid nods. "Must have shifted. I've never seen a burial like this before."

The trench fills with cautious excitement, but Nell steps back. She turns over a small piece of charcoal in her hand.

It had been sticking from the sanguine peat near the head. With a brief inspection, even in the dawn light, she recognises the tip of a sharp grass leaf. A grass that would have been very tall, would have brushed against shoulders and ears. She tries to imagine the owner of the bog body, walking through this field in its ancient state. Did the air bite with cold or heat? She can't quite reach it yet, can't pull an image into view.

But this feels like something. She can't tell if it is heavy or light in her hands, but its fragile texture presses through her gloves. When she was small, she held the plants in the field out back like this, like their delicate bodies could crumble apart under her touch.

A voice snaps her back from the ancient past, and her own past, all of it knitted together. "I'm right on time."

Nell cranes her neck upwards. The dawn silhouettes a man about her age. She takes another step away from her colleagues as he climbs into the trench and holds a hand towards her.

Hair, asphalt-black and metallic when the sun catches it. Complexion, the sandy hue of a Roman ruin, with a hint of pink. Shirt, printed with dark green and plum-coloured leaves. Ill-fitting glasses that sit low on his nose. His sleeves are rolled to the elbow, exposing thin arms that writhe with sinew as he leans forwards. Nell lifts her arm instinctively, wondering without meaning to what this man's hand will feel like.

Tight grip, hot skin. "Gunner," he says. "Everyone's not too mad at me, are they? If I could have gotten here sooner, I would have."

Nell had checked his profiles too, of course: filled with landscapes, taken from behind him so he has the air of an explorer. She tries to think of something reassuring to say, but Ingrid speaks first, without looking up from her notes.

"Let's see how you'll make up for it. Come here, Gunner."

Gunner releases Nell and steps towards the others, loudly introducing himself, which Ingrid answers by introducing him to the inverted body at their feet.

They scoop away the looser earth, then switch to brushes and picks nearer the flesh. And it is flesh: even amongst the small exposed area, Nell sees remnants of leathery, tanned skin stuck to the skull. The conditions must have been optimal, waterlogged from the moment the bodies were buried. She recalls from Ingrid's papers that hard tissue preserves better than soft tissue in fenland, but with enough waterlogging over enough time, the pH stays low enough to maintain softer parts, too.

Ingrid points Nell and Gunner to wherever needs attention. She notes the apparent degradation of proteins, the red ochre which must have been painted on the skin, the tanning process, every detail she can see from half of a skull.

Gunner sighs with satisfaction. "You know, I've read a lot of your work, Ingrid. But can I say what an honour it is to work with you?"

Tender

She waves a hand as if to shush him, but the smile betrays her. "Thank you. I am looking forward to working with you too." Her voice quietens. "Just kids and you've both already done so much."

There is a palpable shift in Gunner, a tightening of the shoulders – animal, instinctual and competitive. "Well, I feel like I still have a lot to learn. Who'd have ever thought there was so much to seeds, huh?"

Nell senses she ought to join in the self-deprecation for Ingrid's benefit. "I'm a complete newbie when it comes to bog bodies. I just wrote a thesis on weeds that got published in some places."

They return to work, though Nell leans back onto her hands for a moment, finding the feeling in her legs, allowing blood to pulse through.

Gunner's cropped trousers and the hairs around his ankles are mud-caked. He digs hungrily, picking things up and tossing them around – perhaps one of those tramplers raised by laissez-faire parents. Nell allows herself a moment longer surveying him, and even holds his gaze when he smiles at her. He has large nostrils like he could breathe in the world, and a mouth that stays open, teeth exposed, even after he says, "Hi." Nell starts, and turns back to the earth.

She eases soil from the skull, and soon scoops her fingers around the back, into its eye sockets. Ingrid and Gunner are exposing the curved neck bones and a butterfly of shoulder blades, fanned inwards.

"They're curled up," Nell says, then gasps. The others stop digging and wait for her to speak again.

As she draws her hand out from underneath the skull, dark pinkish-brown organic material flakes over her gloves.

There is something in the corpse's eye sockets. Nell becomes aware of the dryness of her mouth, her breathing so quick that her tongue sticks to the back of her teeth.

Gunner leans closer, the air moving with him. "Flowers?"

"I think so," she coughs, finding tweezers and pulling something free. It comes loose in a few pieces, and despite its deteriorated state she grabs a Sharpie and labels a plastic bag with the word *Thistles*. "They've stuffed the skull with some sort of thistle head."

"What could that mean?" Gunner says. "Some kind of ritual?"

Nell shows him the charred grass leaf she picked out before, and bags it alongside the thistles. "The plants all seem to have been burned or charred in some way."

"Careful," Ingrid says, "I've been quick to cry 'ritualistic' before. It tends to make people suspicious."

Nell opens her mouth to respond, but closes it again.

By lunchtime they have hit the shoulder blade of the second body. Ingrid deduces it is smaller, perhaps female, or a child, or elderly. The two bodies lie close together, so much so that their arms may interlock somewhere in the soil, but both heads are turned, forced to look down.

Beth hovers at the edge of the trench while Ingrid explains the morning's discoveries. A small tractor hums near one of the outbuildings, waiting to take her back onto the distant fields where she is collecting the first of a vegetable crop. Nell watches in fascination from the doorway of their makeshift laboratory, a small marquee with plastic tables

Tender

arranged in the centre. Beth's face remains calm, even as she agrees with Ingrid that this is very exciting. Today her hair is twisted into a bun, and she's wearing denim overalls covered with greenish handprints. When Beth turns to leave, she looks directly at Nell, unreadable as she was during the barbecue.

They irrigate and cover the bodies, then take shelter from the sun. Ingrid hands around high-calorie snack bars and stands over the group until each has had a cup of water, then puts Gunner and Nell on flotation and sifting until the heat breaks. In the corner of the marquee, Bill makes affirmative noises into his phone.

Nell heaves the samples into a line, and while Gunner turns on the hose, she records preliminary data. Soil colour matching, noting the distinctive ochre redness around the bodies. It's a clay pigment – she's quite sure – that would have been dried, powdered, and perhaps turned into a paste or paint.

A worn calliper juts from the tool pile, so Nell measures some of the large flower heads and leaf remains from the bagged samples. Some are dyed with the red pigment, while others have turned to charcoal. Gunner shows the assistants how to pour their samples into the first sieve and rinse off the worst of the dirt.

"I know it seems boring," he grins, "but it's actually where you get those eureka moments. You never know what a quick clean'll uncover. When I visited the Sonoran Desert in Arizona with my parents, we broke open this rock and there was fossilised grass inside. And when we cleaned away the dust, we even found preserved beetles…"

Nell sifts through the lab tools. "There are no over-the-elbow gloves."

Gunner shrugs. "Use your hands. With such acidic soil you won't get any bad bacteria in there, don't worry."

She knows this, but plunging her hand into the water sends shock waves along her arm and deep into her shoulder. The pain finds the lump and she shivers.

"It's always worse when you're hot, I find." Gunner watches her with a smile.

"You do a lot of digs?" she asks. He seems too polished, too much of a lab person. But he's turning out a catalogue of fragments in perfect size order on a tray.

"My dad was an archaeologist. You might have heard of him actually: Malcolm Bloud? He wrote a bunch of books that get used in university reading lists. We followed him around the world – he gave lectures and taught courses and stuff."

The word "Was" drips from her mouth before she can stop it. One of the assistants, the one wearing a bucket hat over her glossy, dark brown ponytail (Mia, Nell thinks), visibly holds her breath.

"He died a couple of days after my thirteenth birthday. I ended up specialising in pollen and micro stuff – maybe so I didn't, you know, feel like a clone – but I never pass up a chance to get on site if the spaces are there. My dad was insatiable when he was on a dig. It makes me feel, I don't know, closer to him. Dismal, right?"

"I'm so sorry," she says. Gunner shrugs.

Nell shakes her hand through soil clumps, the pumping of blood just enough to keep her from yanking it out from the cold. Gunner talks about his childhood travels – Mexico, Scotland, the Basque Country.

"How about you, Elinor?"

Tender

She scoops the floating matter onto her own tray and grabs the hose. "What about me?"

"Well, you've heard my life story." This is partly true, although she knows more about Gunner's father than about him.

"There's not much to tell," she replies. This is completely true: her childhood was uneventful because her parents didn't relish events.

"But your career is really something," he says. "I read your paper on British wildflower morphology and acidity. And the essay about weeds and society, that tension in how we perceive them? And your rising star feature by the *American Journal of Botany*! Also, I'm pretty sure everyone here follows you on Instagram."

She looks to the assistants. Mia and another student both nod.

"Oh," she says, her heart quivering. "That's really sweet."

Mia pipes up, "Your feed is literally gorgeous."

The quivering worsens. "Thank you, it's really not that big a deal, though!"

At one time, when she was freshly graduated, she had the energy to upload multiple times a day, growing her following into the thousands. She posted intricately pinked chicory flowers with four perfect cuts in each petal, and feathery yarrow leaves adorned in butterflies, and selfies with her lips painted the burned pink hue of plum skin. Moving to Milton Keynes had shifted the subjects towards foliage and trees, but she had bought potted plants and visited gardens whenever she could. That was a while ago, now.

Lauren Du Plessis

A little relieved to let the conversation flow on to other topics, Nell runs the hose around her objects, helping the film of earth to let go. There are shapes she can't identify straight away, but she makes a few sketches to compare with her books in the evening.

"So many thistles." She holds her voice close, so even the lightest wind of her breath can't disturb the buds.

When the assistants take a bathroom break, Gunner inches towards her into her peripheral vision. "Hey, I was thinking of going for a walk later, maybe heading into town to get some food. You want to come?"

She wants to say yes, but the closer her face gets to the flowers laid out in front of them, the more she can see them dancing. The more she sees them waving in the breeze, then picked by earth-hardened hands. Arranged in some pattern, maybe a weave or criss-cross. Why are they there – to cover the smell of dead bodies, to cleanse? Or to line the grave, so the plants might grow into their flesh and remake them. The image of the bodies, freshly dead and buried, is becoming clearer.

"I need air," she says, and stands so fast she almost hits Gunner in the face. She feels his eyes on her as she leaves, and her name sounds odd in his voice as he calls after her. A stirring in her chest coils into her gut. She wants him to say her name again. She doesn't know why – it's not like her to enjoy her name in anyone's voice. Makes her feel like a small thing, so easily labelled. Even when her Google Home does it.

With the infinite blue sky pressing heat through her, she stands at the edge of the trench, then climbs down, so the world disappears again. The bog bodies are covered

Tender

with small tarp squares, but she feels them reaching up.

Nell sits in the soil, letting the moisture into her clothes. Who cares – she could lie down, and the fen would consume her in its passive way, as it did the bodies.

She presses her hands to her chest.

Ingrid calls, "You okay there, Nell?"

"Fine," replies an echoey voice that must be hers. "Just taking it all in."

She wants to take it in like osmosis, a starved stem drawing water. She lowers her right hand, gloveless, and digs into the soil. Her pulse begins to throb in her neck. There is a strong urge to plaster the earth across herself. To plant herself here.

Her job is to observe and extrapolate the relationship between humans and plants at any particular site. To assess whether they farmed, what they might have eaten, if they used plants for recreational or spiritual purposes. She is doing her job.

And yet, it doesn't feel like enough.

"Exciting, isn't it?" Gunner has followed her into the trench. "It's so intricate. Whoever this was, they must have been important."

She nods, swallowing more saliva than should have formed in the few seconds he's been talking. She tries to steer the conversation back towards him, where he seems comfortable, and positions her body to hide her muddied hand.

"How come you had to arrive late?"

He answers quickly. "My roommate was sick. Didn't seem sensible to leave her."

"That's kind of you."

His smile moves from her face down her arm, like

he's realised what she's doing. "Aren't we lucky to be able to do this now? What with all the peat bogs and fens disappearing and getting oxygenated."

"I know," she says, trying to release her acrylics from the squelching ground. They are effective digging tools, spearing deep.

"And the dropping water table around here too, Jesus. All these secrets might disappear, and we won't have learned anything. It breaks my heart. I honestly believe we should be looking to these people, now more than ever. Getting back to an older relationship with the Earth – isn't that what we need right now? Not to go all tree-hugger on you when we've just met. But I'm afraid that's what I am! Vegan and everything." He chuckles.

"Get back," she repeats. The invasive thought flashes through her again. Her, covered in peat, smearing it in sultry lines over Gunner's face. Their eyes stare skywards, pupils void-wide.

"I don't feel good. Maybe we can go for a walk tomorrow…"

She stands, and shakes herself, then reaches around her back to pull the water bottle free and take a long swig from it. It must be the heat and the excitement.

Nell showers in the evening, and again in the morning of the second excavation day. Gunner, now settled into the room opposite hers, doesn't seem bothered by her long bathroom trips. Each time she hopes the steam will clear her out. She's fogged up with something, a denseness in her body. There's something in the air, or the water, or the food here, making her different.

You horrible little girl, her mother shrieks. It's a memory, and Nell is a child. The shower head fleshes out to become her mother's face.

Nell reviews her hands, caked in soil and something sticky like honey. And in the middle of her left palm, the spider.

What have you done, Elinor?

She found the spider in the field. The field – of course – was not their garden. Too overgrown and wild. It was next door to their house. They never knew who owned it. Anyway, the spider had crawled onto her leg, where she slapped it harder than she'd ever hit anything before. So hard that three of its legs became detached from its body, and its body mashed out. She'd brought it inside to stare at it. She had horrified herself, snuffing something out so easily and quickly.

Shower, now. Her mother rushes her to the bathroom, leaves her alone in there. She must be thirteen or so, because she remembers hanging a training bra on the hook alongside her T-shirt and jeans. Too old for such behaviour.

Water rushes down her, steam rises. She scrubs at her skin until she's sure the bits of spider are stripped from her body.

Her mind dribbles back into the present and she is crying. She half-expects to see period blood, a welcome explanation for the slow sensation of being unstitched. But the water runs clear.

With her left hand she rubs her chest again, until a quick jab of pain stops her.

The bump has changed. Like a baby in the belly that has kicked its legs out, and found a low seat on its mother's bladder, unignorable. It is wider at the bottom, almost triangular except for its rounded edges. And the skin at the top is even thinner, pores broken open where the three purple, hair-like things emerge.

She wants to slap it, like she did that poor spider. She has to squeeze it and purge it out. But she can't bring herself to touch it again. It's too horrible.

The clatter of shovels and thundering of boots comes from downstairs. Bill's Land Rover engine growls on the driveway, ready for day two. Nell redresses the wound and hopes that her disapproval of its existence will somehow alert her white blood cells to get rid of it for her.

The weather is cooler by a degree or two, allowing them to work longer hours. Whenever Ingrid and Gunner aren't looking, Nell slips off her right glove and uses her acrylics to scoop peat from the crevices of the bodies. She hates how natural and good this dirty thing feels. It reminds her of the field once more. After killing the spider, her childhood self had expected the field to feel angry with her the next time she visited. But it was indifferent, carrying on as usual and welcoming her back like nothing happened.

It is midday when Mia calls out from the smaller trench.

"We need the botanists, please!"

Nell and Gunner leave their stations to investigate. The assistants have reached a gunge of plant matter, woven like damp tapestry. Brown and red: mud, and more ochre. Despite Ingrid's warning, Nell's mind forms the words *ritual, secret, sacred.*

Tender

She directs the assistants, their bodies flurrying around her. She calls the names of plants so Gunner can label bags, though her voice sounds uncertain and she blushes with the attention. As the others mark up the area and take photos, she sinks her re-gloved fingers into the tangled mess of ecofacts, and feels calmer. Some appear charred, others almost pickled by the acid and lack of oxygen. They all must have been burned before burial. Even with the slowest inch of her muscles she can manage, the sodden cracks of twigs warn her to be careful. A single squeeze and she could turn the material to mulch.

As soon as the team exposes them to the air, the most delicate pieces fall apart. They fill the bags with fragments and flecks. Nell pushes deeper and deeper, still finding stems and leaves and flower-heads, until her middle finger scratches against something hard. She pulls her trowel out to cut a deeper square around the object.

"Oh my god."

Everyone stops. Bill's boots appear in her line of vision, as he leans over her from the surface. She eases her fingers around the object as Mia takes photos for the record. It comes loose, peat tumbling away. Nell raises the skull, turns it over, and stares into its stuffed eyes.

A third body.

Someone squeaks in awe and a loud "Fuck!" comes from Gunner's direction.

Ingrid climbs down and reaches towards Nell's hands. "It didn't even show up on the scans!"

Nell turns the new skull over again, noting its saturated weight. It's far more decomposed than its neighbours.

Lauren Du Plessis

There's a large, jagged hole in the back of the head, with cracks splintering out from it.

Ingrid leans over and fixes her fingers around the skull. Nell senses an upward tug. She firms her grip in response, like a child holding a precious toy, but soon relents.

"It's missing a piece," Ingrid points out. "Seems corroded over here."

Nell wants to ask if the damage might have occurred before death, but the thought seems too morbid to share aloud right now, in the moment of revelation. Instead, she smiles, first up at Ingrid and then towards Gunner. Her stomach whirls, but in a pleasant way, almost lifting her to her feet.

"Do you think there could be even more?" Gunner stands back, presumably hoping the site will open itself up to him with some distance. Nell stumbles to his side, arms raised as if she's still holding the new skull. The air particles quicken around them. When he stirs, the hairs of his arm tickle against hers.

Her hands sweat in her gloves, her shirt sticks to her skin, and the bump in her chest burns so hot she feels it in her nose.

"Maybe it *was* some kind of ceremony," she guesses quietly, her voice shimmering with excitement, and climbs back towards the first trench.

Body number one now boasts ribs and vertebrae, floating on the soil like a swimmer in a lake. The skull, which had been staring into the centre of the Earth for millennia, now lies on its side, eye sockets stuffed with thistle heads, near-bud and round. Body number two curls towards it from half a metre away, head still downturned. What happened

38

Tender

to their eyes when they died? They could have been plucked out in an act of violence. Perhaps all these people had been sick. Or the plants might have been placed gently on the eyelids, and migrated inwards after the eyes decomposed.

Don't cry ritual, Ingrid warned, but when Nell stoops over the bog bodies she feels something very old, something her fibres have forgotten, stirring. As a kid she got it by watching *Time Team*, or standing in a museum as a university student. The closest thing she thinks she's ever felt to instinct (outside of the other times, which she doesn't like to think about). Instinct to do what, she isn't sure.

III

The days quickly become a tide, a back and forth between farm and guest house. Nell looks for the gentle comfort of regularity but finds instead the sense that she is marching towards something. Her acrylics are developing the slightest brown tinge at the tips. She gains a hundred new followers, far more than her recent growth rate. And each day the lump in her chest throbs. The back-and-forth days, rather than embracing her, are making her nauseous.

The first two bodies come out surprisingly quickly; four thousand years of burial, and in four days they are born again. The wet soil surrenders their rust-orange bones and wefts of flesh, which are transferred to a fabric mat. Then, the bodies are lifted from the trench and moved to the marquee to prepare them for packing. Only the third body remains wedged in place, its presence as baffling as ever. It seems to lie in its own separate chamber, suggesting that the site isn't just one grave, but many. In the smaller sampling holes, the assistants find a chip of potential pottery, and carved stone.

These are the first corpses Nell has ever seen, and every brush of her living skin against them sends shivers through her. She's never thought of herself as squeamish, but her mind can't let go of the thought. These are bodies, real bodies. There's something sacrilegious about lifting them out of their burial place.

On the Friday of their first week there is a celebration in the guest house kitchen. Gordon pulls up whatever chairs he can find – a wooden dining set, a striped deckchair, a barstool with emergent stuffing around its seat – then retreats to his room, asking only that they turn down any music past ten o'clock so as not to disturb the neighbour's chickens.

Ingrid stands over Mia's laptop and selects a playlist of music from the seventies and eighties, twanging guitar interrupted by synth pulses that add a driving rhythm underneath the talk. Gunner scrambles tofu on the hob while the others eat thick, creamy egg and cress sandwiches.

"I can't believe this is our first dig," an assistant says, perhaps Alex, as far as Nell remembers.

"I'm guessing they're not always this dramatic?" Mia adds.

Ingrid and Bill look at each other, then Ingrid says, "It's the most exciting thing I've seen in this country, without a doubt."

"Ingrid," Nell says, finding her voice with a small cough, "You mentioned not to call it ritualistic. Can I ask…?"

"You will form opinions as we proceed, whatever happens – that's just human. But you are early in your careers, so I want you to explore all options before you commit to single lines of belief when it comes to translating the past."

Bill says, "It's never too early to think about your academic reputations, and this dig is undoubtedly a fantastic start. Ingrid and I are excited to bring you all through this and see what happens next in you kids' careers, as a result."

"Don't call them kids!" Ingrid laughs. "We can't be parenting them already."

"They don't need it," he agrees. "I've read over your first reports this week, and everything looks in order. I think this team is going to be very strong."

Ingrid's eyes sweep across the group until they find Nell's, and she smiles, holding up her glass of warming beer. Nell feels herself blushing and distracts herself by pinning a wisp of hair behind her ear. She notices Mia mirroring her from across the group, tucking back a stray strand. Her insides flutter.

Perhaps the strange back-and-forth rhythm was in her imagination. Perhaps she's simply adjusting to a new place – she isn't exactly used to novelty. And the thing on her chest: perhaps it is already healing, and she has let her worry get the better of her. Nell stands to get another drink.

She finds Gunner by the open kitchen window, and for a moment they eat their food and watch the sky outside turn orange, while what looks like faint steam rolls over the field across the road. It feels good to stop for a moment, to listen for the occasional bird call and think about the tiny life cycles playing out in the soil and hedgerows, carrying stubbornly and beautifully on.

They arrive to the trenches later on Saturday, and as they set up their tools for the day Nell's phone buzzes with another message from Liz. It's gone from WhatsApp the moment she opens it. *Liz has deleted this message.*

Lauren Du Plessis

"Strange," she mutters.

"What's up?" Gunner asks, tying his laces beside her.

"Nothing. My sister is acting weird in our chat."

"Older or younger?"

"Younger, but she's a housewife and has two daughters. We're sort of backwards."

"You're plenty impressive. Look where you are." Gunner's eyes linger on her face.

She raises a hand to her chest instinctively, then flinches away. The lump – which hadn't been on her mind so much today – feels so large she wonders if it shows through her clothes. She drops her phone into her bag, gives Gunner a polite smile, and peers over the edge of the trench. That dark earth scraped through with red streaks, like black forest cake. She almost falls forwards into it.

"Hey, you sure you're okay?" Gunner says. Nell wishes she could shake him off, take a moment to breathe, but it's also comforting to have someone next to her, as the world turns.

"I feel dizzy." She sits. Gunner follows, and their legs dangle over the edge.

"Let's talk about something 'til it passes. That always helps me," he says. "What got you into botany?"

Nell's chest burns and her stomach feels as though it is swelling. Ready to birth something. She catches her breath between sentences, and the pain is so distracting she gives Gunner more than she would usually give a relative stranger. "Maybe rebellion. I was indoors a lot as a kid. But I read a lot of nature books. Also, plants are beautiful. Being a plant seems simple. It all makes sense."

"Simpler than being a human?"

44

Tender

"Right. A plant doesn't have a nervous system. It doesn't need thoughts. It's just hormones and reactions. Auxin and phototropism. The plant detects light, and it grows towards it. It's that simple. And from that we get roses, dahlias, Venus flytraps…"

Gunner laughs. "You'd be stuck in one place for life."

"Maybe I'm not as rebellious as I'd hoped." Nell chuckles too, but this sends another wave of chemicals through her, a wash of vertigo. She fishes for mints in her bag.

"I'm sorry you're not feeling well. It's so typical. We haven't even got Tria out yet."

"Tria?" Nell opens the bag of individually wrapped mints and offers one to him.

"Oh, I nicknamed the first two bodies with Latin neuters: Unum and Duo. So, the third is Tria. Don't ask, it just came to me." He tears the small packet open with his teeth. "Why do they wrap all of these?"

"For hygiene? Or freshness."

"But it's so much plastic."

"It might be recyclable." She turns the main pack over, searching for cryptic waste symbols.

"Not soft plastic like this."

Nell changes the subject as her stomach lurches again. "I overheard Bill talking to the British Museum and Historic England. Do you really think this is the moment where our careers take off?" She extrapolates in her head: more digs, writing books, having a name that carries weight beyond the arbitrary arrangement of letters. Does she want to be known?

"I hope so," he replies.

45

"You didn't tell me why *you* chose botany," she says.

"Oh no, I'm sorry to say my reasons are more immature – it started with sperm."

She looks at him and he laughs.

"You know, 'angiosperms' for fruiting plants and 'gymnosperms' for the ones that produce naked seeds. That too, 'naked seeds'. Stupid Latin words and plant sex, that's what got me started researching. God, I'll stop talking now."

Gunner doesn't stop talking. He follows a tangent about a month spent with Florida palms, and another with German grasses. He talks more about his father – how he encouraged theories over dinner, and taught his son all the funny Latin words for things.

She can't shake the sense that there's a wall surrounding him that she would like to tear down. Not to disrespect his father, but to allow something messier to burst out, like spores from a puffball mushroom. There must be grief or anger festering under the cap of brazen enthusiasm. But perhaps that would be too forward of her. She wouldn't like a stranger to tear any of her own walls down.

Gunner continues. "I also think plants are the unsung heroes of archaeology. They're not the flashiest discovery, until they are, right? And I just… love beautiful things."

He could not have described better how Nell feels. Botany, like a salon appointment or a final lunch with a pregnant sister, seems unimportant until it is. Nell tries to speak, wants to hear more of her thoughts in his voice, but finds the words difficult to get out. No use. She takes a deep breath, and says, "Gunner, can you get Ingrid? I think I have heatstroke."

Tender

She presses her acrylics into her fingertips as Gunner walks away. Heatstroke is a reasonable, realistic explanation. All living things shrivel under heat.

Ingrid leaves her spot in the trench and fetches a number from the lab. The nearest doctor's surgery is fifteen minutes away. Gunner offers to drive while she calls ahead, insisting to the receptionist that a last-minute weekend appointment is, in fact, essential.

The surgery is a small building with an excessive pitch, giving the impression of an ancient roundhouse. Trees spring from its edges, roots presumably knotted into the foundations.

Nell's eyes itch as she leaves the car and approaches the door, where a lavender bush has overgrown the pavement. Its herbaceous scent reminds her of potpourri bags her mother would tuck into the corner of each drawer in a chest, so their clothes smelled of the meadows they were never allowed in. Bees surround each heavy-laden stalk, butting each other away, coating their legs with pollen. One approaches the folds of her skirt before she jumps away, elbowing someone behind her.

"I'll be okay, you don't have to come," she says to Gunner.

He raises his hands. "I'm making sure."

The waiting room air is like toffee, and a fan pushes its way back and forth with futile effort. It's a relief to be called in. Nell leaves Gunner reading posters which predict his prostate's future in blue bubble writing.

"Elinor," the doctor says. No greeting or platitudes, not even a quick gesture showing her to a seat.

Lauren Du Plessis

The doctor curls over in her chair, as if wilting. She blends into the neutral tones of her office habitat: latte-coloured hair frothed with white, milky skin, a beige pinstripe shirt marked with small sweat patches and a camel skirt. On her desk is a mug printed in a vaudeville font: *Don't talk to me before I've had my coffee.* From her demeanour, Nell assumes this was a gift.

"I'm Doctor Shaw. What's the problem?"

Shaw is the sort to want a clear, direct conversation, Nell guesses, so she states, "I have a lump on my chest."

"A lump?" Shaw's eyes are the tunnelling kind.

"Yeah, some kind of reaction."

"Show me, please?"

Nell does as she's told, unpicking the lilac buttons of her shirt. She points, but Dr Shaw doesn't react to the red bump and its unfurling growths, at this point resembling thin, tubular petals. Released into the light, they move like a wake-up stretch.

"Underneath your sternum but between your ribs?" Shaw's eyes dart around the area. "It could be a pulled muscle – especially if you have had a cough, or carried something heavy. Describe the pain."

"It's this lump," Nell says, "it's quite painful and makes me feel sick."

"Let's have a feel." Dr Shaw snaps a glove onto her hand while Nell steels herself against the prospect of being handled like meat.

The rubber is warm, a ring of five points that presses once to the left, once to the right. As Shaw nears the lump, Nell steadies her breath.

The pain is bright. It is hot like red, then hot like blue.

48

Tender

Her eyes water and she tries to hold herself together.

"I'm not feeling anything concerning," Shaw says, even as the purplish hairs curl back on themselves under a thumb.

"Really?" Nell stares at the protrusion. It almost looks alive.

"And I don't see anything."

Nell digs her fingernails into her shirt cotton. "You don't?"

"Any other symptoms?" Dr Shaw returns to her seat and makes a scooping motion with her hand. But Nell doesn't re-button her shirt right away. She stands there, chest exposed, for several seconds. The walls of Shaw's office recede, the floor expanding. She feels small and unbelievable. How can there be nothing there?

She stares at it. As goosebumps rise across her torso, the area around the protrusion puffs up even more. Her skin is so thin she can see into herself. Capillaries, pulsing, cloying for attention.

"I guess I'm dizzy, but I think that's from working under the heat. We're on a historical dig. But if you don't think this lump is a problem..."

"When you say 'lump', do you mean a feeling of tightness in your chest? That sounds like stress."

Nell begins to rebutton her shirt. "No, I mean the lump."

"I don't see any lump. If it persists, come back and we'll look into it further. For now – from what you've told me today – this sounds like stress from the heat and hard work. When was your last period?"

"I'm due on."

"Might you be pregnant?"

"No."

"Well, you can get cramps in your lower and upper back, almost anywhere in your abdomen. Menstruating may relieve the pain. For now, take paracetamol. There's a pharmacy down the road."

Nell nods and excuses herself, but not before she catches Shaw's frown in her peripheral vision.

In the sauna of the waiting room, Gunner scrolls on his phone.

"Making the most of the signal," he grins. "Everything okay?"

"Fine. I think I've been overreacting."

She has been informed of her tendency to overreact before. Nell began therapy at ten and finished at fifteen. The sessions were not weekly, or even monthly as far as she remembers. Her parents treated them like top-ups for her good behaviour.

The hour-long sessions felt more like days, and she always left exhausted. The questions were repetitive, her answers unsatisfactory. Her therapist was a young woman with shiny blonde hair who seemed like the kind of person Nell's parents wanted her to be. So, she took note of every movement, analysing this woman as much as she was analysed herself. Hold the neck tall, back straight, corners of mouth upturned.

They talked about why it was okay to have dark thoughts. Dark thoughts didn't always translate into dark actions. Still, it was good to be prudent, to assess herself and deduce whether she was about to do something bad.

Nell suspected that in private her therapist was as unbothered as Shaw. A patient to a doctor was surely like a petal under a microscope. You had to be careful with it, and be interested in its finer details. But at the end of the day, it was just one of the thousands of bodies littering the earth. Alone, it wasn't truly important.

Tender

*

They return to the smell of geosmin, wood saturated with beeswax sweetness. There are people everywhere. Parents hold children back from the drop, while teenagers turn back on themselves to get selfies with whatever has emerged from the ground. Ingrid stands in the smaller trench, in a hole where Tria once lay.

"They're all out," Nell breathes as she and Gunner cross the field.

Bill calls them over to the marquee, where he's standing guard. "Someone has snitched. I'm going to see everyone off in a while, but Ingrid made the good point that it might help funding if we let some buzz happen."

When they enter the marquee, Nell forgets her chest for a moment. The central table now hosts a wide, wooden pallet lined with tarp, which forms a base for the bodies. They're laid out to resemble how they looked on discovery, saving Unum's hand, which was mauled by the peat cutters. And they're woven with plants. Stems and flowerheads so close to them they may as well have been part of their bodies, too. The flaps of skin are imprinted with botanicals, like engravings.

Tria is incomplete, their cracked skull accompanied by some red shoulder flesh and the bones of their torso. Unum is in the middle, the largest of the three. His shoulder bones have collapsed into a hunch, and the only skin on his body is the fragment that flaps over his skull. Below his pelvis the bones grow scattered, legs entangled and feet a sprawling collection of reddish dregs. Duo faces him. Her skin hugs her torso but ends at her chin, peeling like a calyx from where her skull blooms. One arm from each of them overlaps, meeting in the middle. This finger or that could belong to either of them – they'll need to attempt DNA tests to unravel them.

"It's like they're holding hands," Nell murmurs.

"Perhaps. Or the decay creates that illusion," Gunner says.

"Hang on." Nell steps back, grabs his wrist to pull him level to her. She holds one hand nearer her face, the other beside her stomach, and gestures for him to copy. Their arms form the shapes of the originals, not touching but weaving between each other mid-air. "Something like this."

Gunner stares at their tangled limbs, then straight at Nell. "Can I ask, how on earth do you keep those nails so perfect? It seems a strange choice for a dig. That sounds rude, but do you get what I mean? With your nice clothes, and your…" The pitch of his voice rises with each sentence.

"I had acrylics done right before I came," she says. "My real nails are gross."

He presses one hand to hers, back to back. The air thickens in Nell's lungs, her fingers kindling.

"I'm sure that's not true." Gunner rotates to his palm, and she follows. "Anyway, perhaps their arms were like this, as you said."

"Yes," she says, dropping her arms with the sudden realisation that she just grabbed someone's wrist without asking first, without eye contact, without a thought.

"We should…" he says, and he doesn't need to finish his sentence. They pull out their notebooks and Nell unfolds her colour-matching chart.

Tender

The plants bedded into the skin and orifices are dark: chestnut, cocoa, umber. Still, it's obvious that they constitute a couple of species.

"Are they local, you think?" Gunner says, making his own sketches of the chaff, stems, thistle heads. His work has a roughness, as if he's drawing in charcoal rather than pencil.

"I think so. These look like sedge, rushes, and of course thistles. But only the buds. Which makes sense – for the bodies to be in such good condition, they'd have to have been buried in early spring, before flowering season. The ground would have to be four degrees or lower to stop bacteria, isn't that what Ingrid said?"

Nell stands over the bodies and closes her eyes. They smell of the same sweet rot as the trenches. But here, inside her mind, she can paint them in more colours than sepia. She feels the breeze, carrying smoke from a pyre. She smells the plants, fresh, and the bodies, heady. Rustling ferns, crunching thistle stalks. The bodies are in the ground, sinking, given to the acid. Nell slaps her stomach where an insect crawled onto her, leaving a shock of pins and needles.

"Nell, Gunner," a voice comes from the entrance behind them, "someone wants interviews or something."

Nell spins to catch Beth's back as she leaves. They follow her into the yellow heat, where work has stopped around the disruption of the crowd. Bill herds the visitors while Ingrid bickers into a phone. The assistants chatter excitedly with whoever will listen.

Beth hasn't glanced back, marching towards the farmhouse. Nell calls after her.

"What's this interview? They want both of us?"

"Don't know. It's some guy from a local paper, on a video call. I think Ingrid organised it. In the kitchen." She points ahead. "Just general questions, he said."

"Fantastic!" Gunner says. Nell squishes her acrylics into her palms and jogs after him.

She hasn't actually been inside the kitchen before, so Nell pauses at the rotted doors. Alternating strings of garlic, chilli and beans garland the bricked-up fireplace, where mismatched glass jars and bottles line three handmade shelves. Pickles, conserves and other substances cloud their containers – some labelled, some not. The air pricks with herbs, and looking over towards the industrial sink, Nell notices thyme and other dried stems sitting half-cut on a chopping board. Beth returns to the counter and resumes chopping.

Nell relaxes her shoulders and drinks in wafts of fragrance, watching Gunner take a seat at the dining table, where a laptop is propped on a cookery book. He pats the seat beside him, and she shakes her head. *Sure?* he mouths. She nods.

Gunner plugs in some earphones.

"Hello!" he says to the person on the screen. Nell watches from the doorway, feeling like a kid at a party, level with the knees of the world.

"Well, honestly, the last few days have been such a rush, I haven't had a chance to reflect!" Gunner smiles. "But more than anything, it was humbling to connect with such an ancient piece of our past. That's a soundbite, huh?"

He nods along with a question.

"Ah, but their lives weren't necessarily that short, or full of hardship. These people were shifting from hunter-gatherers to settled communities. Their society was difficult to imagine in some ways, but I don't think it was so different from our own."

Nell smiles. Perhaps the interviewer can't imagine that Neolithic or Bronze Age people could have been satisfied, or wise, or world-loving. That their anatomically identical brains experienced the same fear, desire, and love.

Gunner's eyebrows raise in anticipation of another question. Nell scratches her stomach – the insect from earlier must have bitten her.

"Well, as an archaeobotanist, I consider how people interacted with their environment. And what I can see so far is that these people searched for meaning, in life and in death. They revered the land around them. Of course, it won't be until we do lab work that we can find out perhaps what they were eating, and from pollen we can deduce which crops they were growing nearby…"

He smiles wider, almost a laugh, sharp canines slipping into view below his top lip.

"Too soon to say. We haven't seen any signs of violence yet, but it could be that the evidence has decomposed. As for any disease, we'll need to rely on the DNA analysis for that."

Nell scratches again. Gunner dictates his email address, then says goodbye, before staring straight at her. She begins to raise her arms, wanting to give him a thumbs-up, a grin, but instead an aching wave draws her into herself and she doubles over.

"Elinor?" Gunner's voice is distant.

Nell heaves, trying to put enough pressure on her stomach that the waves of nausea ripple out into nothing.

A hand touches her back. She turns slowly, like a flower towards the sun in the morning. It's Beth.

"I'm fine, don't worry," she assures her, making her way out of the door.

"You don't look it. May I?" Beth takes her arm and leads her into a small living room. "Wait here, I'll get you some water."

She hears Gunner closing the laptop and his chair squeaking. He arrives at the threshold with furrowed brows.

A rush of the tap from the next room. Nell sits on the threadbare sofa. What is happening to her? She presses against the front of her shirt and feels for the lump. No different. What about her stomach? She prods her fingers around it in a similar motion to Dr Shaw.

There is another lump. On her hip, trying to breach the surface, skin stretched thin like latex. She gags.

"Here's your water."

Beth holds out a slippery pint glass, which Nell drains.

Her phone rings on vibrate, and she checks the screen while the others suggest medicines, teas, a cool flannel. *Mum.* If there's anything worse than cryptic messages from her sister, it's a call from her mother. Suddenly she feels overwhelmed by it all, the conflict between wanting to hide away and wanting to pull Gunner towards her, sit him next to her and lean against him until she feels normal again. She brings her knees to her chest, tries to find words over the conflicting feelings.

"I'm sorry," she says, "I'm really sorry. I think I just need to lie down quietly for a while."

Tender

*

When the heat breaks, around eight thirty in the evening, the fen releases pent-up hisses. Nell sits in the garden of the guest house, barely breathing; because of the lazy air, and because of the ache that travels in a wavy line between the two lumps. She doesn't dare reach under her top to touch them, but she knows from the sensation of catching and brushing that they are both growing, both now the size of blueberries.

Something tickles at her ankle, and she leans over. An ant, skittering along her leg as if it knows where it's heading. She swats it away, but finds another on her calf. She searches the grass beneath her for a nest. Nothing.

"Hey, don't forget this." Something plastic taps her shoulder. Above her head, Gunner dangles a bottle of mosquito repellent. "You'll get eaten alive."

Nell rings it around her ankles, then her wrists, catching wafts of lemon and spicy clove. Perhaps it'll keep the ants away, too. Gunner takes a heavy seat, lets himself fall onto his back.

"Ingrid's pissed at me," he grins.

"What happened?"

"I think she set up that interview so *she* could give it. Oops."

"Are you in trouble?"

"We're all adults here. She'll see the interview, and then she'll know it all worked out okay. Forget about it. Are you feeling okay?"

Holding her hair so it doesn't splay into a wild mess, Nell lies back to join him.

"Not really," she says. "I think it's the sort of thing that might get worse before getting better."

"It's not contagious, is it?" His voice is light, and Nell turns her head to see his jawline cut a sharp silhouette as he smiles.

"The doctor thinks it's," she cringes, "hormonal."

She draws one hand to her chest, the other to her belly. Something stirs. It's growing inside her, like a possession, a poisonous idea. She rolls onto her side, facing him.

"Do you feel different here?" she says.

Gunner rolls his head to meet her eyes. "I guess it feels like the beginning of something. I'm really ready for a change. As much as I love lab work, there's going to be a lot more to this and it's exciting." He rolls to face her more closely. "This is the kind of thing I've always wanted."

Perhaps it's the hundred points of contact she has with the ground, blades of grass touching her back, arms and legs, but Nell feels an unsettlingly familiar current rush to life. Like joy but not, too unbridled and unknowable. Whatever is growing inside her is communicating with her. *Go on, take what you want, what you've wanted since you first saw him.*

Her muscles tighten. Knotting into each other. She lifts a hand to cup Gunner's chin, turns his face to her. "Did I misunderstand the question?" he asks, their lips so close he barely gets the words out before they touch.

It feels natural to kiss Gunner. Her hand creeps, like a vine, over his cheekbone and into his hair, which silks around her fingers, gossamer smooth. His arms wrap around her waist.

Then his mouth grows more eager, tooth against lip.

Tender

And Nell feels the same hunger gnawing through her, the need to tangle into him, to press; but pressing her stomach against his sends pain beating through her.

She pulls away, sits up, throws her head between her legs, and vomits. This time it is so wrenchingly violent, she feels as if part of her soul has been purged with the phlegm.

IV

"**Y**ou might be willing to risk your health, but I'm not. Nobody dies on a dig I'm running."

"Doctor Shaw said there was nothing to worry about," Nell tries, as Ingrid marches her to the marquee the next day. The artefacts she washed with Gunner are displayed like butterflies in museum cases.

Ingrid hands her a battery-operated fan. "Put this on the table, and make sure you stay cool. Bill wants an ecofact summary while the rest of us are sampling."

Nell sits on the wooden stool, and nods at Ingrid, unable to voice her disappointment. She's struggling to explain it herself. Analysing plant samples is her job, and she is excited to begin. But she also feels as if she has been put aside, like a naughty kid pretending to be sick. She must be pretending.

The tug Nell felt on the day they uncovered the bodies persists. As if her body is a plant, with low water potential, and the trenches have high water potential. Her veins and arteries – which become phloem and xylem – reach for equilibrium.

After a few minutes she stands, sneaks to the entranceway. She startles at the sight of Mia, walking back from the trench. The usual marigold warmth of her skin has turned faint, and Nell guesses what's wrong. Anyone would think, from the embarrassed waddle and gritted smile, that it was her first time.

Even though nobody else is around, Mia keeps her voice low. "You don't have pads, do you?"

Nell has two in her bag. It is always good to have one, in case of sudden spotting, and a second, in case you get stuck somewhere overnight. This has never actually happened to her, but she would rather be prepared.

She hands Mia a pad, who smiles with such gratitude Nell almost wants to hug her. Her open smile reveals a gap between her front teeth, and another on the bottom set, between her canine and first molar.

"You're the best!" Mia chirps, and shuffles in the direction of the house. Beth has left the back door open, so they can use her bathroom. For someone who claims never to be lonely, and who seemed annoyed at having to give them a field, Beth has been surprisingly willing to let them traipse mud through her home. It was after she used the bathroom for the first time that Nell discovered the carpets are so trodden and timeworn that it doesn't matter how muddy you are. Beth's house is a continuation of the farm.

Nell and Mia's conversation prompts Bill to look over from his seat, so Nell returns to her station inside. She stares at the Picasso-ed plants, trying to classify anything she recognises. She photographs and sketches.

Nell is stuck here, but that does not mean she can't imagine the outside world. She tries to envision it as it would have been thousands of years ago – the light on her skin, the soft earth beneath her. She draws a long breath

Tender

and lets the dialogue of researcher and subject flow. One by one, the ecofacts give her a story like oral myth: invented, but surely based on a kernel of truth.

She begins in the water, an ash-white sky hanging low over her head. Here the water is knee deep, almost still. Wetland birds pick at the edges, and fish squirm by her ankles in a panic. She reaches down, the surface touching her as much as she touches it. Her reflection shudders into a thousand ribbons.

A green algae, like stonewort, is first to brush her finger. It has clumped around a mound of substrate and comes loose with a sharp tug. She puts it in her basket with thick, strong hands.

Closer to the bank, stems of whorled water milfoil tickle her legs and she stoops to find the submerged leaves – feathery and soft, each dense with leaflets which she adds to her collection. Wind catches in her clothing, making her shiver. Though the season is turning, the air maintains a spring bite.

There are others here, gathering materials for the ceremony. They make plans for dinner, wonder how the rest of the village is doing on the hunt. Someone offers her a handful of spearwort.

As the ground rises beneath her, she climbs the bank and kicks water from her feet. It's too early for the flowers, but she pulls up delicate stems of orchid and fen violet.

Her toes spear into the mud, easing her drenched body away from the water's edge. Here she recovers her boots, and straps the fabric around her ankles. Her calf muscles are angular, her skin tanned and freckled from the sun. This person, whoever she is, is not quite Nell. She is stronger, sharper, and doesn't clean out the dirt beneath her nails.

Some of the younger ones, racing to collect the most, have already arrived at the fen meadow. The rush is waist-height, reinflating after winter like an overdue breath. But she is looking for thistle. While the others cut swathes of rush to line the chambers, she parts the undergrowth, waiting for the leaves to prickle her skin. The meadow thistle's slim stalk is topped by swelling heads. She spends extra time here, clipping each one with a small knife.

Before the village walls, there is a patch of enormous, knotted trees with winding trunks. Sedge grows well here, the sawgrass with its razor edges. She binds her hands with cloth before applying her knife low on the stems, cutting away and arranging the results across the top of her basket, so that she might carry them lengthways to the burial ground.

It is on the final cut that she finds herself distracted, her mind elsewhere, and her hand catches against the sedge. When she tries to tug herself free, it cuts clean through the fabric and tugs open the uppermost layers of her skin. She recoils and walks to the village wall, where she can examine the wound in full light.

It's superficial, bleeding only because of the proximity to her wrist. She reties the fabric to cover it. What she has collected is enough. It is time to visit the burial ground.

Whatever kind of flesh, the red is the same. Nell looks at her hand, which she unconsciously laid palm-up on the table as she imagined this ancient person, who (now she thinks about it) resembled Beth. There is a dot of blood on her middle finger pad. Like she dabbed away a wound. She searches her face, her shirt, for any sign of where it could have come from. Nothing.

"What's going on with me," she breathes. Finding the two lumps on her chest and stomach again makes her want to cry. Last night, when she kissed Gunner and felt poisonous, she was wrong. Whatever is inside her isn't a spreading poison. It's already rotten. When she pulls her hand out, there is more blood. The lumps are bleeding as they grow. At least, that's what her brain tells her. She stares at her hand. Is it possible to lie to yourself so vividly?

She pushes her notes on milfoil and sedge to the side, clears a space to lay her forehead and listen to the rustle of marquee plastic in the breeze. Nell tries to go back to her imaginary Neolithic realm, to follow her Beth-like counterpart through the village with her basket, where *something* important was happening.

But now she's remembering kissing Gunner, and wants to curl up on her chair with lingering embarrassment. After she had been sick, he'd taken her inside and put her to bed. She thought he might kiss her cheek, but when she looked into the bathroom mirror later, her face was ghostly, feral, not sexy. He had left a note on her pillow, though. *Being a plant might be simpler, but only humans can go for a walk tomorrow. If you feel better.*

Nell pushes her fingers through the front of her hair, trying to arrange it in a satisfying wave, but her hands are clammy and she couldn't bear hot water on her body last night, so she hasn't showered. She brushed her teeth several times – that's all she has going for her right now.

But who's to say she won't vomit again, the moment she gets Gunner alone.

Her phone rings from inside her bag. It's her mother. Perhaps now's the time to answer, while she feels nauseous anyway.

"I saw your thing on TV last night. Rotten bodies? I thought your job was about plants."

Nell sits straighter. "Of course, but it's the plants *surrounding* the bodies—"

"What's wrong with those?"

"Nothing! It's very rare to find such amazing preservation."

"Of course." She almost sounds sarcastic. "Mud is good for the skin, isn't it. A bit like the hotel we went to, do you remember? With the mud baths. I'm thinking of going back there. My skin has been dry this year, and this heat doesn't help. Makes you believe we're living in the end days."

As her mother talks, Nell becomes aware of a buzzing behind her ear. Before she can swat it away, a honeybee lands on the table beside her.

"So Mum, how have you been?" She tries to ignore the bizarre stare of its segmented eyes.

"Existing. You've spoken to your sister, I hope?"

Nell sighs. "Yeah. You told her I was coming." She tries to nudge the bee away with her little finger, but it's determined to sit next to her.

"Well, you're so hard to pin down. I thought she ought to know so you two can see each other. You're actually talking at the moment."

If riddles and deleted messages count as talking, Nell thinks. "Yeah, seems so."

Tender

"Good. It's better when we all get along. And you're going to Charlie's party? What did you get her for a present?"

The bee takes another step closer. Nell presses her lips together, then pops them open to say, "I haven't had a chance to get away from the site yet."

"Ah, you'd much rather be working, wouldn't you? You were always like that."

"Really?" Nell asks, watching the bee inch ever closer. "I was the same when I was little?"

"I used to prise you out of that field, I knew nothing good would come of it."

"The field by our house?"

"No matter how many times I told you it was trespassing and we'd get in trouble... you'd go there anyways. All I had to do was leave a door open! It's too bad they didn't make those toddler harnesses for older kids."

The line goes silent as the bee traverses Nell's wrist. She's been stung before, knows she isn't allergic, but it's unsettling to watch its pollen-dusted feet settling into her skin. She stays still, and tries to figure out if her mother has gone.

"Mum?"

"Why are you asking about when you were little?" she asks lightly.

Nell feels her forehead wrinkle. "I've been feeling a bit weird. Maybe it's from being back in the countryside, or what happened with my job."

"What? Is this dig-thing not for your usual job? Were you fired?"

"No, I was made redundant."

"Oh no! What are you going to do about the flat?"

"Mum, I'm good. I've got this job."

"They're paying you enough for digging?"

She lies. "That's right."

"You know, you can always borrow some from us if you need it. Or do you have a nice man who could treat you to a couple of things?"

"No boyfriend, Mum." Nell and the bee continue to eye each other.

"I don't get it. A gorgeous, well-kept girl like you, who is whip-smart? They're missing out."

Nell has no idea who 'they' are. "There's another botanist here. He's nice."

"Oh? Someone into the outdoorsy lifestyle too?" Nell's mother places heavy emphasis on *outdoorsy*, as if it's a euphemism for something else.

Nell prepares her thumb, ready to hang up. The bee watches from her other wrist. "I'll tell you about him at the party. I should get going."

"You take care out there. Don't touch anything that looks dangerous, don't eat anything weird."

"Um, okay." She dismisses the call, and stares at her companion. As if it was waiting for her to finish talking, the bee lifts its wings, beats them into a blur, and sets off amicably.

Over the years, family and friends have hypothesised why Nell doesn't have a boyfriend – why she's never been with anyone longer than half a year, at twenty-eight years old. The explanations often contradict each other. She is too beautiful, and this intimidates men. She is 'unusual-looking' (large ears, and a small, down-turned mouth), and men are vain. She is too smart; this could make a

Tender

man feel inferior. But she doesn't earn much, so the man would feel pressure to provide. At the bottom of this ever-branching list of why Nell is not with someone is the only thing she's ever known to be her issue: instinct. A chaotic, unpredictable force of nature which she envies in others but fears in herself. For some reason, she has always been cautious about being too much herself, or too much of anything, in front of others.

Her vision of the ancient fen is fading. She closes her eyes, and listens to her breath, an anchor to the present. She tries to hear the turning of the Earth. Surely it makes a sound, rumbling around its core.

The marshlands sweat under seven o'clock sun. Above Nell and Gunner's small bodies, the sky glows in rivulets of pink and purple. On the horizon, mist rests in patches over the field like hot breath. Nell follows Gunner down the road, where his phone suggests there's a locally renowned pub and a convenience store where they can buy ice cream.

Gunner is wearing another of his notable collection of patterned shirts – repeating crocodile heads, poking out from indigo water. Nell looks at her patent shoulder bag, her white plissé skirt dotted with pink flowers. They are both overdressed.

"How was excavation today?" she asks. She'd been so drained that she returned to the guest house ahead of the others, even though Sunday was a shorter shift anyway. She still feels raucous inside.

He minimises the map on his phone and shows her the headlines resulting from their work so far.

Lauren Du Plessis

Astonishing "Flower People" Uncovered on Somerset Farm.

Archaeologists Stunned by Ritualistic Burial Site: "How Many More Bodies Will We Find?"

"Where's that quote from?"

"Me, who else? I'm getting overexcited." Gunner reaches towards her, and she doesn't pull away as his fingers weave into hers. "I'm sorry if you feel like you've missed things. Are you getting better?"

"I don't know. I'm hungry, though. What will you get at the pub?" She can't make decisions in this heat; she'll have what he's having.

"I hadn't thought about it. Let's hope they have *something* vegan, aye? Out here, I guess they don't always cater to different diets, even in this age."

"Well, there are farms everywhere. It's just people living off their land, right?"

"No way." He squeezes her hand, waving his phone around with the other. "Agriculture destroyed the fen. I know they don't peat cut here nowadays, and it's made new habitats, sure, but people forget *how* damaging farming is to the environment, before you even consider the animal cruelty."

"What about crop agriculture?"

"That sucks too. We have to change all of it, like a proper food revolution. We need vertical farms, lab-grown stuff. Otherwise nature will never recover."

Without Beth's farm, they would never have found the bodies. And ancient farming is just as responsible for the

Tender

existence of the fenland as its destruction. Nell doesn't dare say this. It seems a weak point in the face of killing animals.

Gunner continues his argument, his voice always on the edge of bubbling over into shouting. He cares a lot about the planet. He believes people can fix it, with pluck and ingenuity. He could be right. All the same, she wonders, can humans extricate themselves from nature in this way? Behaving like we can fix it from the 'outside'? The questions are loud, and snake in circles underneath her skin.

"Shit, we missed the turning." Gunner unlocks his phone. They have been walking a while, the sun low enough to be hidden behind nearby woodland, orange twinkling gem-like through the canopy. "Maybe we can take a shortcut through this field."

Nell finds a stile in the hedge. It feels good: hands on rough wood, feet hitting the cracked earth. It's like jumping into the wildflower field by her house as a six-year-old, waiting for the day she could take her little sister out too. She only ever managed to bring Liz a couple of times, when nobody noticed. But here she is now, watching Gunner avoid splinters and climb over.

"So, you mentioned you weren't working. Are you studying?" he asks as they set out down the side of the field.

"I was made redundant."

He groans. "What happened?"

"It was a small firm, too dependent on one client. They went bust, so we had to cut back on staff. It wasn't even my speciality, I just had a degree in archaeology. I spent most of my time writing labels and getting coffee, so I was expendable."

"Expendable?" Gunner takes her hand again. "I refuse to believe it. You were wasted there, if they were making you get coffee. You're a wildflower expert. How did you end up in construction?"

Nell flinches in his grip. "I guess I'm not a career ladder type. I don't have big aspirations."

"If you're lying, you're a terrible liar," he smiles.

"What?"

"Your brow gets all wrinkled and furrowed when you say something you're not sure about," he says. "I think you want more than you think."

Nell laughs nervously, and pulls ahead. "You're a PhD candidate, right?"

"That's it. Evo-devo of seeds in domesticated plants, so this dig isn't my usual kind of thing either, but I pulled a few strings because I figured using plants in burial is a step towards domestication, right? I couldn't lose this chance, it's too damn good and I needed to be a part of it."

Gunner is so hungry, Nell thinks.

They go quiet for the length of the field. Freshly cut, the stalks are cornsilk-yellow spikes, too short to be moved by the evening wind. But amid this stillness, the ground comes alive beneath them. As they near the black streak of woodland at the field's edge, Nell's footsteps grow more strenuous as her feet sink. Shaded from the heatwave, the ground here has kept its nutrient-crazed softness. Ragged Robin flowers bloom in riotous jumbles of pink confetti. The further in they go, the more the trees distort and loop around each other, no two alike in shape or size. Before long they are ducking and clambering.

"Have you got signal?" Gunner asks. "I've lost my bearings."

"I think I know where we are," Nell finds herself saying.

Tender

Her heel slides into a small hole. The spongy consistency of the earth here has preserved a large animal footprint.

"What could that be," she wonders aloud.

"One of those phantom cats?" Gunner jokes. "The ones that look like jaguars? All English cryptids are suspiciously similar, have you noticed? Big black cat, big black dog, all with glowing red eyes."

He chuckles to himself. Nell shrugs and presses on.

"You're a real country girl, huh? I've never seen you so relaxed."

"It's been a long time." She takes a break on a near-horizontal branch. "I live in Milton Keynes. They call it a 'garden city' but there's a lot more concrete than there is garden, that's for sure."

Gunner joins her on the branch. "My parents were based nearby in Bletchley for a while. I'm sorry, we've known each other almost a week and I hadn't even asked where you live."

"Maybe you asked. I just didn't answer."

"What d'you mean?"

She casts her eyes back towards the footprint. "I'm not good at talking about myself. And when I do, I end up talking nonsense."

"I want to get to know you better."

"I'm not a puzzle to be worked out," she snaps. Gunner shuffles closer, saying nothing at first.

"Sorry, I must be tired. I don't usually snap like that, promise." She hates that she can hear her mother in her head, even in her late twenties. *I won't have children who shout.*

"Don't worry. I'm an oversharer, I forget other people aren't."

"What makes you overshare?"

"Oh god, a desperate need to be liked?"

"I understand. I want people to see the best side of me."

Gunner squints a little. "You've got a lot of good sides."

She loves how he looks at her, even as it makes her nervous. "So, where's your mum now?"

"Who knows. She travels on Dad's life insurance. Probably Italy, we've got family there."

Morbid curiosity forms her next question. "What happened to him?"

"Oh," Gunner says. "He got encephalitis on a trip, which then revealed an undiagnosed heart condition. After he was discharged, he kept getting sick. It took a long time. And boy, did he get mean." Gunner's laugh doesn't sound like a laugh.

"You don't like to remember that side of him."

"It wasn't him, at the end." Gunner swallows. "It's some bullshit that such a big life can end so small."

"Does dying scare you?" A hand slaps her in her mind. Her cheek goes hot.

"I don't know, I guess. I've seen how awful it can be. I'm not sure human beings are cut out for dying. But *omnes una manet nox* – I think that's Horace. The same night waits for us all. I like that saying. Very final, however much we fight it. This is a heavy conversation for a date walk, isn't it?"

The bog bodies are beautiful, Nell wants to say. They are in a frozen state of constant dying, but after the dig is over they will go to a museum, to be admired by millions of people. Both could be true: that death is awful and death is beautiful. Perhaps death is nothing, something completely neutral. She's never thought this way before,

Tender

always a little unsettled by the certainty that she will one day be eaten by microbes and that the rest of the world will grow through her, and erase her.

"This is a heavy conversation," she agrees, and takes his hand to lead him further into the woods.

The farmhouse is a white splotch in a parting through the trees.

"Oh," she says. They've gone in a circle. Another fifteen minutes and they'll be back.

Gunner laughs. "You know what, I'll drive us!"

She wraps her tongue around four words, consonants bursting like tart cherry. "Let's stay here awhile."

She pulls Gunner away from the clearing, instead finding a shallow slope leading to a ditch, where the earth has collapsed in on itself. A dimple in the long, sloping back of the woods. Bedded with early leaf fall and hardy shrubs, those that don't need so much light, it crunches beneath their steps.

Nell sits, Gunner follows. She takes his face in her hands again. His lips part and he's about to fill the silence with words, always words with this man. Nell wants to absorb his blind enthusiasm along with the mushroom puff of pain she couldn't resist prodding.

Nell's ribcage expands with relief, inflating around a vacuum as they kiss. Gunner makes noises, soft moans and sighs that she muffles as soon as they begin. His hands are in her hair, then between her shoulder blades. Her hands wrap around his wrists, where veins bunch together and thud.

There's something delicious and horrible in her. This week has done something, watered a seed, something that was embedded in her gut after all. She wants to shout, can't quite bring herself to, even when their lips break away. But when Gunner's hands slide to her hips, play with the hem of her skirt, hers spider down the buttons of his shirt. She's smiling, her teeth feeling huge in her mouth.

"Nell," he gasps. It barely sounds like her name. The body that was Nell has expanded, its walls thrown out, a field of charged air around them. From her core, branches reach and crawl, breaking and breaking into smaller and smaller divisions, sharp spikes.

They are breaking through her skin. Dark jabs through her pores. She draws him closer. She wraps her legs around his back. She ignores the sting of the lumps, which are no longer lumps but buds – of course, buds! – and at last they're bursting open. Purple tendrils, purple florets unfurling like claws.

Something has risen in her like dawn, sending her into a wonderful bloom. Her hands itch. She has felt something like this before, in another time, another life. Powerful, yet out of control. Somewhere between joyful and dangerous.

Gunner begins to kiss her neck and, tugging her shirt fabric, her collar bones. She feels trapped, but in a somehow pleasurable way. She wants to bite him back, to pull at his skin. It's never been like this before. She'd grown so used to positioning herself carefully when she was with a man, making soft noises. The moment he breaks from her, she lowers her head and presses her lips to the skin of his neck. It is dry but a little salty in the heat. She swears she can feel his pulse.

Gunner recoils. "Nell!"

Tender

She pulls back. "What?"

He breaks into anxious laughter, blotting blood from his neck. It is a sharp, startling scarlet on his skin.

"Oh my god." She wants to tear her gaze away but can't. "Gunner, are you okay?"

He dabs it again. "It's tiny. Looks worse than it is. But – well – maybe we got a bit carried away." He laughs, clearer this time. His pupils dilate as the adrenaline passes.

Gunner might not be afraid of her, but the power she felt seconds ago has drained. Nell apologises again and again, and disentangles herself from him.

"We should head back."

His voice echoes behind her. "We can still get dinner! Nell, I'm fine, you didn't mean to!"

She can feel it now. The way the earth is warm through her shoes. How the darkening sky presses the horizon. How everything bends with pressure. And how all her eyes can focus on is the white smudge of the marquee, the tiny scratches of markers above the trenches.

She checks over her shoulder. Gunner is still getting to his feet. She undoes the top buttons of her shirt, looks down. Her vision tunnels around the impossible flowers. Actual flowers. Growing out of her.

Her skin peels away where they tore through. Lurid purple, firework petals, with spiny bases that disappear back into her. They are thistles. The pointed leaves and stems must be furled over inside her.

Curiosity grips her for a moment, and she tugs on a floret as if to pull it loose. It stings quick, makes her body whirl. She lets it go, and it settles back into shape. She rebuttons her shirt, and runs.

Root

V

The skin thistles don't scrub away. Fresh blood slithers down her body under the guidance of hot water, but the flowers don't.

As the steam clears, Nell stands in front of the mirror and brushes her hair, tucking away any white strands out of habit. But she can't stop scrutinising the thistles.

In her hallucination – because that's what it *must* be – two thistle heads burst from the wound in her chest, while one emerges from the wound on her hip. Her skin turns paper-white where it peels back from the holes. Each head measures a centimetre in diameter, and extends half a centimetre out from her.

She holds her breath and touches one, again, trying to convince herself they don't exist. Thistle heads have two parts – the magenta florets, soft, and the distinctive wide base, a firm, greenish-white pod. These bases are where the thistles meet Nell's flesh.

They are meadow thistles, not unlike the ones knitted through Unum, Duo and Tria. Not unlike the one she picked after the barbecue. In the wild, the meadow thistle has runners: delicate green arms knitting an interconnected web. The upright stems are usually hairy and soft, like human skin. Running her hands over her body, she's sure the skin is puckering, disturbed by new veins growing inside her. There could be hundreds. She gags, presses her hands firmer into herself. Perhaps, if she dug her acrylics in, or smashed her hand into them with enough force, she could rupture them, force them back inside.

"Stop it," Nell tells herself. "Stop being silly. It's not real."

But her hands claw at her stomach. Her face grows hot. Maybe if she gets back into the shower, one more time, she could wash them off. She turns the water on again.

After another hour she returns to her room, having put on the most oversized shirt she packed. Her entire torso flares beneath the fresh plasters she applied.

Gunner is waiting by her door.

"Hey. Can we talk about what happened?"

She shakes her head. "I need to... I don't know, Gunner. But I would never hurt you on purpose. I didn't mean to. I swear." She waits for him to open his own door, before opening hers. "Maybe we can talk in the morning?"

He nods, clearly working to keep his expression casual. And then he's gone, and she's left with the terrible thing she did this afternoon, and the terrible things growing from her body.

She knows it's rude to send him away. She ought to offer him the first aid kit and tend to him. She knows she's done something wrong, so why won't she fix it? Perhaps, if she knew the right thing to say, she could undo the last few hours and reassure both of them that she is perfectly normal.

Nell drifts between fits of sleep and her phone screen, which feeds her endless videos of immaculate smoothie

Tender

bowl recipes and meditation tips read by robotic voices. She tries to fill every moment, to avoid any second of consciousness where thoughts of Gunner or the thistles could seep through. Liz sends her another message, which reads: *There are a bunch of pressed flowers in your boxes, and plant books. Pick them up when you come?* While Nell navigates to WhatsApp, she sends another message and deletes it. Nell only catches, *I remember.*

Her resolve wavers. She almost calls Liz. When they shared a bedroom, back before they were sick, they would lie on Nell's bed together and tell each other secrets. Liz had four-year-old secrets, like *I don't like tomatoes,* and Nell had eight-year-old secrets, like *a boy kissed me in the playground and his mouth was like a scaly, cracked lizard, sticking out its tongue.*

But nobody would believe her secrets now. She researches the likelihood of plants growing through epidermis. From her first search term, frenzied hours pass, her research branching into ever more niche content. As a teen she got a fungal nail infection which lasted months and annoyed her so much she had nightmares about amputating her toe. She begins there, remembering what it was like to have something distinctly not-you growing within you. She learns about candida yeast infection of the mouth; thrush; and tinea versicolor, in which stark circles of ash-white or purple grow across the skin. Eumycetoma presents as wet nodules and bone disfigurement. When the photos of fungus make her nauseous, she moves onto learning about a man who inhaled a sweet pea, which sprouted into a shoot in his lung. Toxic plants recolour blood vessels and birth weeping ulcers, while seeds become lodged in intestinal tracts and burrow their way into vital organs.

Lauren Du Plessis

By the time Nell falls asleep, old tears crust her eyes. She feels as sodden and eternal as the house itself.

Sunday inches into Monday, and the routines reset: the morning chatter, the car engine barking as Bill turns the ignition, the guest house groaning around its residents.

All night, more thistles tried to break through. Nell's skin stretches in taut points like a circus tent. She squashes a large, red lump – under her right breast – to stunt its growth. Pain flames through her torso, and she presses harder anyway. She reminds herself that pain is only electrical signals, and that all of this is only an invention of her mind. But by the time her colleagues' voices are audible outside, the lump has swollen, as if out of spite. She fights to control her breathing. Long exhale.

It is Monday, this pain does not exist, and she must get back to the real world. She will go back to the site, and she will do her job, and she will find a way to apologise to Gunner. Nell goes to the bathroom.

She ties her hair into Dutch braids, the way she and Liz practised on each other during long, eventless weekends in their preteen years – starting high up and gathering as they went. This was after their relationship began to cool, and Nell always sensed Liz would have rather done makeovers with her friends. However, like Nell, she didn't have many friends. In primary school, Liz came home with swears scrawled by other hands on her exercise books, but in secondary school she came home with bruises. Nell didn't understand why the other children bullied Liz, and not herself. Both girls were equally weird, by society's standards. But Liz was small, fragile since her illness, and an easier target than Nell, who was tall and bandy, had learned makeup techniques to appear older and untouchable, and who once hissed at a classmate. Occasionally the neighbours' kids would come over to watch TV for a couple of hours, but either they never wanted to overstay their welcome, or the welcome was cut short by their parents. *Off you go, your mother will be worried!* And so, Nell and Liz were each other's whole worlds.

Nell sprays her perfume and tries to refocus on the present, gathering the scattered petals of her mind. Because it cannot be real, can it? She can't *really* have a skin condition that makes thistles grow out of her. She must have heatstroke, hormones. Is there such a thing as hormonal psychosis, she wonders.

Nell dots a pink colour corrector beneath her eyes – her mother always said she had a suggestion of green in her complexion, and it only seems worse now. She massages BB cream into the apples of her cheeks, and carves out the V-shape of her chin. Next, some concealer. A dusting of highlight wherever her bones protrude. She strokes clear mascara onto her lashes. A dab of lip balm, and done. She creeps back to her room with her makeup bag and towel, which is beginning to smell of damp.

There's a knock at her door, and Gunner calls through. "Nell? We're going."

She extends her exhale and follows the breath to its end. Perhaps she learned the technique from a book, or her therapist. She doesn't have many useful memories from her teen years – just Dutch braids, and the long exhale, anchors she can always return to. All she needs, to ride the hallucination out, is the assurance of her own breath.

Bill stops her by the car. "Good to have you back today, Nell! Do you feel better?"

"Much better, thanks," she says.

Gunner sits in the passenger seat, Nell in the seat behind him. The scab sticks out above his collar, on the right side of his neck. A speckled clot of blood. So close to the arteries around his jugular. Nell plays with the word *jugular* in her mind as the path roughens beneath them, before coming to her senses and shaking the heavy syllables away. As they approach the farm, patches of dawn-red flash by Nell's eyes, like lanterns lining the borders of the fields.

When the team arrives, they can see Beth spraying crops from a small tractor in the distance. They cross the field with their tools under a curious sky. Blears of orange-scarlet, like burning fingers reaching down to stroke their heads. Nell feels the heat penetrating, reaching down and down for whatever grows beneath their feet.

It's week three. The original trenches now have a range of stepped excavations within them, and more shallow test pits have been opened around the field. Ingrid points at the assistants.

"We'll have you lot on the first burial location. Botanists, work on the second. Now the fuss is over, I want to see random sampling like it's going out of fashion."

Bill nods and sits in a folding chair near the head of the trenches with his tablet, making notes.

The bodies are gone now, leaving behind the mat of plants. Gunner climbs into Tria's trench and squats to begin measuring spots to take samples. Nell lowers

Tender

herself to join him, sucking the smell up her nose and letting it nestle in the cavity inside. Everything in the trenches is cast in dark brown, almost too dark to make out her colleague's silhouette. With the safe cover of dim light, Nell can stretch and dig and not worry about the odd jab of pain from her body.

"So, I assume that was the first time you've bitten someone," Gunner says, so quietly it takes Nell a moment to register the words. She stops digging.

"Gunner, I don't—"

"I'm going to keep bothering you until we talk about it. You don't have to be so embarrassed."

"I'm not embarrassed. I'm," Nell searches for the right word, "mortified. Horrified. If there was some way I could just disappear…"

"Don't disappear. Who would motivate me to get up at four in the morning?"

"*You* knocked on *my* door," she reminds him.

"Ah, but it was the prospect of waking you that woke me up."

Nell's voice falls to a murmur. "Are you flirting? Don't you think I'm a freak?"

Gunner laughs shamelessly, and says, "I think I'm only here once. And okay, I didn't *expect* you to bite me, but I'm also kind of… intrigued. So, now that's out of the way, here's a question: what is your favourite ice cream flavour?"

"Ice cream flavour? Are we done talking about the biting?"

"Well, if you bite me again, maybe we can talk about it again. For now, answer the question."

Lauren Du Plessis

An unsettling shiver thrills its way through Nell's stomach. "Strawberry. I know: boring."

"It fits your aesthetic, though. After work, I'm buying you strawberry ice cream."

"No, please let me pay. It's the least I can do."

Gunner leans close, and Nell can feel him smile against her ear. The thistles throb, and she fights the waxing urge to turn and kiss him.

In the fourth hour, the heat sets in. The ground reacts by drying out, moisture retreating downwards. Even with the early start, it won't be long before they're covering the site, irrigating it again. The forecast is over thirty-two degrees celsius.

When no one is looking, Nell sets down her tools. She needs distraction from the itchy idea of her work partner's lips. And there's more to be found here, she knows, and they won't find it in five weeks with a soft brush and tweezers.

The peat crumbles and seeps into the maze of her fingerprints. She begins to pick, then to shovel with her hands, now adept at using the scoops of her acrylics like tiny trowels.

"You've gone rogue!" Gunner reaches over to punch her arm, but she flinches away. "Bill and Ingrid would have something to say."

This idea is both anxiety-inducing and laughable. "So don't tell them then," she replies.

The ground comes up like tofu, filling buckets. Gunner pauses now and then to sift layers through a net basket, but Nell can't peel herself from the ever-darkening earth beneath her.

Before long they turn up another bone. A shoulder

Tender

blade. They call the others over, take photos, find more pieces. It isn't Tria, Ingrid says. This one is the earth's half-memory of a body, missing most of its skeleton, missing the bigger picture.

Later, Ingrid finds a vertebra and a pelvic bone in one of the new test pits. She glorifies their astonishing preservation and makes sure everyone beholds them before laying them out in the marquee. The quickness of the discoveries lights a fire beneath their feet, and the whole team begins to move like one, flickering thing. They talk as quickly as they work, sharing flashes of their lives far away from here; how Ingrid's 'long-suffering' husband puts up with her list-making, how Gunner's next dream destination is the Grand Shrine of Ise in Japan's Mie prefecture, how Bill has missed his monthly delivery of journals and will need to drive into Birmingham to pick them up when he gets back.

Nell listens, and progresses downwards. She digs so far that the ache of her forearms and back are enough to dampen the root system of pain webbing across her chest. It is some time before a heavy hand lands on her shoulder, as she climbs from the trench.

"Nell." It's Bill. "Look at the state of you! I think it's time for a break."

Ingrid places a foil-wrapped sandwich in her hands, and Nell sits. There are even more flowers beneath her shirt now than there were in the morning. Four, perhaps five, she guesses from where the cotton catches and tugs. So, what's the trigger? She can't risk inspecting them, but she senses how much worse they are, and is no longer convinced that they are pure delusion.

Lauren Du Plessis

"Hi? Are you in there?" Mia's hand blinks past her face. "Beth said there's a stream at the edge of the farm. Want to come with? It might cool us off."

Nell's shoes crack through the stubby grass of their field, and the next, until she and Mia reach the stream. Beth has beaten them there, sitting on the bank and tugging steel-toed boots off her feet. A vein on her forehead rises with the effort.

The stream is so quiet you wouldn't know it was there, though it is over three metres wide, and runs all the way to a false horizon formed by hedgerow. Nell remembers the patchwork of fields she drove over to arrive at the farm, like so many chloroplasts. Yet again, she gets the sense of being observed, like everyone on the farm is a speck on the surface of agar jelly in a lab. She tries to blink the thought away and refocuses on the grass beneath her. She pauses where the ground softens, while Mia dumps her mac and her shoes.

Mia wades knee-deep into the water, and Nell watches. They haven't spoken much, beyond *good mornings* and the sanitary towel incident. She's a Masters student, as far as Nell knows, but seems far too energetic for it. Her gait is light, her voice eager.

Nell leans over the edge of the bank. It's deep enough to wash, or play, or even drown in, if you fell. She privately speculates about how many feet have stepped in, over hundreds if not thousands of years.

Mia hitches her corduroy pinafore to her hips, and bunches the fabric, securing it with hair bands. Her legs gleam golden and spotless: laser-treatment spotless.

Tender

Probably a similar routine to Nell's. She stands on her left leg, swirling the right from side to side.

Jealousy sweeps quickly through Nell. She wishes her body was as smooth as a pebble, and able to jump into a stream with blissful abandon. She dips her boot into the water, watching the surface tension dimple around it. She can't get in, however well-protected the thistle wounds are. That would be asking for trouble.

"Is it clean?" she asks Beth.

Beth nods and shrugs at the same time. "Better than a pond. Worse than a swimming pool."

Nell sits, the needlelike ends of the grass poking her. She takes a photo of the light on the water for Instagram, then pulls off her boots and balls one sock in each. Her legs are nothing to be ashamed of. They are hairless and as elegant as Mia's, with no sign of any impossible flowers. Taking a deep breath, she taps the water with her big toe. It is pleasurably tepid.

"Come on," Mia says, "lunch break will be over by the time you're in here."

Nell drops her toes, the sole of her foot, then her ankle. She tries to relax her shoulders, but her teeth remain clenched. She searches for any bumps, and hardly trusts her eyes when she doesn't see any.

"This feels like the summers before the pandemic," Mia says, dropping to a seat in the water.

"How so?" Nell watches every movement of her shirt as she takes a step from the bank, making sure the cotton doesn't catch on the shape of a thistle.

"I used to go wild swimming. Something about the coldness of a lake makes your body feel alive like nothing else I've ever experienced."

Lauren Du Plessis

The riverbed is softer than Nell expected, silty and unstable as she walks out to where milfoil and other aquatic plants tickle her skin. Goosebumps rise all over her body. She hugs her elbows, holds herself small and close, hopes the other two won't be able to detect the petals curling underneath her shirt. Surely no more will bloom? She checks for new eruptions with every step.

As they wade towards the centre, she leans to avoid splashes; one misplaced drop carrying the wrong kind of bacteria could infect the wounds, if it gets through her bandages. Mia gestures for her to go further. She shakes her head and tries to distract herself from the nerves with a new topic.

"How are you finding the dig?"

Mia's expression turns soft and luminous. "Brilliant. I've never done anything like this. I wondered if digs would happen anymore after the last few years! The present is so all-consuming, nowadays. Do people still care about the past?"

"Did you find the lockdowns difficult?" Nell asks.

"Torture. I'm an extrovert, at least an ambivert, so not seeing my friends for a year and a half almost drove me crazy. And my flat – oh my god, my flat! I was an absolute mess for the entire time, 'cause I felt very low. When my parents came over, I think I shook them to their cores. And it's not got better, either – I'm still a mess, it's like some kind of trauma. How d'you find it?"

"I guess I never reflected on it. Maybe I was relieved." She regrets her choice of phrase as Mia raises her eyebrows. "Obviously not at all the suffering, all of the terrible things that happened. It was terrifying. But I mean, relieved I

Tender

didn't have to keep up a pretence?" The words won't stop coming and the goose pimples harden further, the flowers stirring. Nell presses her hands over them, playing up a shiver. "I've always found the world quite overwhelming."

"Wow, really? I'd never guess you were an anxious person." Mia reties a loose strand of hair. "I actually read your paper about weeds during research for an essay once. I could so easily be intimidated by you and Gunner, Ingrid and Bill. It feels so weird being all the way out here with you all."

"You're from London, right? Are you homesick?"

She tilts her head. "I guess." The movement loosens her hair, half of which tumbles down. She gives up, releases the clip, and shakes it out. "Is that dumb? We've only been here a couple of weeks. But I've never been away for work before. I'm used to people everywhere. It's so *quiet* here."

Nell lets her eyes drift over the playful reflected light to where it catches Beth's legs. Unlike Mia and Nell, Beth leaves a fine down of hair on her skin, which catches tiny spheres of the river. Of course she does – she is a farmer, not a model, Nell reminds herself. But the hair is silken, and shines in the light.

Beth leans over the bank and picks at something. Plants. She tugs them free, bundles a few into a bouquet, then places them on the bank before starting on a new batch. Nell wants to ask what they're for, but Mia speaks again.

"How are you doing? How about you and Gunner?"

"What about me and Gunner?" Nell doesn't think they've touched each other in front of the others the entire time. Everything has been hidden in the trees, in the undergrowth. Perhaps, if anything more was going to happen between them, they would have to keep it to their floor of the guest house.

"Nell! It's obvious how he follows you round, all puppy-dog eyes."

Mia means the comparison to be endearing, Nell knows. But puppies are all tooth and saliva.

"He likes you. He told me so."

Nell could be gossiping with a sister – not Liz, of course, by their teenage years they didn't speak much. The flicker of control, of being wanted, gives Nell the kind of mid-teen excitement she never really experienced. The largest thistle, the one on her pelvis, resists its gauze and oozes with growing pains. She turns and wades to the bank.

"Maybe we should head back."

Mia isn't done, though – she sighs happily and lets herself sink into the water.

"We should all hang out one day," she says. "We could invite Ingrid, too. Wouldn't it be fun to have a girl's day?"

Beth laughs. "Not if you catch a cold. Did you bring a change of clothes?"

"A cold? Even in a heatwave?" Mia weighs up the risk for a moment, looking downstream, but shrugs and sinks deeper.

Checking back every so often to ensure she hasn't been abandoned, Mia paddles back and forth. Even at its deepest the stream is no more than hip height, so she can claw along the bottom with her toes to push off, and doggy-paddle short distances. Her hair, now half-wet, spills behind her in iridescent brown-black waves.

The moment is picturesque, Nell thinks, and feels like it needs protecting. Mothers must feel like this while they watch their children. Some mothers. No, she decides, all mothers. They just act on the feeling in different ways.

As Nell watches, her mind wanders back to her flat during the pandemic. She had rarely invited people over beforehand, but as the lockdowns came and went she had no visitors in almost a year. Even then, she kept the place sparkling clean. Her clothes were folded in the drawers, the dishes stacked on the draining rack and put away as soon as they were dry. Who had she been trying to impress? She talked about not wanting to keep up appearances, and yet had kept up every appearance at home. A place where she should have felt safe, where she should have been free to be as messy as Mia claims to be.

Underneath their plasters, the thistles twitch, runners tugging on each other. What would she experience if she let everything inside her run free? Nell can't remember going so quickly from elation to curiosity to panic in her life. She wonders if this is why the thistles are growing: an overabundance of emotion. She has always tried to keep her emotions in check, because harsh facial expressions cause wrinkles, but also because life is easier when it isn't powered by drama.

She focuses on her exhale, and checks her watch to find that lunch is over.

A couple of metres away Beth collects her bounty in her fists, stems dangling behind her, dripping much-needed water onto the parched ground.

The road to the shop is lined with hedgerow, so Gunner and Nell bear left, searching the road ahead for cars. Gunner tells a story about the Sonoran Desert.

Walking behind him, Nell clasps her hands under her armpits. She can't remember whether she put deodorant on before leaving the guest house. She was either too distracted by the thistles, or her skin has absorbed it. She draws one hand to her face to sniff, getting a sting of body odour. She keeps her arms glued to her sides.

They first pass the cluster of cottages, which are stitched together with archways leading to effusive green gardens. Then, the houses dip back from the road, marked by tall wooden gates with even numbers, and names like Meadowview and The Old Barnhouse. These houses are large, detached, and several have been freshly rendered, perhaps to hide the same ivy damage that afflicts the cottages.

Nell gasps and raises her hand to her chest when Dr Shaw steps out from the final gate, a grey one, cut with a glass slit.

"It's the archaeologists," the doctor observes. "Are you better, Elinor?"

"Doctor Shaw," Nell says. "This is Gunner, the botanist who came with me the other day."

"Yes, hello," Shaw says, before turning back to Nell. "Better?"

Nell reaches for Gunner with her little finger, brushing his hip. "Can I meet you at the shop? I want to check something."

She endures the childish sense of abandonment as he walks away. The growling tiger print of Gunner's shirt blends into the bushes and vanishes, before her heart begins to shudder against her ribcage.

Nell takes a step towards Shaw.

Tender

"It's worse," she says. "Something is happening to me – something weird. I can't find anything online like it, I didn't even know it was possible…"

"Listen, I'm popping to the market today, but I'll be back in my office tomorrow. If you call when the phone lines open, we might have a slot."

"Can't you look now?"

"Look at what? Have you developed a rash?"

Nell reaches for her top button. "It's the lump… and now there's more than one lump. But they've opened up…"

"They what?" Shaw frowns, waving her hands as if warning Nell not to open her shirt.

She disobeys. Nell pulls the fabric apart and lifts the topmost plaster. "Look! Look at them! I have flowers growing out of me!"

Shaw releases a single exasperated sigh, and pulls Nell through her front gate, checking around in case someone saw. "Pull yourself together, please. There's nothing there."

Nell stands on the tidy gravel of this stranger's path, holding her shirt open in some combination of shock and defiance. It feels like she is eight feet tall, revealing herself as some sort of fantastical creature.

"Yes, there is," she says.

Shaw reaches forward, closes Nell's hands and her shirt together. "Please make an appointment for tomorrow, Elinor. I don't see *anything* to worry about. But if you would like to discuss some sort of mental health support…"

Blood, or whatever noxious substance is inside her, rushes to Nell's head. Her cheeks heat and her brain flares. "Doctor Shaw, they are right there. The thistles."

Lauren Du Plessis

"Who can I call to come and get you?" Shaw threatens.

Nell's arms fall to her sides. She forms the words *you don't see them*, although she isn't sure they make a sound. Shaw gives her a cursory pat on the shoulder, and recites the surgery's phone number. The sounds float around them, landing nowhere.

Nell absorbs the facade of the house: clean render, and floor-to-ceiling windows, which frame a Peloton, largely empty bookcases, and abstract pendant lights. It's too much like the house she grew up in. As the silent seconds pass, she imagines Shaw has a daughter, and one of the upstairs rooms belongs to her. In Nell's teenage room, there were pink clouds painted on the cream walls, and a poster that read, in pastel calligraphy, *Give a girl the right pair of shoes, and she can take over the world.*

Shaw is not going to help. From the moment Nell arrived here, her reality somehow branched away from everyone else's. To her, and only her, the thistles are real. She draws a deep breath, tries to accept this in one sour gulp, and closes her shirt.

"I'm sorry for disturbing you," she says, her throat constricting.

VI

Nell wakes to wet sheets. Her sleep-drugged thoughts wade through the possibilities: she has wet the bed, or the guest house has finally capsized – her room submerged in the fen. Now it's everywhere, in everything, the waters risen once more, eating the hamlets and leaving islets of the larger towns. She imagines Glastonbury-on-sea.

But a draught through the window cements reality. She sits up, and even in the early dawn the dark red circle is undeniable. She's two weeks late, but her period has begun.

Sunday arrives as she rinses her sheets in cold water, as quiet as she can, while the others sleep. She hangs the result beside her window, and sits on her floor with her phone propped against a bed post, sucking in her stomach in time with a deep-breathing ritual.

Tuck the pelvis, activate the core, extend the spine. Find length in the back of your neck. Imagine a string from the crown of your head, pulling you up like a puppet. She fights the searing of the flowers as she stretches. *Nobody can see you*, she tells them, *so disappear.*

She was hoping that with her period, the flowers and pain would evaporate, as Shaw had suggested in their first meeting. But as she runs her hands over her body, following the massage routine on screen, her skin pimples and distorts under her touch. Pale bumps on her stomach and back join into twists, like bulbous veins from one flower to the next bud. Traitorous lines encircle her chest, advancing towards her neckline. Ornate whorls of spiky leaves sprout along them, marking where the next thistle is threatening to appear. The leaves are new, a deep emerald green, and their sharpness terrifies her. They catch on their plasters, harder and harder to hide. She has to apply the adhesive tabs so carefully, tucking foliage under plastic. It seems pointless to bother so much after Shaw made it clear that only Nell could see them, but she can't leave the nauseating things alone. Perhaps she is mad, but the madness is growing and she can't think of another way to stop it.

When she has settled her breathing, and her aching pelvis, Nell scrolls through Instagram. Gunner has added a photo of himself with Unum and Duo's trench. No identifying details, but his huge smile informs his followers of a successful day. She pauses on his face for a moment, then clicks through to his profile. Before she met him, she saw vistas and landscapes. Now, she sees women. His hiking friend has elven features and a forest of brown hair. His 'London crew' features a snowdrop-white girl with a reddish bob, who wears bras with suits, and nothing else. Contained within each landscape is a triumphant Gunner and a companion. He does love beautiful things.

Other than the moans and shuffles of sleep, the guest house is silent. Gunner is a heavy sleeper, the sort of person who could sleep on a plane, or during a loud thunderstorm. Though he wakes up early, whenever she

Tender

passes the door at night she hears snoring. This is why Nell can sneak through his door across the hallway, which is open, without panic overriding her.

She doesn't go in, not completely. She clutches the door frame, and peeks around to look at him. As if he knew he was going to be observed, Gunner is lying on his side and facing her. His full lips are parted even now, revealing his incisors. His nostrils flare every few breaths, as he inhales the sunrise. Unruly hairs curl at the side of his face, near his ear, and his thick eyebrows are mussed. He is carnal and luxuriant.

A few minutes pass, then Nell goes back to her room when he stirs. She is a noiseless fire. It has been a long time since she has wanted someone the way she wants Gunner. She wants to graze his cheek tenderly and bite his neck again. She has felt this way once before, with a man she slept with a few times near the beginning of university. Sex was a fresh discovery for her, and she had been the perfect plaything for a fuckboy. She didn't tell anyone about it, and when they were having sex she disappeared into him, in the best possible way. She split open into a half-her, half-him thing, and she was suffering the brief belief that she could be someone else, so she never said no. She didn't make any noise during sex, beyond tempered breaths and cautious gasps. It was him who broke things off, saying he was seeking that special connection, which Nell was not. Marco the physicist had been kinder, and she felt safer in his arms, but she did not burn for Marco. Sex with him was even quieter, a bored kind of quiet, although she would never have said anything like that to him. He was sweet. They bought little gifts for each other in a constant back and forth. But she always felt like she was acting, rather than being, the perfect girlfriend.

It is the end of their third week, which they allocated to be a 'girl's day' for Mia. After scanning through Gunner's online presence until she hears everyone else getting up, Nell ties her wrap dress, knee-length with pleats, with shorts underneath to thoroughly conceal the growths. She pairs it with pink ankle socks and trainers. They might go for a walk, take in some sights with Beth as their local guide.

Across the hall, Gunner answers his ringing phone, murmuring at first, then bickering. He rasps like a threatened cat, back arched. She has never heard him like that before, and it replaces her desire with intrigue for a moment. She decides to shake off her nighttime fantasies and go downstairs.

The assistants' and Ingrid's rooms are on the floor below. Through the open doorway, she peeks at Mia's outfits hung from the curtain rail in a cheerful yellow room with a floral printed suitcase lying open by her bed. Next door, Ingrid is sitting in bed with a mug of tea, a book printed in small, dense text open in her lap. On her bedside table sits a pile of novels with dark covers and one-word names.

"Is your book good, Ingrid?" Mia grins, joining Nell in the corridor.

"So-so. I'm usually a fan of this author, but there isn't enough tension in this one."

"That's a shame. I like a good domestic thriller."

"Oh, do you? I prefer eco, or political. Fiction is the only place I like danger."

"Are you coming today, Ingrid?" Nell asks, noting her pyjamas.

Tender

Ingrid bites the skin beside her thumbnail. "Sorry, ladies. I had one too many drinks last night on the porch. Beauty sleep is in order."

Nell hadn't even noticed the chatter which must have risen to her window from the back porch last night. They pass through the kitchen on their way out and there are five glasses drying beside the sink. It would be the first night that the group weren't all together to drink, and Nell wonders briefly who got an invite and who didn't.

Mia doesn't drive, so they get in Nell's car. Nell pushes the car into reverse and backs out of the guest house driveway.

"Do you have any tips for thesis proposals? I want to make a start on mine soon," Mia says, settling in the passenger seat where a bar of sunlight catches her left eye, lighting it topaz.

"I don't know. I was always told mine were flowery. Oh, pun unintentional. But I guess you should be direct, and concise."

"I love a pun! Do you have any good uni stories?"

"Sorry to disappoint. I just wanted to fit in, so I guess I didn't get up to much."

"Come on. Field trip drama? A hot professor? Nothing?" Mia checks the gap in her teeth in the side mirror, then smiles at herself.

Nell thinks. "I lived with three other girls. We did each other's makeup, got blackout drunk on Friday nights. Uni stuff." She remembers lights in her eyes, endless limbs, bodies overflowing with booze and blood. It had been a little like the feeling of kissing Gunner. All the edges thrown out. But then she had to wake up the next morning with dread smeared under her eyes. What had she done, who had she been?

"Do you keep in contact?"

"With two of them, for Christmas brunches, picnics in the summer. They live in London with their partners. I wrote a chapter for Billie's book about flowers."

"Oh! *The Secret Life of Wildflowers*? I've been meaning to read it. What about the other woman?"

"Well, the last time I saw *her* in person she pulled some of my hair out." Nell doesn't mention she scratched Stephanie across the face. Or that the fight happened because Nell had been using Steph's expensive perfume to calm her nerves before exams.

"I think a friend can hurt you more than a romantic partner. Maybe it's worse because we understand each other better, so we know how to hurt each other. Kind of unfair, right? The people you're closest to are the ones who can hurt you most."

It's then, two minutes before they reach the farm, on a narrow corner turning, when the car lurches left. The suspension jars, and something tangles around the wheel.

"What was that?" Mia says.

Nell brakes. "I don't know." She opens the door, peering back with dreadful, instinctual awareness in her throat.

A small body lies in the road.

"It's a rabbit! Or a hare?" Mia leaps from the car and approaches it. It's huge, definitely a hare. "Oh my god, is it alive?"

Nell walks towards the body, watching the last puffs of air leave the hare's lungs. Its eyeball scrolls up and down, side to side, before stopping on Nell, where it freezes.

Tender

She echoes the same words, again and again.

"Oh my god."

She squats. The hare is on its side, front and back legs outstretched like it was paused in the act of running. Mid-brown fur with a white belly, crops of dark brown around the face and shoulders. The eye is a deep, glassy orange, brighter than Mia's but similarly innocent.

"I'm so sorry," she says, her voice flatter than she means it to be. She feels remorse, of course. She says it again. "I'm sorry." The thistles flex in her skin.

"What do we do?" Mia asks. "Do we have to tell someone about this? Should we try and move it?"

Nell's voice still sounds disembodied to her. "I guess a fox will come and eat it."

"Maybe Beth will know."

They get back in the car, drive the final minute, and turn towards the farm. Beth is already out front, watering plants.

Nell pulls up and edges out of the car, hiding behind the door until the last moment. This is Beth's world, and she has killed a part of it.

"Beth!" Mia calls. "We hit a hare! What do we do?"

We, Nell notices. Mia doesn't implicate her. She even puts a hand on Nell's shoulder.

"Shit, that's rough," Beth says. "You sure it's dead?"

Nell nods.

Beth strokes her chin. "Was it big?"

Nell holds her hands fifty centimetres apart.

"Let's not waste it, then." Beth puts her gardening gloves back on, strides over the path and turns out of sight. Nell finds herself following with unsure steps.

Returning to the scene feels disrespectful at best, gross at worst. Shouldn't it be left for predators and bacteria to gnaw through?

"I know," Beth says over her shoulder. "Not how you thought girls' day would start. But we'll sort this. I've done it before, don't worry."

She squats to inspect it, then pulls a plastic bag from her pocket.

"I didn't mean to kill it," Nell says. "I didn't even know it was there. It must have jumped out so fast."

"Nell, you look like you're about to throw up. You clearly didn't mean to do it. Besides," Beth lifts it by each set of legs, transferring it into the bag, "he's huge, probably lived a great long life. It's sad, sure, but this is Mother Nature, right?"

"How is my car Mother Nature?"

"Way I see it, humans can't escape being a part of this. We are natural, ergo everything we do is also natural. All the horrible stuff, all the great stuff, it's just *stuff*."

Nell isn't sure she's ever done anything so wrong in her life. She watches Beth walk back to the house, dead hare knotted in the translucent bag.

"The important things are: fresh, not allowed to spoil in the heat, no sign of disease. This time of year, you get it gutted quick so no bacteria can spread. Then you cook it, a lot."

Beth slaps the hare down on a wooden work surface in one of the sheds and cleans it off. Mia has already gone into the house to make tea, leaving Nell and Beth alone with the dead creature.

Tender

Beth makes the first cut. The slit runs from between its back legs up to its collar bones, a thick browning line. The body flops as she turns it to check for other wounds or issues. Then, without warning, she applies her knife to the top of its right hind leg, finds the meeting of skin and innards, and gently rips the skin from the hare. Within twenty seconds, its torso is a blue-white, hairless nightmare, and two wads of fur bunch at each end. The body turns black-speckled-red towards the neck, and after clearing the last of the fur from the area, Beth beheads it.

She splays it on its back to cut off the four feet.

"It's clean," Nell mutters.

"Won't bleed once it's dead," Beth says.

She makes large cuts for the back legs, snaps off the front ones, then massages the torso, clearing out a dark sludge.

"This is where you hit it," she says. "See here? That's blunt force damage I reckon."

Nell inhales, exhales. *I didn't mean to,* she repeats to herself.

Beth finishes by removing four neat fillets from the breast and stomach: dark and uniformly pink meat that could be shrink-wrapped at the supermarket. At last, it doesn't resemble an animal anymore.

Beth leaves and returns with a Tupperware box and a plate. "I'll freeze the legs. Put the breast on here, I'll use it for dinner."

Nell holds her breath and uses the tip of a knife, its handle still warm from Beth's touch, to transfer the meat onto the plate. It is soft and malleable as a tongue.

Lauren Du Plessis

*

"I'm sorry, I didn't know what to make tea with!" Mia laughs, holding up the boiled kettle and some empty mugs.

"Ah, sorry. I've started drying my own," Beth smiles, veering towards the bricked fireplace display. She assesses two large mason jars and chooses the second. The dense, dried mixture within it is a tangle of large, dark leaves and small, white flowers.

"Nettle," Nell guesses, "and camomile?"

"Close. Daisy."

Nell and Mia sit on the sofa while Beth takes a seat in a tall chair with frayed armrests and spoons the fragrant mixture into tea strainers. Nell takes her saucer in both hands, then lifts the teacup to take a smell as it brews. It has the greenest smell she could imagine. It is so green her stomach lifts, and the thistles ache pleasantly, like pulled muscles.

"Did you grow up here, Beth?" Mia asks, getting a nod in response. "What was it like?"

"Like any other countryside childhood, I think. Quiet, not many friends around. We had a dog for a long time, when I was small and we still kept sheep. The farm's been in the family for generations."

"Do you have any animals now?"

"We switched over to crops when I was a kid. The marshes change over time. Certain parts become dryer, others get boggier. For us the ground softened, and keeping animals wasn't sanitary."

"Did you help out on the farm as a kid?" Mia blows across the top of her tea.

Tender

"Oh, yeah, everyone was expected to help. My two older brothers did too. But one moved to Bristol, and the other's travelling now."

"But you didn't want to leave?"

"No. After my dad died, he left the farm to us. My brothers weren't interested in keeping it up, but for me, I don't have any other talents, and to be honest I'm not interested in anything else either. We've downsized obviously. And like I said I have some local lads who work for me. But on some days it's me alone on the farm, and I like it."

"I remember you saying when we first met," Nell says, "it's not the kind of place where you get lonely. What did you mean?"

"I mean that exactly. There's way too much going on around here. You saw what we did with the hare. This is what it's like out here."

Nell studies the kitchen, which seems overgrown with herbs and vegetables.

"Nell's jealous." Mia smiles. "She was just saying to me how she's always been quiet, too. You guys are very similar, but under different circumstances."

"Oh, yeah?" Beth says, looking at Nell. "Would you ever want to move out somewhere like this?"

Nell turns her gaze out of the back French doors, over the grass, the trench and marquee in the distance, and the crop fields beyond that. "As a kid I used to go into this field by my parent's house, though I wasn't supposed to. It's up the road, actually, but my sister lives there now and I haven't been yet, she's busy with her kids. I used to run around in there and feel... free. Maybe I could live somewhere like this again. I guess it never occurred to me."

"Why weren't you supposed to go in there? Was it someone else's?" Beth asks.

"Abandoned, I think. It was the only rule I always broke. There were a lot of rules in our household."

"Same. My dad used to scare the shit out of me sometimes. He loved us, but he had no idea how to be in good relationships. He and my mother used to hit each other – never us – but she got out as soon as we were grown. They were messed up."

Mia, who has been sipping her tea, stops to say in a more anxious voice, "I'm sorry Beth. That's horrible to deal with. It's like what we were saying in the car, Nell. People you love can hurt you most."

Beth shrugs. "Probably because they care *too* much and they don't know how to show it. I think when you don't know how to express something, nature takes over. But your nature is something that can always been tended to, and worked with. My parents just never got round to that whole self-improvement thing."

"You think violence is natural?" Nell asks.

"All I can say is what I've seen. Seems pretty ingrained to me. Like I said, you can try to transform it, but I don't think it can ever go away completely."

Mia's cup clinks against her saucer. "I don't understand why anyone would ever harm someone else on purpose. I wish…" She trails off. All three fall quiet and sip their nettle and daisy teas. Then Mia speaks again. "Who wants to go for a walk? I want to see the fifteenth-century cottage you were talking about the other day, Beth."

On the way out the front door, Nell catches Beth. "I feel

so guilty, it's kind of making my body panic." She wishes she could stop thinking about the hare, but she can't.

"I think that's a healthy reaction."

The words keep coming. "It's almost... like I've done something like this before. I was lost. My sister Liz was there. It was when we got sick, and it was my fault somehow. I just felt, like, fear and shock. And my mum shook me until my brain hurt. Sorry, I don't mean to..."

"Whoa, it's okay," Beth soothes. "Sounds like your parent's reaction was worse than anything you did."

Nell grasps her stomach, and whimpers against her will. The thistle runners twist over each other. Beth touches her arm. Nell puts her own hand on top. Pressure builds in her fingertips, as if the runners want to reach out from her body to Beth's.

"I'm okay."

But Beth knows she's lying – it's obvious from her eyes, which permeate the surface of Nell's skin and threaten to expose whatever horrors lie beneath. Still, this is Beth. Unclear, unreadable. The look passing between them feels like a tangible weave of admiration and caution with no certainty as to which will win.

"Hang on." Beth pulls away, jogs to the kitchen and back, puts something in Nell's hand. "Now, you're going to think this is weird. But keep this in your pocket. Old Celtic folklore thing, something about hazelnut trees representing knowledge and protection from things to come. It's what my mum always gave me."

Nell strokes the smooth surface of the hazelnut, then slips it into her pocket.

Lauren Du Plessis

*

It began with one, which scrolled serpent-like into the first body, and changed itself to fit them. Before, it came from something else, something humans could never understand. But now, within its debut host, it shifted, and grew.

Then it spread, and ravaged. It moved through the bodies of the town. It was the first seed of an awful thing. Perhaps it was a quick-ripping virus that put Unum, Duo, Tria and their companions in the ground. But what if it *was* something more? Something from deep within the soil, exposed by low-lying heaths and fens, where people dug and were remade? And what if, like a retrovirus preserved in Arctic ice, this thing was still in the ground, waiting for new victims?

Nell rubs her eyes. It's two a.m. on Sunday night, and she's lying in bed thinking about violence. She can't forget Beth's words, about violence being inevitable. Could the bog bodies have been placed there with bad intentions, she wonders. Or could it have been to protect the rest of the village, from something in the ground itself?

She cannot shake the image of the hare's dead stare, of Mia's sunlit eye, of the hazelnut. She is feeling too much, again. The thistles react. Beneath her nightdress, the burning rings around her navel.

She lifts the dress over her breasts and observes as the skin turns white, then translucent, revealing the red-purple growth. Her breath catches as she braces for pain, and is surprised when the area numbs instead.

Her navel shifts, the deformed skin from where her cord was cut rippling and remaking itself. But then the

Tender

bloom sets in. A prickle comes up like a needle through fabric. Her skin stretches like latex, then rips open.

Nell finds her breath again, and counts through her exhale. The thistle edges through, complete with an unfurling leaf beside it. Its florets reach upwards, then outwards. It's large, almost two centimetres across. Tears bud at the corners of her eyes and coat her eyelashes as she blinks. The world turns hazy as the pain sharpens.

She always heaved at the brutal sensitivity of her navel, which produced a strange, bottomless pang when she pressed it. She won't miss it. But she might never get it back, not if the thistles are a permanent part of her.

The new thistle settles against the others nearby. It is a thickening cluster, and she knows it won't be long before the thistles spread beyond her torso. As soon as the growth slows, her stomach rumbles.

She hasn't eaten all day. Perhaps she was hoping that not-eating would leave her body too weak to sprout any further. She rummages through her suitcase and takes out a packet of crisps. The squeak of the plastic makes her flinch. She allows silence to settle once more before she sits on her bed and begins eating at last.

She's cleaning the salty mulch from her teeth when a knock sends fresh jabs through her. She hasn't showered, looks a mess, but covers herself and cracks open the door.

"Gunner."

"Hey. Can I come in?" He enters before she can answer. Nell closes the door and walks him to the bed, where he sinks, the metal feet groaning against the wooden boards.

Something is wrong. She sinks beside him, letting her thighs spread to brush his. Perhaps it's stupid to invite closeness when he is upset and she might be turning into a monster.

Gunner pushes his lips against hers. She buckles at first, then pushes back. He's upset, but she can't break away to ask why. They can only fight each other for breath.

Gunner wins: Nell eases herself back onto her elbows and he leans over to push her into the bed. Her thistles prick upwards as if reaching for him. Can he feel them through their clothing? If he can, he doesn't react. His weight is pushing her into the mattress, but he isn't forcing her down – he's daring her to retaliate.

When she does, wrenching upwards from her abs and putting a hand on his chest, the pain is gone from his face. Her reflection ogles back at her from the curvature of the moon on his eyes, irises turned jet black in the night. The deep breath she takes lights an acid burn under the thistles. The movement, again. It's undeniable. The harder she presses against Gunner's solar plexus, the fiercer the sting, and the more she thrills.

He's wearing the tiger print shirt, and as her hands fiddle around the buttons she stares at their gaping, toothy mouths. The silky fabric rolls off his shoulders, where lean muscles warp from his otherwise small frame.

Her hand almost snatches his away when he reaches for her nightdress, but the fabric lifts too easily. She squeezes her eyes shut, holds her breath.

The guest house air is cool. When she finally looks, Gunner is staring up at her.

"Sorry, I didn't get a chance to shower." She doesn't know what else to say. Suddenly her body is exposed, displayed for him. She has no idea what he can see, hardly

Tender

knows how to ask. The sounds of the guest house around them make her wonder what noises they must have been making together – could someone have heard? What kind of noise is she supposed to make now?

Gunner stares right at her navel, where her new and largest thistle head stares back.

"Can I?" He holds his hands a few centimetres away. Terrified, Nell nods. He places them on her waist, thumbs stretching either side of the thistles. They collapse and reform under his exploration. His fingers disappear and reappear, weaving like snakes through undergrowth. It's been a while since she totalled them, but in the silence Nell sees fourteen heads, and many more leaves.

"What do you see?" she manages. His hands are clumsy in places, pulling on the petals and making her wince, like he can't fully connect with what's in front of him.

"I don't know," he says. "Eczema? Scars? It's sort of like a pink web, like filaments. What happened?"

The acknowledgement that something truly is there is both a relief and surreal. Is Gunner really seeing more than Shaw? Nell stammers, "I can't explain it."

He releases her body and props himself up to sit. "It's okay, you don't have to."

He kisses her again. Nell relaxes. Maybe she has been overreacting after all, her mind distorting a simple rash into flowers. She kisses him back, smiling against him.

"Nell," he says, voice breaking at the end of her name, "I need… I need you. Do you want to?"

"Yes. But I'm—" She cringes. "Shit, I'm on my period."

He pauses to consider this. "How heavy?"

"I can't."

"Okay."

They return to kissing, although his hands grip tighter.

"Touch my neck," he says, eyes closed. She walks her first and middle finger up his arm, relishing the dimple of skin with each second of contact. Then she brushes them up and down over his Adam's apple.

"No, it's okay. Use your nails. It's good."

Her acrylics are claw-like in the moonlight, the thistles standing sharp on her skin. She enjoys the power of pressing one talon into the dip where his collar bones meet. Gunner makes a sound, a loud and satisfied hum that seems to come from beneath his voice box, somewhere deep in his chest. It's a bewitching sound, and she's certain that anyone awake would hear it if they listened closely enough. She wants to reply but doesn't know how yet. He sounds so free. She presses harder into his skin and waits to hear him again.

VII

When Nell is with Gunner, she understands what it is to be a flower under a botanist's eye, observed in all its beauty and strangeness. They exchange roles, from researcher to subject, depending on where they are. When they have sex in Gunner's room, which gets morning light, she takes note of the pores around his nose, the scar above his left eyebrow, and a large pockmark near his right shoulder. He tells her it was from chicken pox, and it makes her feel even safer with him, the idea that he too has had alien life growing in his skin. When they have sex in her room, bathed in carmine sunset, she lies back and allows him to study her. He cups her face, bites her lip, draws his hands over her body. Their fourth time, he presses his thumbs underneath her floating ribs, and she releases an uncontrollable laugh. He smiles so wide, and she wishes they were somewhere else, somewhere they could laugh and shout from their bellies with nobody to hear.

When they leave their floor of the guest house, they try to stay apart. From Mia's side-glances it's obvious that the others know something, but nobody pries. They are professional, until the next time they are alone.

Lauren Du Plessis

Gunner examines the thistles in the same way as they do the bodiless bones in the trenches, knowing they are something, but unable to know the full truth.

"How long have you had them?" he says on the evening of their twentieth day.

"Always," she lies.

His grip often catches on them. Even at his most gentle she twinges and smarts, and Gunner is rarely gentle. He isn't rough, either, but searching, always searching. His fingers scour through her leaves, as if he's working his hands through thick grass. Now and then, he flinches, pricked by an unseen spike. Somehow, his mind glosses over it, and he never takes his hands away.

In the week before the dig began, Nell had brushed up on her knowledge of bog plants. This is why the image of *Drosera rotundifolia*, the roundleaf sundew, is in her mind when he folds his arms around her again.

The sundew family uses an uncommon method of coping with acidic, nutrient-poor ground. They are carnivorous. The flat, round leaves form a rosette, which lies in wait for insects. Its leaves are covered in red, glandular hairs, which secrete a sticky substance sometimes called *rosa solis*, or dew of the sun. Visiting bugs become trapped in the dew, and the leaves curl in on themselves to encompass and digest them. If Nell finds one out in the fenland, she will show it to him.

Nell isn't trapped in Gunner's arms, but held. He curls himself around her and holds her tight enough to burst her. Then, when his arms tire, they fall apart and tear into a can of tinned peaches he bought from the store. It has become a strange habit of theirs, to take it in turns providing

Tender

saccharine post-coital snacks. The lady at the store knows them now, and she always gives Nell a funny sort of look that lands somewhere between recognition and wariness.

Heavy syrup clots around Nell's teeth and she lies back on her bed.

"I got you this, too," Gunner says, dropping something into her hand. A small tealight candle, the tin topped up with dried red petals.

"The shopkeeper said it's from a local brand. I thought you'd like it, it reminds me of your perfume."

He kisses her. Everything, from the window to her skin to the peach slices, glows in juicy gold and amber.

She is almost asleep on his chest when her phone buzzes. The messages arrive a few minutes apart, as if Liz isn't even imagining her at the other end of the encryption – only a void she can shout into.

At the first buzz, Nell rolls over and picks up her phone. It reads, *Do you remember how Mum used to decorate the living room for our birthdays? Do you think the decorations are in the attic? I don't think we have a ladder. I want this day to be perfect for Charlie.*

That reminds her. "Gunner, this might sound weird, but would you come to my niece's party? About a twenty-minute drive away. My family is… intense. I could use the company."

Gunner's voice fills her ear through his chest. "I'm always up for a party."

The second message arrives when Gunner leaves to shower. It reads, *Something's going on with David. I'm lonely.* Then she adds another, *I'm scared he's cheating on me.* But she deletes it.

Lauren Du Plessis

Nell taps the call button.

"What's going on? You should talk to David if he's upsetting you." She would never have the guts to do this, in Liz's shoes, but it sounds like appropriate advice. Liz had a boyfriend cheat on her in secondary school. She cried for a week and Nell had no idea how to comfort her, so she watched from her doorway. It must have left an emotional scar.

Liz's voice is scratchy. "Just ignore me. I can't talk right now, Elinor. I'll see you soon." She cuts the call.

The thistles tense in Nell's chest and pressure grows in her head, inflating to a sharp pain behind her eyes. Could the thistles grow there, too – burrow through her nerves and take control? She's relieved when Gunner returns, smelling of mint, and she can fold back into him once more, knowing he will be with her when she goes to the party. She won't come face to face with her strange family as her new, strange self, alone.

They lie together in the dusk air. She quakes with new growths, but having a warm body radiating next to her is soothing.

"Bristol tomorrow," he whispers.

Nell, exhausted, moans an affirmative reply.

"I can't believe we're halfway through. I'm glad we get to work together after the dig. Imagine you and me in the lab…" His arms reach for her again, folding her into position and pressing her into his body.

Halfway through. The thought makes her ache again. When they are done with the dig, and a few weeks of lab work, she will return to Milton Keynes and walk through the concrete underpasses, cross over the wide grey roads, stroll

Tender

through the gleaming shopping centres, and catch rickety buses. It feels like a betrayal to the surreal new self emerging here, this woman who is unafraid to dig through soil with her once-perfect acrylics, and who unearths new sounds from within herself each time she fucks the man lying next to her.

The first thing Bill says as they leave the front door of the guest house is, "Nell, Gunner, best behaviour, please."

"Best behaviour," says Gunner, flashing Nell a conspiratorial grin. Bill gets into the car and closes the door hard.

Nell cannot remember the last time it rained. One step into the direct sunlight cleaves her blood vessels open, fills her with fire. Ingrid's back is marked already with a growing sweat patch, deepening the coral of her blouse. Her arms blotch with sunburn, pink and red as camellia flowers, stretching around the notebooks and reports she and Bill have been preparing over the last week.

They have collated their findings so far into clear, palatable explanations for the general public and university newspapers. There will be two interviews when they get to Bristol, and a tour of the lab.

And this is my chance, Nell thinks, *my chance to make myself known here. To share how significant nature is in our history, how inseparable from our bodies.*

"Chop chop." Ingrid ushers her to an open door. She puts a hand on Nell's shoulder as she passes, almost pushing her into the seat. "There's a time and a place for everything," she says, and Nell can't meet her eyes, but stares at her drumming fingertips.

Lauren Du Plessis

When she gets in, she looks at Gunner. His eyebrows are raised, mirroring her confusion.

"What's with those two?" he murmurs.

The drive is an hour long and smooth, cutting their way back out of the Levels. They arrive over the suspension bridge, the city spilling out under the dazzling morning beneath them. The river is low, silty at the sides, like a loose seam holding the earth together. The buildings range from a sandy limestone hue to coppery and dust-brown brick. Bristol feels prematurely autumnal, with parched leaves dropping from the trees.

After they park at the bottom of Woodland Road, with the university up the hill ahead, Bill escorts them on a tour in the direction of the museum, then down streets lined with cafes, takeaways and vintage shops, to the cathedral. Between his running commentary of historical anecdotes and Ingrid's constant reminders to watch their step on uneven paving stones or grass, there's no space to talk. Still, Gunner brushes her hand whenever the others aren't looking. The broad stones beneath Nell's feet are stacked in a brick design, but they wrinkle like a great subterranean plant is stretching its roots for air.

As they cross the narrow, busy roads, Nell learns that the city's Old English name was *Brycgstow*. There's something more phonetically pleasing about the guttural catch in her throat. *Brycgstow* cuts its way through the earth, the 'bridge' as it translates. A bridge between what and what, she wonders – the rivers, of course, but maybe something else too. *Bristol* is leisurely on the tongue.

Nell leans around the others to catch glimpses of colourful graffiti, murals splaying over any wall stepped

Tender

back from the main roads. The city is handmade, hand-adjusted over time, even organic. It makes her wonder if maybe cities aren't so different from the countryside. Every corner reveals another street of stepped Georgian and Victorian buildings, like caps of a sprawling mushroom growth.

Bill continues to spew general knowledge and even raises his hand to rest against a pillar – too sentimental for him, like he left his colder, managerial side in the car. Nell feels a paradoxical fondness.

They arrive at the waterfront, a tree-lined square chunked into by a rectangular quay, stretching out towards the harbour. An unexpected gust of wind barges through from the water, taking the humans and trees by surprise. Leaves whip away while passersby grab at their caps and skirts. It's coming from the south-west, where they drove from. The trenches. Even here, Nell thinks, even here.

After lunch they return to the Department of Anthropology and Archaeology. Bill shows them through the doors and flashes his card around, then points Nell and Gunner to the laboratory.

"The supervisor is a great friend of mine," he says. "I know you're going to love it here, and she'll do everything she can to support you both. Who knows, she might even have a seminar slot for you to present our work at the beginning of the new academic year."

Gunner peers through each window like a child at a zoo, pointing out wet and dry benches, large microscopes, and endless floating bookshelves that line the walls. The ground-penetrating radar and gradiometer that Bill and Ingrid used at the beginning of the survey are pointed out, as is the archaeological chemistry laboratory with its radiocarbon mass spectrometer, which looks like a living thing itself, a system-jumble of silver cylinders with a sprawl of winding blue wires.

"I think what *you'll* be most excited about," Bill says to Nell, "is the reference collection."

He takes them into a quiet room and pulls out a long sliding drawer from an enormous filing cabinet. Inside is a grid dotted with hundreds of charred leaf fragments, all labelled with numbers and their genus. He closes it, pulls out the one below. Another tray filled with leaves, then another.

"Bristol is better known for its osteological collection, of course. They say there are over six hundred bodies here. But I'm sure you'll agree this is something special, too."

As they leave the room, Gunner catches her hand and squeezes.

"Have you ever seen anything like this? I got so used to excavation I forgot to get excited about this stage. We could work out what these people ate the day they died, how their day was going. Jesus. I bet Ingrid is going to find out how they died, too."

Nell nods, not wanting to sound arrogant, but she's been thinking about their cause of death. She can't help but suspect the evidence has been in front of them the entire time. All the time they've sunk their hands into the mud, they've been sinking into a morbid and inevitable truth.

The first interviewer is a Masters student, about Mia's age. He offers them each their seats in a plastic row, while another student tests a camera and boom mic. Ingrid leans over, asks, "May I?" Then she tugs Nell's sleeve straight and checks her hair is even on both sides. Nell struggles between two expressions: a grateful smile, or mistrustful, tight lip. There is something different about her supervisors today, a current between them charged by serious glances and extra sharpness to their movements.

The interviewer flips his notebook open, unclipping a pen from the spine, but as he begins his questioning Nell can't help but notice his eyes meet with Bill's and Gunner's. He directs his speech at them before turning to Ingrid or herself. This is nothing new to her in an academic setting, and perhaps it's nothing at all. Perhaps she's lying to herself. But the thistles are eager to deepen her sense of injustice. She opens her mouth, twitches her hand as if to raise it.

Bill and Ingrid follow the script, and for the most part Gunner does too, though more excitedly punctuated.

"What kind of experience has it been, working on such a high-profile project?"

Nell wants to answer with something reverent. *Life-changing, self-changing.* Bill answers, "A privilege. We look forward to sharing our findings with the community."

"How does this compare with your other work?"

Nell wants to explain that the budding silence of a farm is a world away from the hum of a digger on an industrial site. She'd like to say how low the wages are, compared with the importance of the discovery, and how the field should be made more tempting to new blood – more hands in the dirt, discovering stories and truths. Or how even her superiors don't understand the magic of the bodies. Ingrid says, "It is similar to bog bodies discovered in the Netherlands and Germany, but it's exciting to do the work at home."

Lauren Du Plessis

"How do you feel about funding in the field right now?"

Bill and Ingrid don't answer, so Gunner raises a hand. "Not enough. We need to invest not only in new green technologies for the future, but learn from the technologies of the past."

He nods at Nell, as if encouraging her. But when she begins with a "Well", Bill and Ingrid cut in. They let Gunner talk about water flotation, and the delicate task of removing seeds from the mass of the soil. But when it comes to the macro plant samples, they talk for her, and she nods along. "That's right." The thistles throb. The air around herself and her team has shifted. Had something happened in the past few days, some disagreement or pressure that would scatter and rearrange what she'd learned about her colleagues without her even noticing?

When the interviewer addresses her directly, asking her area of expertise, she presses against the whorling new thistles beneath her cargo trousers, and prepares her voice for battle.

"I'm most interested in how ancient people used plants, as food or something more." Ingrid's eyes snap to her. "And... I think this is an elaborate and purposeful construction of deep graves for ritualistic purposes; perhaps to keep bad spirits away from the bodies as their souls passed on, or to cleanse bodies which the village may have perceived as bad or diseased. With the grandiose detail, it's like... a ceremonial purge."

Bill clears his throat. Ingrid drums her fingers on her knees while maintaining a tight smile. Nell continues.

"Based on my knowledge of the thistle plant – the most abundant plant present in the graves – there is clear

Tender

symbolism. The thistle is known for its sharp prickles, but has a soft down after flowering. Harsh, yet gentle. They're essential for biodiversity: providing materials for all kinds of other creatures, and the people likely recognised this. The burial was sealed off as the plants were budding, probably in spring. To me, it suggests a planned occasion. It may even indicate the deaths were premeditated. Everything about the burial seems immaculate, from the bodies being placed in curled, foetal positions, to the selected plants being summer bloomers and therefore only in their bud form. I feel like this burial design is meant to represent renewal."

She catches herself. The interviewer's eyebrows are raised. Two of the bumps on her thighs crack, heads oozing through. She tries to smooth her trousers over them, but the fabric creases and bunches. The words flowed out of her like water, and it felt good. They were the most interesting spoken so far.

Ingrid smiles. "There is a lot more research to be done here. Nell, our archaeobotanist, is newer to the site. These are her initial impressions. Of course we will entertain all possibilities, but as an expert on bog bodies myself I'm excited to get back to the lab with the osteological *evidence*, and develop informed theories."

Bill claps his hands together and starts talking about a lab elsewhere in the building, where they will be working on samples from the skeletons and skin.

The interviewer does not make eye contact with Nell again.

Between interviews, tea and biscuits are brought into the room and passed around. Nell leans around Gunner and stares at Ingrid until she meets her eye.

"What did you mean when you said I've not been on site as much?" she asks.

"Well, you were ill in the first week, weren't you? And in week two you took longer lunch breaks than the rest."

"So, what are your theories?" Nell asks, feeling unusually bold. "You're not offering alternatives."

"Because that's not how it works. You can't make assumptions at this stage – that's what you learn from a full career. You need to be methodical. Especially with the media nowadays. They latch onto misinformation like vultures."

"I never said I was sure. Shouldn't we inspire people, tell them the amazing stories, and get more people into the field?"

"We are scientists, not science communicators. I'm trying to protect us all."

Nell finds one new thistle head in particular, and presses the heel of her hand into it. "I know what I'm looking at. I know what plants can mean to people."

The thistles flex and relax as she sits back in her chair.

Bill and Ingrid stay quiet until the next interviewer comes in and begins to ask the same questions.

This time, Bill and Ingrid focus on the bodies, steering the conversation away from specific discussion of thistles, and towards generalised *biomass*. Ingrid tosses her hair, which she has loosed from its claw grip.

By the time they leave Bristol the sun is achingly low in the sky, blinding them all in flashes on metal signs and on the mirrors. When they arrive outside the guest house, Ingrid takes Nell aside.

Tender

"You and I need to talk."

Nell's stomach drops. After the slow but peaceful drive back, she had assumed the tension had passed.

"We invited you for a reason. You're a bright spark. But if I don't say something now, I worry what will happen later."

Nell stares towards the red sun, an ellipse slumping over the nearby treetops. The sun casts her body in hot orange.

"First, there's your behaviour today. I'm not your boss, but I also am. If you're going to spread unscientific rumours in interviews, we're going to have a problem."

Nell balls her hands into fists.

"Then there's your unorthodox use of tools, or rather, your refusal to use them. Don't think we haven't noticed you digging in the ground with your bare hands. You're *going* to get sick again." Ingrid pauses, her sunburn tinging redder. "Then there's your... You don't appear to be taking care of yourself. I've noticed you're not using the washing machine much. I don't see you eat, if it's not from a plastic packet. And your *relationship* with Gunner... Well, I'll remind you that my bedroom is directly below yours. So, you know, if you could keep it down. We'd all appreciate it."

Flares, like lights in her eyes. Every thistle in her skin, and runner beneath it, snaps to attention. Nell slams her car door so hard the metal body rocks. Her own strength shocks her. She can't find her voice.

Ingrid's eyes widen for a second, almost like she's afraid, then edge downwards. "It's my job to look after—"

Lauren Du Plessis

Nell wants to be sick. She thinks of every moment with Gunner, every moan or laugh she'd finally let slip. How could she have been so naive, believing the night would protect them? She learned the creaks of the floorboards and echoes down the pipes from their first night at the guest house, and still she allowed herself to make those sounds. Heat surges through her. Her restraint is slipping, something darker desperate to escape her mouth.

"You're not my mother. You think you're looking out for the project?"

"Watch your tone, Nell."

"Ingrid, this is the dig of my lifetime. But you want the sole voice to be yours, or something sanctioned by you. You can't bear that I might have something interesting to say." Every thistle leaf stands on end. She feels twice her usual size. "Just because your time has passed."

The thistles retreat back into her for a second, then explode. The skin around her spine thins and breaks like overstretched chewing gum. She bubbles and tears with new blooms. The pain comes in ripples, lip after lip folding back on itself and inching over until it breaks and the next bud pushes through. She releases a yelp, an animal sound. Ingrid blinks in confusion.

Nell storms away, strangled silent again by shame.

She climbs the stairs, ignoring the calls after her, covers the length of the hallway in seconds and wrenches the bathroom door closed after her. She wedges the door shut with a towel and the doorstop. Runs the shower to boiling point, to chase the blooms back into her. How hot before they wilt? Higher, higher, until steam floods over the top of the shower door and clouds the bathroom.

Tender

Thoughts float in the vapour puffs: of Mia in the river, a soft and peaceful femininity Nell has tried to imitate, and Beth, who never seems to care and is beautiful anyway. Of Ingrid, someone she ought to admire. She feels so distant from all of them now, cut off by the growing thing within her.

This poison has spread despite every attempt to slow its onset. She has eaten only the smallest packeted things, and only when she could bear the hunger no longer, or when she has been with Gunner and forgotten herself. She has exhaled so far, keeping her body calm even as she wanted to claw her hair out with worry. And she has washed, scrubbed, soaped away all she could, day after day. But this thing has still sculpted her into a terrible new shape.

Her teeth grind together under the cleansing heat as she steps into the stream. Is she being warned, or punished? Does the marshland want her to leave, or to excavate deeper? She wonders if a curse has lain in wait for four thousand years, in the bog bodies. She lets the water and the fear saturate her. Her skin prickles. She might be crying, but her tears are erased by the shower spray.

A flower ought not to grow out of human skin. A flower ought to be a gift, a contributing member of a bouquet, a manicured garden, a Van Gogh painting.

Her moans become loud, gargled. When she inspects her hands, they are incensed pink and almost bubbling. No more. She turns the water off and steps out.

A few minutes pass while the extractor fan whirs and clears the air. When her mirror self sharpens through the fading vapour, her flowers aren't even wrinkled.

Lauren Du Plessis

They're impenetrable; thriving even as the rest of her burns. A long future kaleidoscopes in her reflected eyes. How many more flowers will grow before the body known as 'Elinor' disappears? When her hands are pointed stems tipped with buds, and her brain a blow-away mass of thistledown?

The nail scissors are in her hands before she can stop herself. She bought them before coming here, in case she had to remove the acrylics and neaten her real nails. The blades are pristine. She caresses the foliage around her waist, choosing a target. Here, this one, garish magenta.

A slip around the delicate floret. A steeling breath. A slice.

An eruption. It shoots outwards through the root system and lights neurons across her stomach. The dismembered fragments tumble over her shaking body to the floor. She gasps a loud, "Fuck."

Blood oozes through the thistle's swollen base and out where she made the cut. She presses the ruptured flower with her finger to try and hold her insides in.

"I'm sorry," she apologises to the thistles, "Oh, fuck! I'm sorry."

She crouches, and eases herself to the floor, picking the bits of her off the tiles and cradling them in her shrivelled palm.

The thud of fist against door makes her scream.

"Nell, Nell! Are you okay?" It's Gunner, and he's forcing his way in, falling to his knees and cradling her against his chest. Her blood smears on his shirt. The blood trickles.

"What have you done?" Gunner's voice echoes.

Tender

"I don't know," she says, because reality is split and she has no idea what he's seeing.

He pulls reams of toilet tissue from the roll and wads it. "Give me your hand."

She holds out her bloody hand, the other still grasping the cut florets. He guides it towards the wound, pushing her into place and patting her fire-hot skin.

"Hold it there. There's a first aid kit in your room, yeah?"

He's gone. Nell's ears ring. At first the tone is unsettling, but she hums the same note and wonders if the sound has always been there, she's just tapping into it. The hum reverberates in her chest and calms her.

Gunner returns quickly and pulls her hand away. There is sharp, cold wetness, then a "This will hurt", then a dart in her abdomen. Alcohol. She snarls.

"Breathe with me," Gunner says, and she does. The ring fades, and the sound of two bodies breathing grows clearer. Like she's resurfaced, or walked out of a wood, and is back in the guest house bathroom.

"Why did you do this?" Gunner asks. "Is it Ingrid?"

"What did I do?"

Confusion registers across his face. "Were you completely out of it? You dragged your scissors across your stomach!"

"Oh." Nausea hits. "It's not bad, right?"

"It's long, but not deep? I don't know, Nell, I'm not a doctor and I'm not you. If it were me, I'd get it checked."

"It's fine. Help me clean up."

Gunner helps her to cover the wound. They hobble to her room, where he plumps her pillows and helps her ease back against the headboard.

"The doctor's house is so close – you sure I shouldn't call her?"

Nell closes her eyes. "I'm tired, Gunner. If people could stop deciding what's best for me today…"

She ought to rush for help, ask for stitches, get frantic with worry about a new, ugly scar. But right now she could wear the cut like a badge of wild achievement. The cut says, *I'm dangerous*. It says, *Fuck off*.

He sits at her side and places his hand over hers. Her acrylics have finally worn thinner at the edges, with new nails pushing out. Underneath they must be stained with dirt and blood. She hides the other hand, still holding the florets, under the blanket.

"Nell, I'm scared for you." He casts his eyes over her. "I don't want to do anything to make things worse. Maybe we need a change."

Her mind goes blank. "What?"

"Maybe we shouldn't be pursuing anything right now. There's your health to think about, but there's also our work here. Ingrid told me they all know about us. And after today, with how strange and tense we all were… I think things would settle down if you and I were just friends."

Her tongue burns with the words *Maybe I can make my own decisions*, but the weight of his brow tells her he's made his own. Tiredness washes over her. The thistles stir but can't flare as they did earlier.

"You're worried you have to babysit me," she says.

"I don't have any experience with bad mental health stuff. And it's not like we were—" His eyes are panicked as he says, "We haven't been official, right?"

What would have classed it as official, she wonders.

Tender

Fucking eight times, instead of seven? "I guess not." He wanted to immerse himself in something new. And now he's ready to go home. "You're seeing someone back in London, then?"

He leans away. "How did you know that?"

"Heard you on the phone the other day. You were arguing with someone."

"I should have told you."

She nods at him, then repositions herself to lie on her side. Her insides broil as his voice continues behind her.

"I got swept up. You know what I'm like. But I care about you, Nell. I thought things were over with the other person." He leaves a silence. "Okay. I'll leave you alone now."

The door clicks shut. All over, her skin prickles, new heads pushing against her skin. But it's too late, too difficult. Her skin stretches but does not break.

The florets weigh in her hand. She rolls forward to drop them onto the bedside table. Her phone lights up, and she lifts it to check the time. Ten. The sky outside is still warm. She has a message from Liz.

Please, please don't forget Charlie's party. I want it to be a special day for her, so she can have these family moments we didn't get. Here's all the details. A screenshot invitation. *I don't want to let her down. Are you bringing your boyfriend?*

Of course, Nell responds. *We'll see you there.*

VIII

Nell was seven years old, and sucking a bug through a straw. It was a woodlouse, uncovered by her grimy fingers wiggling its log home out of the way. The straw led to a small tub with a mesh layer at the top, so she couldn't accidentally swallow it. It didn't stop her wondering how the crunchy little creature would feel on her tongue.

"What do you think woodlice taste like?" she asked her classmate.

"Gross! Bugs are gross!"

That's true, she thought, holding the tub at eye level and assessing its contents. One woodlouse, two unidentified beetles, and an ant. They weren't too bothered by each other. Perhaps because they were equally gross. Nell surveyed her classmates, who ran in circles, squashed ants, or sat on the benches chatting. She was ready for a moment away from them.

So she walked, enjoying the crack of twigs beneath her.

"Where *were* you?" The teacher stood over her later. "I was about to phone the school!" She sounded half angry, half terrified, a bit how Nell's mum sounded when Nell did something unacceptable.

Lauren Du Plessis

"Completely unacceptable," her mum said over dinner, where Nell picked at her microwaved vegetable stew. Apparently she was missing for over half an hour.

"We were right to be sceptical," her dad said.

Mum wiped Liz's mouth. "How are two adults supposed to monitor seventeen children in an open forest? Of course someone was going to get lost."

This sounded to Nell like they were more angry at the school than they were at her, but then they both snapped their heads to stare at her plate.

"Not eating either?" Mum said. "Think because you've got away with that attitude to your teachers, you can get away with it here?"

"Take your food to the sink," Dad said. "And no reading time after. Go straight to bed."

There was a barstool by the dishwasher and sink where her mum sat to read magazines, a white leather circle on a slender stem. The sink gleamed, used for nothing but running water. Nell spooned stew into her mouth in silence, scraped her plate, and put it into the dishwasher.

In her room, she stuck her hands in her pockets. The peppery-smelling knot of leaves she had picked came out.

She'd spent the time her schoolmates were all calling her name foraging. There were no interesting plants in the artificial grass of her front garden, and her parents hated it when she went into the field next door. This was her only chance.

She had decided that she liked plants, or rather, they decided they liked her. She didn't have much say in the matter, noticing every plant that came into her path as if it were a blaring red siren. She thought this must be the earth speaking to her, saying hello.

Tender

Her mum and dad didn't talk much about God, so it felt like her school had made it up, like Christ on the cross was a unique peculiarity of St Mary's. All it convinced her of was that magic was real, and that divinity could be contained within a person, or spread around in everything, down to the tiniest plant.

Nell liked that her school was named after a mother. As she learned about the planet and how it grew everything out of its atoms, she thought that a parent was a very appropriate kind of god. Documentaries called it Mother Earth. She settled for calling it the earth mama, or the earth magic, or the fairy magic, in her head; she had no more complex or comprehensive words for it at the time, and she wasn't sure human words would ever be enough for it anyway.

Over time, Nell became convinced that it was a sort of spirit, an earth voice who she could feel when she went into the field next door. The earth was a lady, or something like a lady – something sensual, tumultuous, and hopeful for the little creatures living on it. The movement of the ground was the breathing of her chest, and all the people in the world were just children in an enormous, verdant womb.

The plants Nell picked had curls, pinked edges, spikes. One had a round spiny head. She had recently learned of the existence of microscopes, and tried to imagine the ecosystem of living things on the plants. The bugs she collected must feed on microscopic things. Microbes often came from dead things. She could just about make sense of it in her mind. In this world, everything was woven into everything else. The plants got light from the sun and food from the ground, and gave everything else food and air. Animals and humans ate the plant, or they ate each other. The earth mama watched over all of this, waiting for her children to finish their plates so she could cook some more.

Nell put a leaf in her mouth as her mum walked in.

"The floor!" She went pale. "Where did this muck come from?!"

Nell glanced down, chewing on the leaf. The leaf came apart effortlessly on her tongue, leaving a harsh, green taste.

Mum strained through a long breath and recited a line from a parenting book she often reread. "A difficult child does not a difficult day make. Elinor will clean her own mess." She eyed Nell. "You know where the hoover is. Explain where this came from."

Nell said nothing.

"The school trip, wasn't it?"

The room seemed to fold into itself and become small.

Mum continued – she never struggled to hold a conversation with thin air when her daughters didn't respond. "Well, that's the last you're going on, then. What if you'd picked something poisonous? Look at the state of your nails."

"Mum, can we get real plants in our garden?"

"Who would water them? You? Now, I don't want to have to punish you, darling. Punishment is for bad children. Please, prove you're still my good girl."

Nell liked the dirt under her nails, shaped like smiles. She said nothing, but wished she could say something to hurt her mother. Something jabby. She imagined opening her mouth and showing off the mulched leaves, except they would keep pouring out, cascading green that would fill up the room and bury them both.

That night she threw up, producing a knotty splotch on her duvet. This time, her body had rejected its own wildness. Expelled it. In her nausea she feared her mother was right all along. She was too old for fantasy and would never be friends with the magical earth spirit.

Nell looks over the fields from where she stands, half in the present and half in the past. She holds the line of her stomach where she made the cut two nights ago. It still feels like some monstrosity could pour out of it.

She has barely spoken a word since that night. She passed Gunner silently in the corridor before breakfast, and all morning she has worked as far from Ingrid as the trenches allow. An hour ago the thermometer hit thirty-five, and Bill ordered work to stop. The day so far has been a long, painfully held breath.

Gunner reached for Nell's arm when he and the assistants chose to return to the guest house, but she brushed him off. She'd rather not experience the tempting heat of his skin. Now she stands beside one of the vegetable patches, because she wants to be reminded of the stillness of plants, watching the cabbages bloom with waxy radiance.

Her phone buzzes. It's Liz. *Can you bring fruit juices with Charlie's present?*

"Shit."

She'd forgotten. What does a four-year-old want that can be plucked from fenland?

Lauren Du Plessis

At the edge of the field, the figure of Beth leans over to turn a tap. Then there is spray, cool like a shadow falling over Nell. Sprinklers fan droplets over the leafy vegetables. She hasn't stepped back into the shower after trying to burn off the thistles, and the cool freshness of moisture on her skin almost makes her cry.

Beth approaches, and Nell assumes she must be coming to turn another faucet. But she stops.

"I noticed you working by yourself the last couple of days. Something happen?"

Nobody has said much to her since she shouted at Ingrid, although perhaps Beth doesn't know that. Nell asks, "Is this ready to be harvested?"

"Very soon. I supply a couple of farm shops nearby; the rest goes to supermarkets. Not enough this year, though: with the weather and your trenches. Council money won't cover my losses."

At the other end of the field, two farm hands continue their work. Nell peers towards them, backed by the punishing blue sky.

"I think you were right the other day, when you said everything humans do is natural," she says. "You can't separate us from the earth."

"Nope. You fuck with part of the system, and the rest shows the effects."

Nell looks at Beth. "Can I hang around here this afternoon – do you need help with anything?"

Beth gestures for her to follow, collecting a bucket full of tools on the way. "Help me with the blackberries."

*

Tender

Stepping across rocks in the stream, they cross two small crop patches before arriving at a grassy field with dense hedgerow.

"This is the best kind of year for my blackberries. They grow like mad."

Beth hands Nell a pair of gardening gloves and then tugs a prickly, red branch out from the tangle to demonstrate. It buckles, laden with deep green leaves, and a rainbow of berries from pale green through pink and red to midnight purple, swollen with juice and ready to drop.

Beth places a wooden stool on the ground to reach the top branches, while Nell works at the lower brambles. Even with gloves, prickles stick through and surprise her. While pulling the weighty shears from their bucket, she notices small glass jars and labels.

"Do you send these to the farm shops, too?"

"Sure, sometimes. But they also make good gifts."

"Can I take one, as a gift for someone? I'll pay."

"Take a couple. And no you won't. Who's it for?"

"One for my sister, one for my niece. She's only four, she won't get it."

"She'll love them. These are the sweetest blackberries you've ever tasted. Try one."

Nell removes a glove and plucks a large cluster from her punnet. The drupelets burst one by one, juice spilling over her tongue and around her teeth, registering sweet and pleasantly bitter. Nell's skin stirs and she finds herself grabbing another from the branch, and another.

"They *are* the best."

They are almost enough to throw off Nell's eating habits, make her lust for crisp apple and bursting orange vesicles, not from cans or packets but from the sides of roads and from orchard glades. She and Beth pick and eat alternately.

After some time, Beth climbs down from the stool and sits on it, looking out over the field. The grass seems to burn under their gaze, heat radiating off in ripples. She sighs.

Nell can only imagine what it must be like to have your life at nature's mercy, at least in such an obvious way. She grips the shear handles tighter. Something like hunger coils up her throat. She wants the earth to decide what she does and when she does it. She sits.

Red veins stain Beth's lips, as if she has been bleeding. The undersides of Nell's nails are the same. Someone ought to scold them, comment on their mess. Beth grins at her, berry-bloodied, sluiced vampire teeth. For the first time Nell notices a dark spot on the inside of her bottom lip.

Beth notices, and pulls her lip open like a snapdragon. A tattoo.

"A clover?" Nell guesses.

"Lucky four-leaf." Beth closes her mouth and leans back to pull a low branch free. "Fuck!" She picks a thorn from her forearm and flicks it away.

Nell reaches out and touches the small but flaring mark.

"It's no big deal," Beth says. "Don't worry."

"Can't you get tetanus from plant pricks?" Nell searches her mind to try and work out if the risk applies to plants other than roses. She places a thumb either side of the wound, a prick of blood with a red ring.

"What are you…"

"Just checking it," Nell says. It is surprisingly easy and

unselfconscious to touch Beth's arm. It is like touching her own arm.

"I think I've got something to soothe it." Beth stands quickly.

They pack up and return to the white-hot farmhouse. After thumbing some salve and a plaster over her cut, Beth begins filling jars with the best of the berries. Nell mimics her, tying paper doilies over the tops of Liz's and Charlie's gifts with twine.

"Are you and Gunner together?" Beth says suddenly.

It's pointless to lie to Beth, Nell senses. "We had a moment, but it passed."

"I think that's for the best. Maybe I should've said something sooner, but I'm telling you now. I know his type. They don't know what they want, and they take too much. Like when I planted squash and cabbage next to each other. The cabbage took all the nutrients and the squash didn't grow."

The thistles burn and Nell's throat tightens like she might cry. Watching her friend work, she wonders if she'd rather *be* Beth, or stay with Beth, where things make sense.

If Beth is a bog plant, like Gunner is sundew, then she is sphagnum moss. Growing in easily, forming a bed that spreads quickly over a marsh. It doesn't even need roots – it absorbs nutrients directly into its leaves. Simple, nothing required below the surface. The moss creates peat, turning the inhospitable into a soft and welcoming bed. Sphagnum lines hanging baskets, but also protects – where it grows, the environment acidifies, killing bacteria. It absorbs moisture quicker than cotton, and can even be used to cover wounds.

Beth lines Nell's mind like sphagnum moss. This is the only reason, she thinks, that she has the strength to get in the car with Gunner and drive to Liz's.

Taking Gunner to her sister's house now seems just. They haven't mentioned the break-up – if what they had could even be termed a relationship – throughout the twenty-minute drive, but as Nell pulls onto the private road, Gunner speaks.

"I know I upset you. I was an idiot."

"Well, I shouldn't have said you were my boyfriend."

"I probably deserve an awkward evening. Call it just deserts. And who knows, we might have fun tonight."

"Shit!" Nell stamps the brake, and they lurch to a stop. A scream strangles away as a small figure in a white dress runs from the car and towards a door. A woman scrambles from the house to meet her child, scooping it into a tight embrace. Her choked scold is loud enough to hear from inside the car.

"Never, *ever* do that again, Charlie!"

Nell bumps onto the kerb and stops. A new thistle cuts through the top of her thigh. "I nearly hit her."

"But you didn't," Gunner says.

She nods to herself as they walk up the path, approaching the tangled bodies of Liz and Charlie. Liz's russet-brown hair is bound into a skin-pulling French twist at the back, and flyaway wisps blow in the breeze either side of her ears. Her long, delicate stem of a neck is flushed with fear

Tender

and adorned with a dainty silver chain. She wears a knee-length cotton dress, puffed sleeves gathered around her sharp shoulders.

Any tenderness in the reunion is already snuffed out. Liz can barely get a greeting out between panicked breaths, still clinging to Charlie and stroking her hair. She rushes in ahead of them, leaving Nell and Gunner to admire the latest incarnation of Nell's childhood home.

Each house on the close is the same: semi-detached, built in the nineties, with covered porches and large door-knockers and flat, white render. The lawn ends before the houses, so no roots can even approach the brickwork. Not much has changed about her old home, save two olive trees either side of the porch and the knocker being a curling black leaf, rather than a bland rectangle as it used to be.

Voices erupt from a room at the end of the entrance corridor. Gunner gives Nell a final reassuring nod before they enter.

They lose their coats and shoes and pad over the vinyl to an open plan kitchen-diner, the old wall knocked through and a glossy breakfast bar in its place. The walls are so white, so bare, every memory ever splattered, drawn or spilled is painted over. This house is a tabula rasa, until Nell takes her first deep gulp of the air and the buried feelings come back. The time she ran in from school and squealed about winning the spelling trophy, and her mother said she was too old to make a noise like that. If she won a spelling bee, why was she speaking in baby talk?

"Elinor." Her mother gasps, as if they didn't know she was coming. She mouths a hello while Gunner extends a hand to each of her parents.

Lauren Du Plessis

Her mother is unchanged by the year since they've seen each other: brown hair slicked back in a ponytail, tailored black suit, chemically peeled skin, and a flatlining mouth. Her father shakes her hand like they're new business partners at a pitch meeting, and waits for her to speak. It is, of course, Gunner who fills the space with small talk.

They eat dinner around the dining room table with the back doors open. A wasp pays a visit, and it is Charlie who swats it and looks to Liz for approval. Nell watches her with fascination. She eats her pizza with a pink, silicon knife and fork, and attempts to join in with the adult chatter. Her high ponytail twists into perfect ringlets at the end.

David sits at the end holding Genie, the baby. He is wearing an inappropriately warm twill shirt, looks like he'd rather be anywhere else, plays on his phone whenever he isn't being spoken to. His hand is affixed to the baby's stomach, but she has no back or head support, so lolls around whenever she tries to move. She ends up resolute, head back against his torso and staring at the ceiling. Nell fights an urge she would never act on anyway: to take the baby into her arms and sing to it, replacing the echoes of this house.

"Elinor, will you help me in the kitchen?" Liz says.

They prepare the cake as secretly as possible in the large, bright space. Liz moves away while Nell lights the candles.

"Oh, one moment," Liz says. Nell stands in front of the vanilla sponge, shielding it from the breeze, while she takes a pill bottle from a top cupboard.

"How've you been?" she says, not making eye contact.

Tender

Her voice is low and serious, and there's clearly more to the question but she doesn't elaborate.

"Tired, I guess. Hot summer, isn't it?"

"Mm-hm. Somerset suits you. You've lost that city fug."

"Oh? You're more…"

"Anxious. I know you're going to say anxious. What did you expect?"

Her frown breaks the second she catches Nell's eye. She puts the pill bottle away and takes a sip of water.

"Sorry," she says. "Ready?"

They sing happy birthday, Charlie joining in until the cake lands in front of her and she understands that it's her they are singing to, after which she beams golden up at them.

"It is so *nice* for you to have come," her mother says from over her teacup. They are sitting in the living room in tall armchairs, resting their feet on a fluffy rug that must be a nightmare to keep clean. "What's it been, three years since we were all together?"

Gunner attempts to cut in. "I barely saw my parents over the pandemic either…" But he shuts up when all eyes dart to him.

"I come to the things you invite me to," Nell says in a pleading voice that she regrets slipping into in front of Gunner. She grits her teeth even tighter as she realises the implication of those words, which despite their timid delivery are also an accusation. But this accusation goes unrecognised.

Charlie begins opening presents. A shiny, kid-friendly

tablet. Big hair bows. Ruffled dresses. Contemporary versions of all the sorts of gifts Nell and Liz used to get on birthdays. When Charlie gets to the blackberry jars, she holds them towards Liz with a screwed-up nose. "What is it?"

"Wow." Liz's fake fascination is grating. "These must be from Auntie Elinor."

"I picked them myself, from the farm where our dig is. They'll be good with cake or ice cream. They're like sweeties," Nell says.

Charlie smiles. "Please can I have one, Mummy?"

"In the kitchen later," Liz responds.

They don't go back to the kitchen until after Charlie has gone to bed. The sun has set outside, and the adults move onto the deck to drink around a large outdoor table. The rest of the garden is paved, ending in a fence of solid wooden slats, obscuring their view of the field beyond. Liz puts out crackers and dainty slivers of cheese, then goes inside to tidy. Happy to let Gunner fan her parents with stories, Nell heads in too.

"Dad is looking old," Liz says. "But I think Mum has had botox."

Nell lets her talk about them while they tidy. The kitchen has gone cool in the dark and she watches the hairs on her arm rise while trying to ignore the whisper of the thistles underneath.

Liz clears her throat. "What do you think?"

"I don't know," Nell says. Her sister's question – whatever it was – has flurried away into the air.

"Ellie, I invited you here in the hopes you'd make an effort. You didn't even pick up juice."

Tender

Nell fidgets with her ponytail. "I brought presents. What else was I supposed—"

"An effort to talk to us! To tell us about what you actually do. At least to tell me not to gossip. You know... be with us. I wanted to help."

Part of her wondered if a member of her family would ever speak to her like this. There were times, when she was a teenager, that she longed for questions, instead of instructions. But tonight the questions feels like intrusions. She thinks about Unum, Duo and Tria on their trays, plucked out and prodded. So all she can say is, "Why would I need help?"

Liz puts a plate down with a clatter. "For god's sake."

Nell stares into the mirrored glass of the table. She doesn't know what to say to make the conversation stop. The thistles begin to heat, heads unfurling.

"*Everything* changed when we were in hospital. You know it did. *Everything.* Because it's two decades later and every meeting still feels like a wake. That's almost my whole life! Maybe you remember a time before, but I don't. My therapist suggested I talk to you."

"Why are you seeing a therapist?"

Liz pauses, exploring the air between them, before reaching out and pulling on Nell's sleeve. Out of the kitchen, along the corridor, up the stairs. The first floor is a similar story to the ground: grey plush carpets that could be new if it weren't for the subtle dimpling down the centre, undoubtedly pressed in by clean white socks and light steps.

Liz leads Nell into the master bedroom, another open space with a mirror and bespoke built-in wardrobe on one side, and a bed with an upholstered headboard on the other, flanked hotel-style by two lamps. On the left is some sort of co-sleeping contraption, a white mesh box where the baby is asleep under the watchful eye of a monitor.

Nell follows her sister through the soft evening blue, and they crouch at the bottom of the wardrobe.

"One time at school, when I was fourteen – right after you left us – we were in a swimming lesson and Jenny pointed out my IV and food pipe scars. She said my witch sister cursed me. And you know what? I half-believed her."

She opens a drawer, her back to Nell so that the contents remain hidden, then turns back holding a strip of white plastic. There is a name printed on it, a date.

"I found these in the attic," she whispers. "If Mum and Dad are never going to talk about it – which they aren't – then the only person who knows what happened to us is you."

"When, you mean in hospital? You don't remember?" Nell takes the hospital band and holds it between her fingers, the sharp claws of her acrylics fitting into the staple holes where the band was once fixed to her little sister's wrist.

"Keep your voice low. What do *you* remember?"

"Do you want to go in the hall?" Nell casts her eyes to Genie's baby-blue shape.

"No! I don't want the others to hear."

"Well then, we got sick. They took us to hospital and pumped our stomachs. I got better quicker, maybe being older helped. You took a while, but Mum and Dad visited you most days. Are your scars still…"

"That's it? That's all you know?" Liz has to rein in her voice. The baby's head turns, but she stays asleep.

Tender

They fall into silence, but inside Nell's brain the roots are pressing on her nerves, forcing them to fire. None of the memories were completely lost, but holding the band – a tangible link – illuminates them.

Tree trunks, ancient and coarse, bound her into a tight shape. She was dropped into a river. There were loud wails, either wailing voices or sirens. Then, lightning flashed and doors thundered, and the tree bark warped into knotted faces. She was half-conscious when a fire ripped down her throat.

Nell remembers not wanting to go back after being discharged, because her little sister remained in the trap, transparent vines sticking out from her on the bed.

"All I have is a blur," Liz says at last. "That's why I didn't want to believe what I saw on the discharge papers I found with the band."

"Why, what did—"

"That it was you." Her voice breaks from whisper into venom.

Nell says nothing.

Over the years she had told herself different versions of a story. *Mum and Dad became so protective because of that day. Mum and Dad were always like this.* But this is a lie. The truth had grown up with her, a seed in her belly. Many seedlings grow best in the cool and the dark. The doctors had tried to cut it out, but if you don't kill the roots a weed will keep coming back. The truth has always been with her. Their parents were the way they were because of Nell. It had always been her fault.

"We ran away – no, *you* ran away and took me with you – and they found us days later. I was nearly dead. You almost killed me."

153

Lauren Du Plessis

Nell's breath catches, her insides held together tightly by the writhing body of the plant. It squeezes her oesophagus, fills her stomach with blooms. Prickles skewer her intestines, and push out through the pores of her shoulders and arms. The pressure releases and she explodes forwards to wrap herself around her little sister. Liz's bare shoulders are unrealistically soft, the skin barely a membrane.

The baby stirs, then releases a wild scream.

Nell and Liz sink into a heap. Genie screams louder.

They remain perfectly still as the voices from downstairs approach, growing less muffled until the door creaks on its hinges. Nell turns to face her parents, her brother-in-law, and Gunner standing in the doorway. Under their gaze, the full weight of Liz in her arms becomes apparent, and she realises her sister is shaking and heaving.

When Nell pulls back, there is resistance. She finds her acrylics skewered into Liz's shoulder. There is an awful sensation, like fingers in softened fudge. Too much give. She has to extricate each nail from her sister's skin, freckled now not only with the effects of sunlight, but the effect of her witch sister.

Liz backs away on her hands until she hits the wall. She screams. *"Get out, get out."*

Nell tries to form words, tries to find an excuse that will paint her as equally helpless, equally the victim of their situation. But it isn't true, is it.

She stands, every muscle twisted with thistle runners. Pulling herself to full height is painful.

"Sorry," she mutters.

Her mother rushes past her to Liz's side. "You're bleeding!"

Tender

Gunner steps back, and she can't meet his eye.
Her father stands in the corridor.
"I didn't… I just," she begins, but he raises a hand.
"You can't change what you are."

Gunner opens the passenger door ten minutes after Nell got in and put her head on the wheel. She drives them back. He says nothing, keeps his eyes out of the side window. The house, the road: they all disappear in the rear-view mirror.

When the car stops, she lets the words spew from her like pollen in an early summer field. "Please don't hate me. I didn't mean to. I never would have."

They go to their separate rooms, but Nell hears Gunner's door open some time later. He goes downstairs.

She gets into her nightdress and tucks her feet under the covers. The whole place smells of damp, so strong she can taste it. Her breath catches as she notices the bedside table looking wrong, a crack running down its edge that hadn't been there when she arrived, or even a few days ago.

She gets up, crouches and searches the side of it for the source of the damage. It's deep, too deep to have happened in a day.

Then she finds them. The florets she cut from her body have embedded themselves, a sliver of a root system tucking into the wood and splintering it. She smacks her hand over them, crushing the new sprouts and mashing them with the heel of her palm. They fold and tear into a moist paste, then she wipes the remains onto the floor, pulls the roots out of the wood, and shreds their tissues apart.

Prickle

IX

S he turned the main light off because the pink glow of
sunset on the walls felt good, and because her little
sister had fallen asleep. Whenever she thought of darkness,
she thought of the corners of their bedroom, where the
light faded away and another world began. She imagined
a tunnel that burrowed into the wall and reached down to
where the bricks met the soil. Beyond that was nothing but
flowers and grass stretching out into the marshes.

They're called the Avalon Marshes, her dad told her,
the wettest part of the Somerset Levels. Once there was
probably water everywhere, and all the towns were
islands. She was glad it wasn't the case anymore, as that
would mean she was trapped there forever.

She read by her bedside lamp because it was reading
time and that's all there was to do. If it wasn't for the distant
sounds of other bodies moving around other rooms, she
could have believed that time was paused.

She had read *The Legend of King Arthur* more times than
she could count. It was the last of her early reader books,
because her mum replaced all the others with harder ones.
But she hid this one under her bed, even though that was
a messy thing to do. The cover had a blood-red border

that made her think of scuffed knees and bee stings, and within this frame was a watercolour painting of a woman with wings holding out her hand to a knight clad in silver armour. This one ended in a place called Avalon, where the fairy witch Morgan le Fay healed Arthur with her powers.

Nell had to keep this book because she knew that real fairy witch magic was out there, in the woods beyond the field. She could see Morgan's eyes in the gloom, moonlight circling her black pupils as she sat on her throne. She was frightening, really, and she did a lot of bad things to Arthur and his knights. But she also helped them. She was free to be bad or good whenever she liked, kind of like the earth mama.

Nell put her book down and went to the window.

The field was a big square of very tall grass with speckles of colourful flowers like splattered paint when she flicked her fingers through her brush in art class. But these flowers were not a mistake – she knew this because the flowers told her. They communicated through their colours and their smell when she crouched down to sniff them. They smelled like green, chemicals, and soap. The smell was sharp in her nose at first, then sweet. And when they told her to do things – strange things, wild things – she knew that she must have the fairy witch magic of the earth mama, this oldest and most apparent deity, in her heart. Now as she watched the wind move through the grass and rustle the woodland beyond, the rushing sound was like a whisper through the window glass that told her to come out and play.

She was too old for play. Too old to wander through the grass and pick flowers and turn them into potions. Too

Tender

old to use herself as the canvas when she painted. Mummy and Daddy said so, Mrs Graham said so. She pressed her forehead against the window.

What if they were wrong?

She got that funny feeling in her tummy – the one she got when she cuddled her sister, or the time she pushed the neighbour kid into mud when he hit her.

Her little sister lay on her princess bed in a tiered dress, ruffles displaced this way and that. She had pulled out her hair ties so her curls covered her face. As if she knew what was about to happen, she opened her eyes and pushed the board book off her chest.

Nell said, "Can you keep a secret?"

Her sister rolled onto her belly and regarded her with sleepy eyes. "Yeah."

"I go outside sometimes when you're asleep."

Her sister looked unconvinced. "How?"

"I know where the key is. And I know how to undo the child locks."

"You're lying."

"Am not. Watch by the window."

She unclicked the door. At the top of the stairs, she held her breath and edged down step by step. The back door was in the kitchen, so she crossed the living room doorway on her hands and knees. The sofa where her mother sat had its back to the door, so she could pause for just a moment, watching her mother's oblivious head. Barely moving. Barely breathing, as if she was barely alive at all.

When she crossed the threshold, the world started up again. Her feet wobbled, sensing the ground crawling along underneath her like a great creature. She was just a smaller creature on its back. Like lichen or a parasite, except the earth didn't mind her being there. This huge earth creature was where she would get her powerful fairy witch magic from someday, if she figured out how.

Once she was over the fence and in the grass, the boundaries disappeared. She dusted off her hands and scooped through the tall grass like swimming. The blades tickled until she found her favourite corner, where the grass was trampled and she could lie on her back and spend time with the clouds, which were like the earth's breaths.

Since she started junior school, they didn't have lessons outside anymore. When she got dirty in the playground, the teacher scolded her. All her classmates perched in their red plastic chairs. When they fell on the tarmac and it razed their skin they cried. They didn't like to eat bugs or plants or mud at lunchtime, even if she made them into the shape of cookies or cake.

She and all the people around her were human beings. This was the truth. But human beings are animals. And animals are just a type of life, living on the Earth. Humans and cats and roses and ticks are all the same. When she realised that it was like a light bulb coming on. But nobody else wanted to be like the animals or plants: they wanted to use knives and forks and take showers. Be quiet when they were told to be quiet, and loud when they were told to be loud.

Is this how it always was? Would she one day learn to hate the field like her parents did? She didn't want to become an adult. They were so afraid of everything. They had so many rules that she wondered why they didn't get tired.

Tender

A cry sounded out over the field. The wind carried it to her ears, as if to make sure she knew about it. She sat up but the grass here was taller than her, so she could still see only earth and sky. She walked back to the edge, searched the windows of the house.

In the downstairs living room, her mother was watching a cooking show filled with glossy foods she would never make herself. Her father was nowhere to be seen.

Tiny handprints pressed against the upstairs window, which was cracked open at the top to keep the girls cool.

Why don't you get her? the earth mama asked through the rush of the grass.

Nell whispered, "I've never brought her here before."

But now you've told her, she's just like you. She wants to come and play.

She climbed the fence, walked back towards the house and went inside. When she unlocked the bedroom door once more, and went in, her little sister remained pressed against the glass. She scooped her up under the armpits and pulled her across the room.

It took a few minutes to push her to the top of the fence and show her how to scale the other side without getting splinters or falling and hurting herself.

"I'm here with you," she said in her nicest voice. "I know what I'm doing, trust me."

Liz wiped away angry, silent tears and allowed herself to be led. When their feet hit the floor, she stayed quiet. Now the field stretched out from them and into the woods. *Come and see.*

Nell knew her little sister was understanding all the things that she understood. Even the things that she couldn't yet name. They walked across the field to the special place and lay down together.

Her little sister lay on her front, eyeing the ground. She saw a worm, its concertina-body bunching and stretching through the soil.

"Did you know you can cut some worms in half, and they'll turn into two worms?" Nell asked.

Her sister stuck her tongue out.

"We're like bits of a worm that got cut. We're the same but also different."

Liz seemed impressed by this idea, and leaned out to touch the worm, recoiling at its sliminess. Then she pointed out a beetle and some ants. The sun was red hot and all of the flowers around them were open even though it was getting late; bees and flies visited their petals and pollen before moving past. Her little sister stood and began to pick them, gathering a bunch of wild colours in her little fists. Nell watched her sister and saw herself and knew that she'd done the right thing, bringing her out here and showing her the real world.

Just a night or two, she thought to herself. That would be long enough to find the source of the earth's magic and escape from the boringness of their normal life.

Liz picked daisies and dandelions and clovers, but shrieked when a thistle spine caught her thumb. Nell's eyes snapped to the back door, waiting for one of their parents to appear. But nobody did. The wind wouldn't carry the sound to them, because they didn't care about the earth.

The girls picked flowers, not caring if they were garden flowers or weeds. Much later Nell would know that a thistle is like a daisy, both coming from the family Asteraceae.

Tender

Where the daisy has a glowing face of ray flowers, the thistle's disc flowers are an explosive clump. It is pretty from afar but up close the prickles reach out from its stem and leaves. It knows how to keep itself safe. The sharpness is self-protection. A thistle does not care if it pricks you.

Nell did not yet know these facts, but she knew the feeling.

The air warmed around them as the sun emerged from behind a cloud, the wind continuing to amplify the voices of the plants.

A long time passed. Perhaps their parents were already scouring the grass for them. But they wouldn't understand. It was much better to stay out here until they found the magic, uninterrupted by bedtime routines.

They had to find dinner, though. What did the things of the earth eat, the plants and animals? Liz liked turkey dinosaurs, but she'd have to eat like a fairy tonight.

"You can eat these," Nell said to her little sister, holding out the flowers. "Why don't you try one?"

Liz looked thoughtful, then ventured further to find a large leaf and placed the flowers upon it like a plate.

"You eat," she said.

Nell already knew which parts tasted good and which parts were bitter and left an aftertaste. She plucked the petals from the daisy, and rolled the heads of the dandelions into the leaves like parcels.

"One day we'll learn to cook them and make potions, but for now we'll eat them like this."

Liz watched as she took the first few bites. The wildflowers were tickly and sometimes juicy, falling apart in her mouth as if they were waiting to be eaten.

Lauren Du Plessis

"You know," she said, "before humans had tools and built houses and things like that, we ate plants like this, and killed animals ourselves. We could eat flowers and little animals for our whole lives."

She held out a dandelion, and her little sister snatched it. The yellow lit her face before she folded it into her mouth, which immediately reopened. Yellow flecks fell onto her dress, and she fished out half of the flower, nose scrunching tight.

The wind dropped for a moment; the plants stopped speaking.

"You don't like it?" Nell asked.

Liz tried to get the last petals off her tongue.

"Blech!" she said.

So her senses weren't quite ready yet. Maybe she was too young to hear the plants and know they were safe. Nell shrugged and took her hand again.

As they crossed the field into the woodland, she explained to Liz about the fairy witch magic and how the earth had always talked to her, not in words but in magical bubbling feelings in her tummy. Liz listened in quiet fascination, until Nell finished. Then she said that she wanted to find the real earth magic too, so they pressed on. Their little feet were carried forward by the cresting and bowing path, marked with pebbles that seemed to have been placed there specifically for them, at the exact right distance apart for a child's step.

Beyond the first short trees, the canopy lifted and the woods became like a pillared cave, all covered over the top. Like hiding in a fort, the girls would be hard to find in here. But the magic would keep them safe, Nell was sure.

Tender

The forest had every flavour she could imagine and more. Sweet and sour and fresh and old and bitter and strong and aromatic. Tastes that got into her nose and behind her eyes and deep into her belly.

Once the houses were no longer visible, she began to touch her hands against the trees and the soil, trying to find a definite voice from the earth mama, to guide her towards the magic. Liz walked behind her, collecting more and more flowers and leaves until the undergrowth turned dense and prickly. Then Nell picked her up, showed her how to cling with her knees. She giggled as Nell's feet crunched over twigs.

Nell didn't know how long it had been when her knees gave out and she had to lower her sister to the ground. It was dark. Warm, yes, but dark like the corner of their bedroom. Liz clung to her leg and wouldn't let go. She had no idea how to get them back to the house.

She spread her arms out and searched for a comfortable nook in the base of a tree. They lay back together. Liz's stomach rumbled. For a moment panic coursed through Nell's chest, and her skin itched. She had done a terrible, terrible thing. Far more terrible than anything she'd done before. But also more brilliant. She held Liz close to her and let herself smile.

It had been another day, and Liz had not eaten. She was so weak she was starting to change colour – they both were. Whenever they reached a patch of light in the trees or came to a new field, Nell saw their skin, pale purple and blistery.

They had crossed into the marshes now, the earth becoming more and more spongy underfoot. Each field was like a giant roasted marshmallow. Nell watched Liz's stumbling path, to make sure the ground didn't swallow her up. This was what her parents always warned her about: the ground really could eat them. But she kept thinking about the earth magic, and nothing terrible happened. As long as they believed in the magic, they were safe.

They stopped in a meadow filled with even more flowers, though they grew from a strange, dark soil Nell had never seen before. It was crumbly and soft, so the flowers were easy to pull up.

"We should eat something," she said.

Liz folded her arms in imitation of their mother and shook her head. "I won't."

"Yes you will, otherwise you'll starve."

"What's that?"

"It means you'll die because you didn't eat enough."

Liz ran forward to hit Nell's side with her grass-stained hands. "No!"

Nell stooped to detach some flower-heads. "Then you have to eat something."

Her little sister went wide-eyed, her short legs bent and ready to flee. Nell grabbed her by the wrist and held the plant to her lips.

"Eat it."

"No."

She pushed the scraps against her sister's mouth while she wriggled.

"Eat it! It won't hurt you because you're like me."

Tender

Her sister growled through closed lips and waved her arms, trying to bat her away.

She must eat it, the earth said, *so you won't be alone.* Nell became strong with the sureness of it, the certainty that they had to be free. The magic, or some weak form of it, sparked down her arm and made the muscles unshakeable.

Then Liz screamed, letting it tear out of her like a wave. Nell covered her mouth. "Shh! They'll find us!"

Her little sister cried and bit down, catching Nell's fingers with sharp milk teeth. When she wrenched her hand free, it was marked by harsh red bumps with white dimples at the centre.

Where did Liz learn how to scream and bite? They weren't allowed to behave like that at home or at school. So, where? It must have come naturally, that thing animals possess called instinct.

Nell grabbed her little sister by the earlobe and pinched hard. "You have to stop crying now. We need to find the magic."

Stunned by pain, Liz relented and they went back to walking. Nell picked and ate as she went, feeling madder and wilder with every passing second. The sky over their heads was now a fantastic deep blue, with no clouds to break it.

By the evening they were barely moving. They crawled for a few metres, then stopped, then tried again. It felt like they had been gone forever, and there was still no sign of the magic, no proof to Liz that Nell had done the right thing.

Lauren Du Plessis

The wind was cooler. Their feet sank lower and lower with each step, as if they were treading water over a depth that couldn't wait to consume them.

Nell's skin was changing, she knew that for sure now. It was undeniable, completely happening. The blisters were kind of greenish in the middle, but red and swollen all around. She felt like a patch of soil about to become a flower garden.

At the edge of a field, Liz fell backwards onto her bottom and went very, very quiet. When she spoke, they were not human words but animal sounds.

Nell sat beside her and rubbed her back, placing her other hand on her own stomach. Her sister trembled, and when she looked at her hands she saw them shaking too. She reached out to catch strands of saliva as they dribbled from her sister's mouth.

They were two little girls in the middle of nowhere. If there was ever a time for magic, or a mother, it was now. Nell felt a pain in the centre of her face between her eyes. The ache of her stomach shuddered into nausea. Liz lay back, making unnameable noises and convulsing.

You need to save her, the ground said.

Nell gathered the scraps of dandelions from around the area, her whole body burning with every step. She could feel something new and desperate trying to crawl out of her. *Please let it be the magic*, she thought.

Liz didn't fuss anymore, when Nell fed her the plants. They ate slowly for a while, and Liz seemed to rouse. Her hands twitched. Her eyes flickered open.

As her insides started to boil and bubble furiously, Nell knew she had done the right thing. Her little sister

Tender

snuggled into her and smiled. She was healing. This was the magic, it had to be.

In the dim light Nell's hands seemed to shift and blur. Her skin cracked, but if she squinted, she could just about make out a green light beneath those fractures, like blood vessels only filled with the magic.

As she lay back, she imagined the flowers of the field growing through her. Not in a frightening way: she was like the fairy witch, inseparable from her earth creature friends. She felt her strength coming back, calm washing over her. She was lying on the back of a great rabbit, or a fox, or a wolf, which was the earth mama, and it was going to take care of her forever.

Welcome home, the ground and the plants and the sky said to her.

She looked one last time into the palm of her hand. There, right in the centre where the middle line is, a beautiful purple flower was nestled. She curled her hand around it and went to sleep, thinking of the magic, and how she and her sister would live with it forever as truly wild creatures.

X

You can't change what you are.

She almost believes that, getting ready in the morning. Defeat makes her lazy. She leaves her pyjamas unfolded on the floor, and goes to shower without taking her mildewed towel, drying herself instead with one of her T-shirts.

The guest house echoes her sluggishness. The shower water won't come hot, however much she turns the knob. When she tries to run the sink tap to brush her teeth, the water takes a while to come on, then gurgles angrily, spitting out a gob of black mould before a greyish liquid trickles out. She doesn't use it.

Nell arrives at the dig site late and alone. The others went without her, leaving only a short note in the kitchen. Gunner must have told them about Saturday, how her perfect facade withered and everyone saw what she'd been trying to keep from splitting through her.

She parks and trudges across the ground, letting the dust coat her shoes. The voices on the breeze are frenetic – they must still be gossiping. Reaffirming the social order. Animals and plants do it through chatter and chemicals. Nell is now hanging from the bottom rung in their minds.

Lauren Du Plessis

And they're right, of course. Her polished and proper exterior was only ever a front, though most of the time she wasn't even aware of that fact herself. For so many years she constructed a new Nell, one who looked and acted like she wouldn't run off into the forest and turn feral any chance she got.

The half-memories she received second-hand through nurses and her parents are so clear now. How she and Liz were found two days after they went missing, suffering from dehydration, poisoning and who knows what else. She became so far removed from the terrible thing she did that she became complacent. That's why, now she's come here, to the dig, and the evil inside her has started to reawaken, that thing she used to call magic, she didn't even recognise it. All this time she's believed it was an alien parasite infecting her. But she is the parasite. Whether the thistles were hers from birth, or whether something from the marsh possessed her the day she and Liz ran away, hardly matters. She should never have come back here.

As she turns the corner and the marquee comes into view, the vague sounds of speech congeal into words. *It's insane. I can't explain it.* Harsh and whispery, it's unclear which words come from which mouth. Even Mia, whose head emerges from the first trench, is talking back to them, matching the anxious tone. *I don't understand.* Beth also stands at the side, watching Nell's footsteps slow as she considers whether she should even have shown up. Nell tries to decipher Beth's expression: perhaps pity, but her lips are just slightly bunching into an 'o', as if she's trying to figure something out.

Tender

At five metres away, the scene shifts. Beth is, in fact, the only one looking at her. The rest are fixated on the trenches. When Mia climbs out, Bill helps her as if saving something delicate from something dangerous. Her denim shirt is pockmarked with holes, and a prickly branch is stuck to her arm, which they unpick.

Nell stands at the edge of the trenches.

It is not her they are talking about. Or – at least – not the part of her that's standing in front of them.

The trench is overgrown.

As if the dug-out interior has been exposed to the air for years, weeds and grass sprout savagely, covering the sample grids in a blanket of muddy green. Grassy plants thicken and knit into dense, wiry brambles, the spines like a child's zigzagging drawing, sharper and sharper towards the middle. There are thistle plants in their early stages, tearing lush from the soil. No order, no sense to be made of it save the cooling Nell feels on the back of her neck. The ground is hungry, eager to fill and overrun. It occurs to her then that maybe the people who created the burial ground might have been appeasing the ground itself. The fen, ever-changing and as unknowable as the ocean: had it been threatening to drink them all in? Did they feel the stirring she feels now, as the plants they relied on betrayed and infected them?

Indifferent to the humans standing over them, the plants rise from the earth to soak in sunlight.

"This is impossible," Gunner says, dismayed. "How can the ground be this fertile? If it's always been like this, we have to date the other plants we found."

"You think they grew after the bodies were placed here?" Mia sits on the bank and gawps at the surreal vegetation.

Bill turns to Beth. "You ever get plants growing like this?"

Beth's eyes continue to bore into Nell. "Never seen anything like it."

"What do we do now, do we clear it?" Gunner gathers his tools and approaches the edge.

Ingrid clicks her finger and points at the spot he's standing in, as if she can freeze him. "This has set us back days – a week, even. There won't be time, will there? We need to talk to funding. We need an extension."

Bill nods, and explains to the rest, "We were considering one, anyway. To search for more bodies before the summer is over."

Beth doesn't say anything, but her jaw grinds. Her train of thought is clear to anyone who would notice: more trenches, fewer crops.

"So what, we leave it until they tell us what to do?" Gunner says.

Ingrid flashes him the same look she's given Nell so many times. *Who's in charge here?* "Of course not. We can't afford to stand around."

"I'll do it," Nell says. They all stare at her from the other side of the trench. But this is the right thing to do, she knows. After all, didn't the trench plants grow this way because of her, whatever she is? She let herself get out of control and now she must rein it back in. She needs to prove that she can still serve a function to them.

"Me too," Gunner says. "We can fix this. I'll work all day and all night if I have to."

Ingrid raps her fingers over her folded arm, leaving sweat spots on her light leather jacket. "That won't be necessary."

Tender

Nell finds the reasoning she knows Ingrid wants to hear. "We might only get one chance here, Ingrid. You know the weather's going to wreck any artefacts before we get approval to come back."

"I'll help too," Beth says.

Bill eyes Nell. But whatever he's heard about the party, it can't be the worst of it, because he says, "That settles it. Ingrid and I will contact the university and the council to discuss extensions. Everyone else clear the trenches. Mia, do the reporting – good practice."

Gunner touches her arm before they begin cutting. "You okay?"

Nell dips away. "I don't want to talk. I want to think about the dig and nothing else. It's like you've said before: this is our chance. So, let's put everything else aside for now."

Gunner nods and clatters through the tools to find a shovel. Nell turns towards the trench and only stops when Gunner adds a final, quiet question.

"Did you mean to do it?"

"You mean poison my sister?"

"And yourself. Why?"

She assesses what reaction he'd want to see. And she takes her time about it, feeling that old, pleasant sensation that she can recalibrate the conversation into something nonchalant. It feels nice, slowing down like she always has, to consider what to show. The thistles retreat, a tiny fraction. She chooses a sad shrug.

"Of course not. I was just a kid, a sheltered one. I didn't know what I was doing."

Lauren Du Plessis

But in her head she's asking, why does lightning strike a tree, why do tectonic plates quake, why do lions tear into zebra flesh? Some questions are just awful, undeniable and true, and don't bear thinking about. She certainly doesn't want to think about how much further she and Liz would have run if they hadn't become ill. Would they ever have gone home?

Nell shuffles between nausea and unsettling calm as they cut through the trenches' tumorous growths. Each snap of her pliers shocks through the nerves of her arm, if nerves are what they can be called now. Her awareness is heightened today, as though accepting the truth about her sister scraped a gunky film off the top of her brain. She can hear Gunner's breathing, and Beth's muttered conversation with the assistants in the next trench.

She hoped it would help, that cutting the trench growths back would tell the earth something symbolic. *You've had your fun with me, now stop.* But the discomfort is so strong in her head that her temples constrict with pressure and she feels it in the front of her face. Building and building as she cuts, until the familiar burn of a new opening begins between her eyes. Her heart rate jumps up – it's never happened here before. But she can't be more of a monster than she already is, so she isn't afraid. All she can do is continue to cut. She takes a deep breath and exhales through the explosion. Being on her face, on such sensitive skin, the pain is worse than usual. She breathes the way actors breathe on TV shows when they are giving birth, but quieter, keeping her face turned from Gunner. The thistle punctures a small hole, then pushes through it, opening on the other side and tickling the skin around it with soft, fresh petals.

Tender

After the first hour, her wrists begin to feel the strain of cutting and the pain in her face becomes overbearing. Gunner works a few metres away from her, dislodging roots with his shovel and throwing branches over his shoulder to the bank. She takes a break to watch him and soak in his unrelenting ambition. She enjoys the sweat beading on his brow, the deepening of his heels into the ground, even when he's destroying something.

Beth's head appears over the top of the next trench. She wrenches herself up over the side to sit over them, boots dangling.

"Nell. What happened to your face?"

"What?" Gunner sticks his shovel into the ground and looks at Nell. A trickle of blood creeps round her nose and pools between her lips. Except it doesn't taste of iron – too sweet, too raw. Blood tastes of old metal, and this tastes of fresh, uncooked meat.

Gunner's eyes widen. "Nell, what—"

"Did you do this to her?" Beth says, voice rising. The chatter of the assistants stops.

Gunner's forearm muscles twist by his sides, hands curling to fists. "Sorry? What are you accusing me of?"

Beth clambers down and walks around a stunned Gunner to reach Nell's side.

"Did he do this to you?"

"No," Nell breathes. "What do you see?"

"Blood. And a thistle," Beth says.

The word leaves Beth's mouth like a thick, fruity syrup. Nell shuts off from the world. She is vaguely aware of Beth's hand approaching her face, a rough but warm touch. Her vision tunnels further. Everything is hazy until the sense of touch fades, and she sees Beth arguing with Gunner. She mumbles over and over, "You can see." But her colleagues aren't listening.

Gunner marches to the ladder and clambers out of the trench. Beth stands to meet him. The sound of their voices oozes back in as Nell's heart rate steadies.

"Maybe you should let us get on with our jobs," Gunner hisses. "Why did you even offer to help?"

"This is ridiculous, can't you see her face!"

Gunner's hand rises to his stomach as if his insides have soured. "I'm the one who's been taking her to the doctor, I'm the one who patched her up after she hurt herself."

"Hurt herself? When did she hurt herself?"

"Look, why are you even here? You should respect Nell's privacy. I can take care of her."

"Like fuck you can."

Gunner grabs at Beth's shirt, wrenches her closer to him. In a second, she curls her fist and jabs his right side. He releases her and hits her square in the stomach. Beth blows out a couple of steadying breaths, and strikes Gunner's nose with such force he stumbles into the trench and falls. The assistants gasp. The crunch of his ankle is audible.

Instinct moves Nell's legs underneath her, and she climbs to his side. Gunner's nose is bloodied and swelling unevenly, the bridge rounding out with skin stretched, while the base flares in purple and brown, flecked with burgundy blood vessels. It looks almost like an orchid. He wipes it on his sleeve. Then, she looks up to Beth. Beth is looking right at her as if the two of them are alone, eyes fierce with apology and fists knotted tight. It's the first time that Beth's emotions have flared right at the surface, clear

Tender

and readable. Nell counts the thud of her pulse to twenty before Beth frowns goodbye, and leaves.

"What happened, Nell?" Gunner stands and assesses his ankle, leaning until the pain causes him to wince. He reviews her exploded face, and once again must see a half-thing, some mark or shape he can't explain.

"I cut myself on a bramble," she says.

"Did you?" Gunner's eyes prick suddenly with tears. "This is all so fucked, Nell. Something's wrong with us."

Nell watches him hobble to the ladder and haul himself out of the trench. A bickering back-and-forth hum comes from the assistants. Then a new sound urges Nell to climb out, too. Retching, uneven and heavy.

She peers over the edge. Gunner is vomiting into the dry grass, on all fours, his chest expanding and contracting like a heartbeat. Mia rubs his back.

She can't watch any more. It hurts too much to see him suffer like that, despite everything.

She wipes the blood from her face, takes a seat in the dirt and threads her fingers around the spiral leaves of a new thistle growth. Did she make this happen, she wonders – the trench growths, the anger? Or did something in this ground make *her* growths happen? Does it matter, she wonders, what came first. This is a symbiotic relationship between her and the fenland. One that needs to end.

She speaks to the earth under her breath. "I'm sorry we have to cut you like this. The sooner this is done, the sooner we'll leave you alone."

She shushes the stems after each cut, strokes the leaves with her fingertips. At each root, she wraps herself around it and leans back with her full body weight, gently, to ease them out. On her third fall backwards, her leg catches on something hard.

She sits up and pulls it from the soil. A fragment of human skull bone. There is a crater in the centre, with cracks around it, and the shape is instantly familiar. Images cluster in Nell's mind like jumbled pomegranate seeds in the flesh, all red with blood and pushing against each other. A blunt instrument to the back of the head, the world fading to nothing, sinking into the earth and staining it red not only from ceremonial ochre but from body fluids.

"Tria," she whispers.

She can see it in her mind. The villagers take Tria into the thicket on a hunt, or so they tell them. They find a deer in a clearing. Tria prepares their arrow. They pull back and aim as the deer looks on, and the villagers stand behind them.

Tria releases the arrow. The villagers launch a stone pickaxe into their skull. They gasp, strangle, and fall forward into the soft earth.

The villagers carry the sacrifice back to the village. They must appease the wrath beneath their feet.

Nell swallows bile and wraps the fragment in tissue, slipping it into her backpack. There is something sour here, something old and capable of distortion.

It's still thirty-four degrees at five in the afternoon. Nell creeps through the guest house kitchen, overwhelmed by everything, every movement of air molecules around her as she walks and every distress call of cut grass coming in like onion fumes through the open windows. Gordon is

Tender

washing dishes in the sink, whistling. Either he cannot feel the shift, or the shift does not concern him.

Nell is wondering how many times he has seen guests transform, when she hears a muffled sob from upstairs. The first floor, she thinks, which means the sound is coming from Mia, because she can't imagine Ingrid having the capacity to sob so outwardly.

She climbs the stairs feeling every creak, hoping she doesn't meet anyone on the way.

There are a few distinct memories in her mind, moments when she heard Liz cry after the poisoning. She otherwise became deathly quiet, but on those occasions she made a noise just like Mia is making now. The first was when Liz was ten, and refused to leave the house in the morning for school. Nell knew why – she was heading towards another long hike through the thicket of nicknames and threat of childish violence. Pulled hair, burned wrists and the like. Nell had offered to cut her hair so it couldn't be pulled, or tell a teacher. Liz had cried louder. The second time was when that old boyfriend cheated on her. And the third was when Liz was barely an adult, nineteen years old, and pregnant with Charlie. It was the first time she'd suspected David of cheating on her, and the first of several, if her mother's gossip was anything to go by.

Nell is thinking of all this, these moments of pain she could not correct, could not erase, and all she wants to do is help Mia to stop crying.

In the yellow room, in the corner, Mia's hair covers her face and arms. She is curled tight. Her room is below Gunner's, so gets little light in the evenings. The yellow is turned a coral orange.

Nell sits beside her, trying to find the words she never managed to say to Liz.

"Who is it?" Mia says, remaining hunched.

"Nell."

She throws her head back, hair still straggling across it, and clings to Nell's shoulder.

"I'm so, so sorry! I tried to talk them out of it. None of this is your fault, none of it."

"What are you talking about?"

Mia pauses to arrange her hair into a large curve, like the lip of a conch, over her shoulder. A fresh tear buds on the outer corner of her eye. "You haven't spoken to Ingrid." Then she looks straight at Nell, and her eyes widen. "Did you fall over in the trench?"

Nell wants to ask all the questions she asked of Gunner – what Mia can see, is it scars or rash or flowers – but she holds back. Mia needs her.

"I caught myself on a bramble. Don't worry, I'm fine. Talk to me, why are you crying?"

"Oh, Nell. We didn't get the extension. Bill and Ingrid said they were thinking of… of firing you and Gunner. But they're moving you to Bristol, to start the lab work instead. In a few days. I'm sorry."

She bends over, dropping her forehead to Nell's shoulder. Nell sits back against the wall and they remain there, as the room turns pink.

"What's going to happen to the dig?" Nell asks. The thistle in her face pounds, the rest of her body smarting like dull menstrual pain. A knotting, barbed tentacle in place of her intestines. But she can't let Mia see this. She can't infect someone else.

Tender

"Ingrid says we'll get some volunteers for the final weeks, to help clean up. Then I think we're coming back next year. At least, I hope we can all come back. I know a lot has gone wrong, and you and Gunner are in trouble, but to me it would feel so weird to come back without you." The conch folds over itself, her face hidden once more. Wet hair catches on Nell's shoulder. "Sorry, I'm a mess today. And the humidity is wrecking my hair."

Nell sits forward. "Do you want me to plait it? I can do Dutch braids."

"Really? I mean, if you don't mind." Mia gets up and approaches her flower-printed suitcase, pulling out a trinket box covered in glitter, which is full of hair clips and bands. She brings over two elastics, and takes a seat in front of the small dressing table that sits under her window. Nell stands behind her, grateful there isn't a dresser in her room. She would never stop staring at her face thistle.

"Does Gunner know? How did he take it?" she asks, gathering the first yarns of Mia's hair from the crown of her head.

"He kept apologising. He had this smile on his face – you know, that really charming vibe he puts on sometimes – trying to persuade Ingrid and Bill that everything's fine. He stopped throwing up once we got back here, you know. Like a one-eighty. It was wild. But Ingrid said her mind was made up, you both have to go find a place in the city and move on from all this... It feels wrong."

Nell works, hyper-aware of every tug and tangle, trying to cause as little sensation to Mia as possible. Because Nell is the danger, isn't she? If Gunner was better almost as soon as he was away from her, then she is the source of all the suffering here. Her fingers tremble.

Mia continues. "You have a sister, right? I bet you did this kind of thing all the time when you were little."

"Sometimes. Did you say you have siblings?"

"A brother and a sister, both eight. I know! Surprise twins. This is the longest I've ever been away from them other than for uni. I miss them so much."

Nell wraps the elastic around the first braid. "Are you very close?"

"They're like... extensions of myself. It's ridiculous how much I love them. I call them my little lychees, because they're so tiny and sweet until one goes bad, and you get a squishy, sour mess!" She laughs.

That this love exists is enough for Nell. She doesn't say anything more on the subject and Mia moves the conversation back to Bristol. She studied her undergraduate degree there, so she recommends restaurants, the cheapest cinema, and a board game cafe. She tells Nell where she can get cookies emblazoned with Banksy artworks. Nell asks where she can get a good manicure, and Mia replies that she isn't sure, but there's a cute salon by the river that she often passed.

"Lots of good Instagram content," she says. "Speaking of, you haven't been updating yours much lately? My feed is a lot less pastel than usual."

Nell is aware that it has been two weeks since her last post, which is the longest break she has ever taken. The last image is of the glittering stream. All the grids of her life are being ripped away: the sample grids in the trenches; her classified, formulated social media self; the framework of her good girl persona.

Tender

"I'm sorry. That wasn't a complaint. It's your IG after all! I wish I could make my life look as pretty as yours, I haven't got the visual eye."

"I wish I could make mine as pretty as yours," Nell says sadly. She has finished her colleague's hair. The style draws attention to Mia's large eyes, which gaze up at her in the mirror.

"Are you taking care of yourself, Nell?"

She is so hungry. And unbearably thirsty, her throat an endless vine. Her vacuoles clamour for moisture, to squeeze and drain it through. She can even feel the thirst in her feet, a feeling she never could have imagined, an acrid, desperate sting in her toes. They lead her up to the bathroom where she turns on the shower and stands under it, hardly noticing the occasional splatter of gunge. The water rinses it away again.

When the stinging dulls, she returns to her room in her nightdress, still dripping. Her towel remains hung on the door hook.

She sits in the middle of her bed, also damp, and thinks about what Mia said.

She is not taking care of herself at all. The thirst has barely eased and the hunger is worse. Her insides feel shrivelled, like all her skin is being pulled inwards to a single kernel. Her breath comes in short gasps as she realises what she needs to do now, the sole thing she can do now.

Nell rips open her bag, and lays everything out. She has two packets of crisps remaining, and a range of snacks from the shop: a paper bag of mint bonbons, a Kinder Bueno,

Lauren Du Plessis

some Melba toast. She begins with the crisps, savoury first. They mulch between her teeth in salty chunks and go thick down her throat, dry as anything. Sucking a bonbon helps, stimulating her salivary glands. So she eats both, a crisp then two bonbons, over and over until all the packets are empty on the floor. Her head hurts with the sugar, but the salt is drying her out again.

She goes back to the bathroom. How can she feel better? She drinks from the tap, long gulps, then returns to her room and uses her acrylics to scoop the nutty centres from each Kinder Bueno segment. The toast is too dry, it crumbs across her tongue and makes her want to claw it off.

It is late. She has eaten almost everything, is enmeshed in nausea, but still feels overheated and undersaturated. She's not sure any amount of water would solve it. It's the thistles. They need something more.

But there is no more food, and when she drinks another gulp from the tap, she throws it back up, clear and barely stomach-touched. She is losing moisture, if anything.

Nell chokes on air as tears rush from their ducts. She curls into a tight foetal position on her bed. All this time she has lain dormant but now her thistles are awake, unravelling the people around her without a second thought. A thistle doesn't care if it harms someone. Nell pulls her knees tighter to her chest and wishes, wishes for the thistles to overgrow and cut her up into little shreds. Physical pain, please. Agony would be so much better than thought and thirst. She wants to *be* consumed; she wants the power stripped from her. No decisions, no thinking, no action. Just the quiet, uncaring innocence of a thistle plant. A thistle plant in heavy, relinquishing rain.

Tender

*

There's a note on her floor in the morning, slipped under her door. *August 29th.* So they have a maximum of two days clearing, if they leave tomorrow night. And that won't be enough. She turns the slip of paper over. *I miss you Nell,* Gunner has written on the other side, *I'm sorry.*

She walks to the farm. Better not to be alone with Gunner – who knows what the thistles would do, or what she would do. Is there any difference anymore?

She doesn't go with a plan, but her mind isn't blank, either. If anything, her mind is full. Not busy, not filled with thoughts, instead full of what feels like cotton wool but must be the mature down of the thistles. There is no space for complex thought, just simple action and feeling.

Nell touches the flower between her eyes. Overnight, another sprouted through her left brow and small lumps pushed through her forehead. They're coming through the back, too: there were thin but noticeable tangles of hair on her pillow when she woke up. There was also vomit in the top drawer of her nightstand, which she thankfully never put anything in. She pumped the spray of her perfume until the last few drips remained in the bottle.

The world is still vivid. The breeze roars, passing cars scream, and her footsteps stab the tarmac. For the first time in weeks there are clouds gathering, so it's now both hot and wet, like walking through a mouth. But she is still parched, and she will do anything to make that stop. It can't go on.

Beth's distant shape on the next field is comforting when she arrives. So much that she's overcome with desire

189

to show Beth the thistles, all of them. If anyone would understand, it's her – someone who knows what it is to have nature dictating your life, who uses plants to heal, who cared about Nell before she started causing trouble.

She pulls off her jacket, allowing the blooms around her wrists to reach the air. But then she sees the lean-to, filled with farming machinery. The small can of diesel fuel. And, next door in the barn, the slats of wood.

And then she has a feeling. That terrible inevitability. She sees Mia swimming in the river, and Gunner smiling while talking about his childhood adventures. Ingrid with her books and Bill on the phone, ordering someone around. She has to protect them all from herself, this other version of Nell.

She labours over the screw to release the lid of the diesel tank, and dips a wood slat into the tarry darkness. It emerges iridescent. Then she takes the lighter from her bag.

She's trying to do the impossible, she thinks. Still, it must be done, like cutting back invasive bindweed and killing its roots, so that other plants can continue to thrive.

She waits, hidden around the corner of the outbuildings, for half an hour or longer. A message comes in from Liz.

Fuck fuck fuck. It's getting worse. He's going to leave, everyone always leaves.

She responds slowly, checking up every few seconds as Beth packs away her tools in the distance.

I'm sorry. Then she sends it again. *I'm sorry.*

Beth goes inside.

Nell dashes to the side of the trench and pulls up the tarp. The ground around it is clear of vegetation for at least a few yards, and despite the heat the ground retains its boggy

Tender

softness. There should be no spread to the neighbouring fields. It's basically a fire pit. Finally, she flickers the lighter under the wood. It takes.

All too quick the smell of burning twinges inside her head, the thistles knowing their own flammability. *Run, run*, they tell her, but she moves towards the trench and drops the wood into the bramble. Red and grey sputters appear like summonings.

"Nell! What are you doing?"

Nell stops still, smoky air brushing between her exposed petals.

XI

She thought the thistles taught her pain, but this is different. Splintering neurons shock up and down the length of her root system. She readies her legs to run but Beth strides over, grabs her wrist, and wrenches her back from the growing flames.

"What the hell are you doing?"

Smoke stings Nell's eyes, which makes her cry more. The words sound insane coming out of her mouth. "The thistles keep growing! I don't know how to stop it!"

She shakes off Beth's hand and fights the pulsing burn inside her to approach the heat.

"Nell, get back! It's not safe!"

She watches the licks of orange as if there could be a pattern to their movements. In the apocalyptic centre, black, skeletal branches curl and break. Leaves shrivel and twist into dust, spat in bursts into the sky.

When a small branch at the edge is exposed, she crouches and snatches it from the jagged mouth of the fire. Leaping back, the burn of hot organic matter sears her fingertips. She keeps still until the thread of smoke dies away, then walks back to Beth and holds the charred result in her face.

Lauren Du Plessis

"Don't you see? It has to be like this."

If only she could make her see.

"What's wrong with you? We need to put this out now!" Beth pulls her further away then dumps her on the floor, sprinting back towards the outbuildings.

Deep, choking smoke now billows up and out, and it's getting worse fast.

"See?" she tells the thistles. "This is what I think of you. What the world thinks of you. So disappear."

She's reminded of a day, a long time ago. She was sixteen, perhaps. In her hands she held the results of her mock exams. Three sheets of paper that her parents could never be allowed to see. Three Es, two Ds, two Cs. The one B wouldn't even matter to them. They'd completely overlook it. She doesn't know how this happened, because she always revised and they always told her what a smart girl she was. So they could never see these pieces of paper. She would do better on her real exams, and these would disappear. She got a match from the kitchen and burned the papers over a plastic sink bucket filled with water, which she carried out to the field. It was a wet day, no chance of it going wrong. So she could just squat over the tub and burn the sheets, watching them curl and erase themselves from existence, winks of ash approaching her fingers until she dropped the remains into the tub. *Your secret is safe*, the grass told her in the wind.

There's a real, perverse joy in watching something burn. Nell sits near the edge of the trench and watches the last few weeks disappear. The soil beneath will be left untouched, ready for any more excavation. She'll be long gone, her and her curse.

Tender

But at the edges of the trenches, where there is hardly any grass, somehow the red licks keep going. Nell sits straighter.

An orange line appears on the grass. It turns into a pool. The fire is escaping the trench.

Beth's thundering feet announce her return, armed with a hose, a shovel, and a stack of plastic buckets clutched in her elbow.

"Hold this." Her voice has calmed and taken on an authoritative tone. She hands Nell the hose and closes her hand forcibly around the trigger. "You need to douse the trench as much as you can. I'll stop the spread up here."

While Nell stands and holds the hose knowing she has won, Beth strides around the perimeter shovelling moistened earth over any flickering tongues that venture out.

There is little difference at first, the flames teasing at their feet. But then the smoke begins to darken and sputter, and the red shrinks away. Beth walks back to her side and orders the buckets to be filled, which she dumps heavily over the remains of the trench. Nell points the hose at the charcoal skeleton bramble once more, and feels hollowed out as if she burned herself in there. *A horrible thing*, she thinks. *This was a horrible thing, an irrevocable thing.* But it had to be done.

The ground is printed with black knots when the fight is over. Sooty lines where the fire tried to spread, and brown worms of wetted soil where Beth contained it.

Beth slumps onto her knees. "I don't even know what to say."

"It's done now."

"What? You could've set fire to my whole life." Beth's voice shakes, the sound new and heartbreaking.

And then it's all gone: the glee of watching the fire, the relief of looking into the trench and seeing only earth again.

Nell swallows back tears. "I'm so sorry. I had to." She claws at her buttons, opens her blouse. "I had to do it because of these."

The petals form a reef across her chest, pink reaching tendrils like anemone. Brushing against her is like running a hand over short-cut grass, if that grass was a drawing, an abstract idea of grass. What little of her skin is left exposed around the thistles is veiny, dry and just as inhuman. The thistles themselves, thriving on her outburst, are the brightest pink they've ever been.

She waits for the scream, a gasp of shock, hand on chest or clasped over mouth. Beth's eyebrows twitch and her lips part, teeth grinding together.

"It isn't just your face. They're everywhere."

"You can see them," Nell sobs.

"They grow near the stream. They're meadow thistles."

Nell makes an affirmative sound, but it's choked by tears. Beth steps close to her and touches a thistle on her clavicle.

"It's so soft."

"You can feel them!"

"Are they real, is this really happening? Or am I dying of smoke inhalation?" Beth says. Her eyebrows are furled so harshly they form a T-shape on her forehead, and Nell reads invisible words from them – taut, tend, truth. "Okay, think. Think. Nell, come with me."

Despite her protests, Nell finds herself back in Dr Shaw's office first. She blinks under the brightness of the strip lights.

Tender

"So, Elinor, you say you haven't seen any improvement?"

She has heard her name from so many mouths in the last few days, it barely registers as a single whole that indicates her. Beth nudges her.

She's lying on the examination table like a specimen, blouse open. Shaw presses on the thistles. She yelps. Shaw presses another area, near what's left of her navel. It burns in her eyes, her feet.

"You're hurting her!" Beth says.

Shaw sighs as if Nell has done something to inconvenience her. "Did you get your period in the end?"

"Yes!" Nell croaks as another corner of her gut lights up. She eases herself into a sitting position, unable to take the examination anymore.

"What does that have to do with anything?" Beth says.

"We have to rule things out."

"But the thistles!" Beth says, walking around the bed to stand behind Nell. "Dr Shaw, can't you see them?"

"I don't understand. Do you have prickling pain? Pins and needles? Have you tried washing your clothes with plain water? Have you used any new creams or lotions?" Shaw leans over, seemingly unaware of the thistles reaching for her face. Her mouth turns down. "I can assure you there's nothing there. How much longer did you say you were staying?"

"Until tomorrow," Nell says.

"These things usually resolve themselves once you're in the right environment."

"Are you kidding?" Beth says. Her fists are tight in Nell's peripheral vision, as if she wants to say something more but won't let herself.

She raises a hand. "Beth, nobody else can see them. It's okay."

Shaw sighs and crosses the office to her desk, pulling a slip of printed paper from a pile which she scribbles a note on. "You could try a cream to reduce inflammation and soothe any itching. But you don't actually need it: there's nothing there. When you get home, I suggest you book an appointment with your regular GP. I'm going to grab my stapler from the other room."

The door clicks shut behind her and Beth immediately pulls away, rounds the examination table, and pulls Nell to her feet.

"This is bullshit. What do you need, Nell?"

"I need it to go away," she says softly. "I need to leave, and everything will come right."

"And if it doesn't?"

"Then I need water. And soil." The words are coming from the thistles, their hunger for growth. But within the urge to bury herself she finds a new idea: rather than chasing them back into her innermost depths, can't she draw them out?

Beth drives them back to the farm while Nell replies to a message from Gunner. She tells him there's no need to come and clear anymore, then types out a few attempts at an explanation before hitting send without one, and staring out at the fields. There are now so many people holding different secrets about her: they must all view her in completely different ways. Like people standing by opposing windows around a house, trying to discern what the world outside is like and all coming to conflicting conclusions.

Tender

The question Beth was holding in comes when they get out of the car and walk around the back of the house.

"Are you really leaving tomorrow?" Beth says, opening a shed door and vanishing inside.

"Yeah. Gunner and I are going to Bristol to start the lab work."

She stands in the doorway and watches Beth march back and forth, each time checking herself as if she's forgotten something, the items popping suddenly back into her mind. She picks up mud-crusted waterproof trousers, a rust-edged shovel, and a gleaming jar of something mysterious and gooey.

Without another word, Beth closes the shed door and walks in the direction of the stream. As they walk, the sky breaks. For the first time in weeks, rain heavily spatters the earth, which seems to relax, finally catching its breath.

The fields take on a new colour palette in the unfamiliar weather. Lime becomes chartreuse, emerald turns sage. Grey and yellow undertones seep through the ground. Thunder murmurs around the horizon. Nell lets tears of exhaustion, stomach ache and gratitude join the raindrops on her cheeks.

They make a new turning down a path she hasn't followed before.

"This is my favourite corner of the farm," Beth says, "but it's not a happy place. It's where I went after my parents split. All the times I was a teenager who thought the world was too awful to put up with. And the times I've thought of selling up and moving."

It is a copse, where the ground scoops into a sharp ditch. A very old, very dark oak twists its gnarled trunk over the deepest area. The ground underfoot is boggy and uncertain. The hedgerows run all around it, cutting this moment off from the rest of the farm. There is only the sound of the rain, and a far-off bubbling from the stream.

"You wanted water, you wanted soil. Here you are."

Beth digs a hole.

"How do you know what to do?" Nell asks.

"I don't. I'm making this up. But if we're having a shared mental breakdown, we may as well see it through."

Nell sits in the earth and Beth begins to pad the gaps around her with soil.

"So, you want to draw these things out?"

"I hope so. Like purging. Like… the fire. I'm so sorry about the fire," Nell says, "I should've said something to you first. I just thought, with the ground being wet from the sprinklers and there being so little grass left…"

"You think sparks don't travel? We were minutes away from it spreading." Beth's voice raises over the rainfall. "I can't believe you did that. Always burning with you. Remember how you wanted the overdone burger?"

"You remember that?"

"It's weird to say this, after everything, but I'll miss you."

Nell almost laughs. "I've been trouble for you the whole time. You can't wait to be rid of us."

"I've had the chance to rediscover the farm through your eyes. Honestly, since our yield dropped and demand started drying up, this job has become pretty mundane. I didn't even feel like I was making a difference to the community. But then I see someone like you, so moved by it. I feel a bit more in touch with that again. So, no, I don't want to be rid of you. You made a mistake. Everyone makes mistakes. Too cold?"

Tender

Nell takes a moment to register what Beth is referring to, before a squelching confirms that the mud now lines her crossed legs.

"This is ridiculous," she smiles. "You are planting me."

The T of Beth's forehead finally breaks, and she laughs. They take it in turns to laugh, nervously, then because they can't find any other words to say. Finally, they laugh until they are breathless.

She should be preparing for her departure, and she is in the ground. Ahead of her is the promise of lab work, and then the vacuum of the unknown. There is a fragment of skull in her bag, and a hundred unanswered questions in her notebook. But beyond that, what is there? She could go back to Milton Keynes, and find another excavation company, some lab. If the thistles do not overtake her completely, life will continue.

Another thought sets in – that she won't be invited back next year. Ingrid will never want to work with her again. And Beth doesn't strike her as the kind of person that would respond quickly to texts or direct messages, if at all. Any hope of keeping in contact with this place might disappear. Suddenly it's like there's a void yawning open between them, one she wants to hold closed.

Beth unscrews the strange mason jar she brought along.

"What is it?" Nell asks.

"We don't have to use it if you don't want to. It's a mixture of salt, apple cider vinegar, and alcohol. I use it to dry out weeds gently. Makes the foliage shrivel."

In her head, Nell hears her mother extol the benefits of apple cider vinegar for anti-ageing.

"Do it," she says, "I want them gone."

They take turns dipping into the jar and applying the solution to her body, Nell on the front and Beth, cautiously, on the back. It glides on smooth as royal jelly. Cool, fresh, and turning her rosy as they work.

It is so gentle that the thistles don't notice its presence at first, busy with their joy at the density of the soil around them. Nell is buried to her waist, legs unable to move now, and she can feel the downwards grasp of her body as roots try to burst from her and keep her here forever.

"Do you need to tell the others where you are?" Beth asks.

"They won't miss me. I'd rather be here."

She misses off two final words, *with you*, her throat closing quickly around them – because how can that be the case, when this place has poisoned her?

"Hey, you probably shouldn't disturb it," Beth says, flicking her hand away. Nell hadn't even noticed her fingers tugging at the tendrils of a thistle under her sternum. She nods and unbuttons her blouse the rest of the way.

"It's definitely for the best that I leave." Nell reaches down to where she placed her handbag near the base of the oak, and takes out the tissue-wrapped bone, kept there since she pulled it from the overgrowth.

"What's that?"

"I shouldn't have taken it. This might be the most important part of this find and… and I stole it." She points to the fracture. "I think these people were killed. On purpose. To try and appease something."

"Shit. So my farm *is* an ancient crime scene?"

Nell laughs despite the sick feeling in her chest. "You seem awfully happy about something so violent and horrible." The laughter quickly dies away inside her. "But the flowers are trying to tell me something. Maybe they were like a deterrent the whole time. They don't want me prying. Or they do, and it's like a cycle…"

"A cycle?"

Nell gasps with pain as the thistles notice the gentle acid twinge of Beth's tincture. "I did something bad. A long time ago. And I feel like it's all connected."

Beth leans forwards, wraps her arms around Nell's shoulders. Everything disappears for a moment, crushed in the darkness of Beth's shirt. There is only her heartbeat and the rumble of her stomach.

"I wish we had longer." Beth's voice roars through her body and into Nell's ear like wind through a forest. "Seems like there's a lot you want to talk about, and maybe against my best judgement, I would've listened."

"But this place is making me change."

"Isn't change good, sometimes? As long as it doesn't involve arson."

"But I can't. Even if I wanted to, I can't stay. I'm making everyone suffer. And I'm suffering for it. It's not worth it."

Beth's words come out slow and unsure, as she holds Nell tighter against her.

"I think this place is bringing out something beautiful in you, actually. Scary, too, but somehow magical."

Nell turns her face, pushing herself further into Beth's stomach. And she cries, ugly, out-of-control tears that hurt so much it frightens her. She remembers each time she and Beth have locked eyes with puzzling expressions, trying to find something unspoken within each other.

When her energy has ebbed out, they lie next to each other, daisy-chained by the arms, in the cold and the wet.

"You wouldn't consider staying?" Beth says quietly. "Or coming back?"

"I don't have a choice. This place has been bad for me."

"I think I disagree."

"I have to go, Beth. If I can't get rid of the thistles, who knows what would happen next? It could be a curse, it could be contagious. My heart tells me I love it here, but I don't trust it. What if it isn't me that loves the farm, the trenches, the bodies, the flowers... what if, all this time, it's been this parasite inside me? Lying to me. Making me something I'm not. I don't know."

Beth pulls their arms closer together.

Nell sobs again. "I don't know who I am."

XII

There is a man waiting outside the guest house when they open the front door.

"You seen the owner?" the man says. Gunner points him inside, where Gordon is sitting in the kitchen, reading the morning paper with a bewildered expression.

"Are you here for the cracks?" Nell asks. The others, standing around the entrance hall, look at her as if she has said something rude. But they must have noticed. Each week there have been more. They're as squirm-inducing as cracks in human skin. The guest house's foundation must be failing. Perhaps, one day, it will sink after all.

Everyone steps out, and Gordon leads the man to one of the cracks, now oozing a brown liquid.

"That's the worst of the discharge," Gordon says. "And there's a gurt big crack right there."

There are several meanings to the word *discharge*, Nell recalls as the two men talk. They are, in increasing order of relevance to her life: a precursor to menstruation; the release of spores into the air, or the release of sperm nuclei into the ovule of a plant; or the release of a person from a place or duty (hospital, employment). As a verb, it is to vent, to let go, to push out.

Lauren Du Plessis

The group seems to remember, all at once, what they are doing in the car park in the first place. The only one who hugs Nell is Mia, wet-eyed and quiet.

"Consider this a fresh start," Bill says, patting the roof of her car as she gets in. "You know who you could be, Nell. I don't want to hear any negativity from Bristol before we join you."

Ingrid hasn't come to see them leave. She's visible through her bedroom window, reading a book. Gunner looks up, then shakes his head as he climbs into his car, and leads out of the guest house driveway.

Nell watches the flat fields recede in the side mirror as she follows Gunner, and tries to picture a seed of new beginnings resting on her dashboard. It is good that she is leaving, isn't it? Things couldn't possibly get worse now.

And had she not known that something like this was bound to happen, ever since she graduated university and was released into the jaws of the rest of her life? As soon as she had received confirmation of its publication and agreed to write articles for several journals, Nell had had the premonition that her Masters thesis was the peak of her career, and from there it was downhill.

The thesis had discussed the ethics of weeds; their treatment, expulsion, and botanical relevance (if any) of the term. The writing was far from revolutionary, but seemed to pluck at some frantic truth that the community had wanted to hear from a young botanist. When she spoke to people about it, she realised that for some of them it was about being a woman in science, or a newcomer to an underfunded, competitive field.

Tender

One line from this thesis sticks with her now, as she tries to match Gunner's weaving path through M5 traffic. *The word, 'weed', is relevant only in context.*

Weeds are all about context. They don't exist until they are assigned that term by a certain person, in a certain place. They sprawl through new habitats, or ones non-natural to them, and are often the first to appear after an environmental disturbance. They are defined as aggressive, fast-growing, invasive.

In the bubble of uni, it was easy to appear a wildflower. Alone in Milton Keynes, it was easy to feel pleasant and organic among the grey walkways. She was living a make-believe life before coming here. But in old family photos she looked undomesticated, out of place. And now, in a lineup of her colleagues – the people who could carry her forward into a prestigious career – it is clear that Nell is a weed.

After her peak, here is the trough. The trench. No, deeper than that. Here is the pit. The kind of place weeds thrive. And somehow, she must climb her way out and play the wildflower once more.

It's an hour's drive until they stop for lunch. As they pass in and out of data service, Nell gets a WhatsApp call that cuts off, and two messages she can't read while driving. When they pull over, at the same service stop she visited on the way down, she finds that the messages are from Liz, of course, and that they have been deleted, of course.

She checks herself in the rear-view mirror before getting out. Her hair does sit better after a thorough wash. She used so much conditioner in the morning that it's edging on fluorescent. Her surreal dermatological therapy with Beth has significantly shrunk the thistles. Before leaving, Nell decanted the solution Beth gave her into more acceptable shampoo and conditioner bottles. Now, when she examines her neckline, she can trace the outline of her bones once more. The buds resemble boils, pink eruptions, but they are smaller. They are retreating.

Gunner locates a table while Nell approaches a salad counter and makes her selection. The bodies around her float like pollen spores on the wind, haphazard and free. The holidays are over, kids are going back to school next week, so the remnant visitors are adults in business suits, delaying their journey to the city.

Perhaps her parents knew something she didn't. That's why they eagled around her. They saw it before anyone else, and the poisoning incident confirmed it. Their daughter was wild and dangerous, and had to be taught how to contain it.

How kind of them to give her those skills. She points with her gloved hand to the baby gem lettuce, grated carrot, sweetcorn, cherry tomatoes and croutons, with a low-fat salad dressing (she has determined that now is the time to switch back to the healthy stretch of her diet). Driving gloves cover her razor nails. She did her best filing them down, but with several weeks of growth the acrylics are now disturbing to look at. She gives the server a toothy smile and tucks her hair behind her ear while tapping her payment card.

"I can't believe how fucked up all that got," Gunner says, after returning with his own meal. "I feel better just being away from that place."

Tender

Nell gathers leaves onto her fork and takes a neat bite. "Me too."

She opens the internet on her phone, to review the flat they reserved. It's one-bedroom with a sofa bed: open and airy, on the top floor of a four-storey building. The photographs leer with a wide-angle lens at the floor-to-ceiling windows in the living room, the Juliet balcony, a brand new white paint job, and vinyl floors with a luxe wood finish. The sort of place that functional professionals live in, and the kind of place that her parents have trained her to live in. The kind of place where a weed would never grow.

Gunner sighs as she checks over the details. "But I feel guilty, too," he says. "Maybe it was selfish to come away when everything got so messed up, even if it's what we were told to do. What do you think?"

"I think," Nell begins, but all the words she could say pool sap-thick in her mouth. She takes another bite of food.

Gunner's knees touch hers under the table. "I've got this urge to put things right. I feel… responsible for everything. I never thought I was capable of that – I've never hit *anyone*. I'm really fucking sorry. I messaged Beth last night and she seemed weirdly cool about it, but still. Something *horrible* came out of me that I had no idea was in there."

Nell presses her knee against his thigh. "Things came apart quickly at the end. We all went a little crazy."

"Feels that way. But I don't want this guilt hanging over me. I'm going to keep talking to Ingrid and Bill – there must be something I can do to convince them we're worth coming back next year." He pauses. "And while I'm putting things right, I owe you an explanation, too. About Erica."

"Erica?" Nell asks, although she knows who this name refers to. She takes a final bite of food, places her wooden fork into the tray, and readies herself to know the woman in the blazers and bras.

"We were the London crew at uni. Different courses but lots in common, so we all ended up in a house in second year. But the first time I met her I was drunk. I don't even remember it, all I have is Erica's version, which she loves telling, of course. She mopped me off the floor outside a bar. I said she looked like an orchid because her dress was a weird shape, and I'd spent the day researching orchid seeds for an essay. She thought that was funny and slipped her number in my pocket when I got in the taxi she called me."

It isn't hard to imagine the university version of Gunner, with over-long hair curling into his eyes as he slumps against a brick wall and shouts funny Latin words at passing strangers.

"We were friends, then friends with benefits. I took her on a date, and we poured all our childhood trauma into each other. Sometimes she'd hang off my arm and every word I said, and others she'd vanish for days and never explain it, like we were just casual mates who didn't owe each other anything. She was only there for me when it suited her."

Nell remembers the roundleaf sundew and its carnivorous, sticky leaves, that she likened Gunner to weeks ago. It seems Erica was even more insatiate.

"You know the weirdest thing? I think you'd like her. She's so cool, dresses in amazing clothes. She's full of stories, she can make the most basic anecdote into a piece of impromptu theatre."

Tender

"Sounds familiar. So what's going on now, is this you letting her go?"

"I didn't want to leave anything unsaid before we got to Bristol. You've shown me a lot and I felt like I owed you that too."

Nell shifts in her seat, feeling suddenly fraudulent. "But while we've been away, she's been calling."

"I mentioned you early on, because I should be able to share things with her, but she got jealous. And when I asked her if she wanted to get back together, she said she thought we were bad for each other... I mean, what is it? That she wants to own me?"

He holds out a hand, and Nell takes it because she's not sure what else to do. He stretches his fingers wide then closes them around hers. She goes hot in the fold of his palm. "I've felt like a ticking bomb since Dad died. I needed someone who I could really be with, and tell everything to. I needed Mum there, but she went all distant and started travelling without me. I needed Erica, and she was always seeing someone else behind my back. I *want* to share my time with someone who gives a shit."

Nell opens her mouth. Gunner's desperate need to spill his insides is frightening, endearing, contagious. But he can't see, she reminds herself. He has never truly seen the thistles. She remembers his eyes that first night, confused and searching for the answer to a question he didn't know how to ask. He called them scars, or something like it. If he can't see the truth about them (unlike Beth), he cannot know her other truths in return. She attempts a gentle joke. "After all this time, it's mummy issues, not daddy issues."

To her relief, he smiles. "Who'd have thought it?"

"Do you need that from me?" Nell asks. "The whole caring thing. I don't know if I'd be any better. I can barely take care of myself."

"At the risk of sounding awful," his voice lowers, "maybe we can take care of each other."

After the runaway, Nell and Liz's mother had a brief but fiery affair with antidepressants. Nell hadn't put a label on it at the time, but the clues had been everywhere, if she was willing to break rules and open grown-up cupboards, which in moments of madness she was. In the upstairs bathroom cabinet, if she shuffled the moisturisers aside, she found one beginning with F. In a kitchen cupboard, above the sheen of magazines by the sink, there was one beginning with S. Each time she checked, these bottles were emptier. They came to the door in plain packaging.

The one sure sign she had was something her mother said one Halloween, when Nell had asked if she could take Liz trick-or-treating. *Moderation is the thing,* she sighed, *you should never have too much of anything, or you'll want more and more, and you'll miss it when it's gone.*

The toilet door slams behind Nell and Gunner. She permits this to happen one last time. She had not known that their last time in his bedroom was going to be the last time, after all. Gunner pulls her into the cubicle after him and grasps at her back, fingertips pressing into her. Her gut turns with equal joy and revulsion. *Moderation,* she whispers in her mind.

If this is her final time with Gunner – and it should be, if she knows what's good for her – she ought to remember

Tender

every detail. Before she restores the former, good Nell, she should absorb every smell, taste and touch. The bleach base, with mid tones of sweat, and notes of the spicy bean patty he ate, and the garlic of her salad dressing. The hot pads of his fingers under her top, massaging invisible pain points.

Nell allows the thistles one more moment to braid into each other beneath her skin, feed off her want, relish the taboo. They are weakened, but still there. In Bristol, she will continue her treatment and exterminate them, permanently.

The muscles of Gunner's face tense against her neck. He's smiling. "God, you're beautiful," he says. Nell brims with pride at herself. Such a beautiful thing, and no longer horrible. After this it will all be out of her system.

There is a satisfying sense of completion in taking their keys from the secure lockbox outside the flat, and adding them to their respective keychains.

Gunner hasn't left his postcoital haze, slumping onto the sofa. She checks around the flat and takes a few photos for inventory purposes. In the bedroom, a spot of black mould in the corner. In the tiny room to the side by the window, a larger closet than she expected. She fills it with her clothes, which breathe fresh, unsoaked air for the first time in weeks. Hopefully they will lose the guest house smell without an expensive trip to the dry cleaners.

The bathroom is small but clean, newly fitted. Gaudy dressing-room-style lights border the mirror. Nell holds her phone up and takes the first selfie she's taken in a month. The thistles, shrunken and paling pink, could pass for some kind of music festival makeup. They're quite pretty, really. But she won't miss them.

She ignores the ring of her phone as she inspects the kitchen before joining Gunner on the sofa. When he closes his arms around her, she nestles her cheek to his chest, her mind singing in time with the quick beat of his heart. Away from the dig, the thick vines of the plant up her back will regrow into a human spine, bone by bone, tempered with willpower. She will wean herself off her tenderness for Gunner. As he sighs into sleep, she raises a hand to her own chest and searches for her slower heartbeat. It is faint but consistent.

"All done," she whispers to herself.

"Hm?" Gunner murmurs. She raises her head, and his eyes are two hellebore-dark circles. She's sure that if you photographed them in different wavelengths, you would find a thousand colours. And beneath them, his smiling nose and mouth, marked by dry cracks but soft at the edges. She will miss being this close to him.

"I like your nostrils. Is that... weird? They're shaped like pears," she says.

"That is fabulously weird. Thank you. I like how your mouth is always slightly open, like you're sipping. It's cute."

"Really? My dad used to tell me to shut it all the time."

"Never shut it. That would be a tragedy."

Her phone buzzes again.

"Please don't let that be Ingrid or Bill, I need a break before I start making amends," he says, before closing his eyes once more.

Tender

She should answer it, she knows she should. What if it is their bosses? What if it's something urgent from the university ahead of their start date? But this moment is so quiet, so uncomplicated by anything. Nell stays where she is.

I thought I could escape.

The message waits on her lock screen. It flashes when she taps the snooze button, checking if now would be a good moment to start chopping the vegetables they bought at a corner shop. Nell senses a rumbling, deep inside her – the hum of life, ebbing in the thistle roots. She almost doesn't open the message. Part of her had believed that was it: that the brief burst of communication with her sister would end like everything else. Another six months of distance between herself and Liz wouldn't hurt.

She wrenches the tap and fills a crystalline glass that weighs heavy in her hand. When she places it on the counter beside her glaring phone, the afternoon light splinters around it in a rainbow. She adds one of her sketchbooks into the moment, and takes a photo. Now might be a nice time to reinvigorate her Instagram.

The phone sounds again.

"Someone really wants you, Nell!" Gunner chuckles from across the room.

She sips once more, and unlocks her phone.

I thought I could escape, but I can't. I've tried everything, therapy, medication, hoping it would go away. I tried so hard and I'm so tired. Everyone said I would be okay. But

Lauren Du Plessis

*I can't do it anymore, so I want you to know that you
started it. Fuck you for waking it up. Fuck you for making
us monsters.*

The glass leaves her hands and lands on its corner,
smashing into four uneven shards. One slides up to her
toes where it comes to rest. Gunner mutes the TV and jogs
around the island to grab kitchen roll.

"Oh shit, don't worry! We'll replace it."

Nell walks past him. She grabs her handbag from the
sideboard, jangling with her keys and the plastic-wrapped
skull fragment. She slips her phone in and opens the door.

The road shudders beneath her. Perhaps she hit something
– a vole, a rabbit, or a squirrel. There's no time to go back
and check for little bodies left in her wake. *This should be
over*, she keeps thinking. She left. She did what she had to
do. Just, maybe, she had been too late.

And so she drives to her sister's house.

After she was discharged from hospital, after they had
gone to sleep with the magic of the earth mama, Nell had
never wanted to return to the hospital to see her sister. Liz
even had a birthday during that time. Their parents took
a balloon and some small, soft-edged presents – nothing
she could inhale or cause a mess with. But Nell wouldn't
go with them. She didn't think her sister would want to
see her, after what she did. That was one explanation. But
the other was a sense of failure. They had come so close
to the magic, but it turned out to be evil. She had clearly
misunderstood the world, expecting to be able to live

wildly in it and be happy. Seeing Liz made her think of the field and the marshes, which now made her deeply *un*happy. So, she never went.

After Liz's discharge she made an effort. She wanted her little sister to feel at home again. She wanted it to be like before. They had always been inseparable. But their parents started painting and decorating Liz's new bedroom, which used to be the office. They moved all her furniture out and Nell's bed and wardrobe became lonely residents of her very own room. They didn't read together anymore, couldn't climb into bed with each other when one of them had a nightmare. There was a wall between them now.

Over the years she watched her little sister become who she was supposed to be. They had their moments of closeness, tying each other's hair on school photo day or going to the cinema. Nell loved going to the cinema with Liz, because it forced them to be near each other, but they didn't have to talk. She hated watching her perfect sister grow up without friends. She hated that she was such a terrible role model. Maybe with a different sister, in a different family, Liz would have been happy.

Overhead, red lines garrotte the sky. The sun retreats further towards the horizon the closer she gets.

When she arrives, there are no cars on the driveway and all the lights are off. The dulling red of the clouds reflects on the windows, as if the interior is on fire. The front door stands open.

"Liz?"

The silence of the house clams on the thistles, which shudder at their first experience of cold. It's true: Nell hasn't been cold in a month, but the house is several degrees cooler than outside. The walls seem distant, like she's wandering instead into the vacuum of space. She wishes a floorboard would creak, just to reassure her that soundwaves can still travel through it.

She enters the living room, where they opened Charlie's presents, then creeps through to the kitchen diner. The back patio is empty, too. All the light of the sky is fading, leaving a soft red-black.

"Liz, are you here?"

No sign of her, the girls, or David. There's a wine glass on the counter near the sink, a ring of brown residue circling its base.

Nell returns down the hallway and climbs the stairs. Under the smell of orange and patchouli air freshener, she detects the familiar scent of stomach acid and part-digested food.

The doorway to the master bedroom is cracked open, a slit of burgundy in the dark wall. She puts her eye to the gap and sees her sister's head, alone, as if detached from her body.

"Liz!"

Liz is lying with her head on the pillow, body splayed diagonally, one leg bent over the side. Her left arm is outstretched, reaching for the door, while the other clutches a tissue to her chest. An empty glass of water and pillbox sit on the side table. It almost looks staged, Liz awaiting Nell's inspection. Another body staring at its discoverer. What is her professional opinion – was this a violent end?

Nell's stomach drops. Her sister's eyes are open, two glossy bulbs staring upwards. Holding in the scream, she leans over to check for a pulse, but Liz blinks.

Tender

Silence, one that a better sister would know how to fill. Then Liz smiles. "I did it. I can't feel it. I did it!"

Nell sits, avoiding the wet patch where Liz must have drooled uncontrollably. She presses on her neck. The beating is slow, but consistent. She wants to ask why her sister has done something so awful, outrageous, unacceptable, or other words their parents gave them. But at the same time, it's all she can do to hold herself back from gathering up Liz in her arms and squeezing.

"I should call for an ambulance."

The phone rings once before emergency services pick up. It will be a twenty-minute wait, they tell her.

For a while they sit in silence and the dread finally inches through Nell, delayed before by adrenaline. The thistles set, so that every movement – even breathing – snags them. But she pushes through to stroke her sister's hair.

Eventually she can't bear the silence anymore.

"What happened?" she asks, although she means, *Did I do this?*

"He left."

Nell fights relief and horror. She isn't to blame, but who cares who's to blame. "Where are the kids?"

"Mum and Dad's." Liz turns her head to shake Nell off. "I never realised how little stuff he had. Maybe he never planned to stick around."

"Did he say why?"

Liz appears to struggle with her words, as if fighting sleep. "You want to know why? Because of you."

"What?"

"He said I was a self-fulfilling prophecy… Left because I expected him to leave. True… I was always waiting for him to go. I don't trust people. You said you loved me, and what happened? Mum and Dad say they love me, but Jesus *fucking* Christ."

"But why this? Did you plan this?"

"You heard me before," she rasps. "I didn't want to die, I wanted to be free. I had to get rid of it. For the sake of my girls. I couldn't bear for them to be like us. And with him gone, there was nobody stopping me."

"Get rid of what?" Nell asks. A siren echoes in the distance, and she rushes out another question. "Does it make a difference if I tell you I'm sorry?"

Liz's eyes are growing heavy again, her body weakening. "Sorry?" she says. "Because my husband left me, for the scabs on my shoulder, or for making me like you?"

Propagation, of the worst kind. To propagate your issues and plant them in another. Nell tries, "I wasn't—"

"Fuck off, Elinor. You think I can't see right through you? With your Instagram and your pink clothes and that dumb smile you wear no matter what? You're an act."

They jump at the knock on the door. Liz turns pale and knots her hand against her chest. When she coughs, spittle catches on her lip like dew.

Then, the rhythm of the world becomes a pulse. The footsteps of the paramedics on the stairs, Nell's heart in her stomach, the thistles savaging back into crevasses she thought they had left. The backs of her knees, the crook of her shoulder blades. Inside her head, they seem to curl around her cochleae and amplify the sound. Someone is coming to get her, get both of them. In that moment, all of her life feels perennial: a bloom when they were discovered in that field, wintering between, and a fresh bloom now.

Tender

"Liz, I'm here, I'm sorry." Nell raises her voice to call downstairs, "We're in the bedroom!"

The paramedics, a very thin man and a beaming woman, are so kind it makes Nell want to cry from shock. The man flutes through their introductions – he's Greg, the woman Susie. They ask Liz questions and she answers in a poisonous tone. When her voice starts to give out, they lie her back and offer to lift her down to the ambulance. Nell follows, grabbing her sister's keys and locking the front door.

The ambulance is cool and bright, blasting out any emotion and leaving only bodily sensations. Tightness in her fists, her torso. Greg prepares an oxygen mask as Liz opens and closes her eyes, slipping in and out of consciousness. He continues to ask Nell questions, perhaps to learn but also to keep her talking. Even in their weakened state, the thistles are strangling her. She answers in a small voice.

"She took this, yes, no, I don't know, I don't know."

Nell reaches out a hand to grip Liz's. She's freezing cold. Nell rubs it to try and create some heat, but Liz's face screws up so she stops. Under the bright lights, she sees red. Flaking, patchy skin emerging from Liz's sleeve.

The paramedic pulls the sleeve up, revealing further scale-like growths. Small cracks.

"She seems to have a rash. Is this new?" he asks Nell.

Nell sees more. Flecks of yellow. Petals. "No," she lies.

As they pull around a sharp corner, Nell squeezes her sister's hand again. The back doors open, and the paramedic steps out to set up the ramp, as other voices approach. She stands, leans over Liz's face.

"Things will get better now. This will never happen again."

Bloom

XIII

In geological time, Britain was young – separated from Europe just two thousand years earlier. Farming and settled community living were novel technologies. The people living at the site would have known transition and transformation throughout their lives. Although slow compared with the advance of modern technology, this shift was monumental, rebuilding the foundations of their society. Our growing understanding of late Stone-Age Britain, now more complete than ever before, reveals a level of mourning, care and spirituality that connects these people to contemporary humans in ways most might not expect. These people experienced both great change and the pull of tradition, each revolving around the natural world. With the further excavations planned thanks to the support of Historic England, we hope that the resurfacing of more bodies – and even a potential settlement indicated by the stone tools and potential cookware fragments found nearby – will enlighten a deep past that teaches us not only about the complexity of ancient lives but modern ones, too.

Lauren Du Plessis

Bill had commented on the closing paragraph of their paper in the PDF they shared: *watch the flowery language.* But he doesn't bother to come to Nell's lectures, even when he's in the building, so she finishes with it every time.

Amid the polite student applause Nell dips her head, slides her notes back into her briefcase, and steps down from the stage onto the block heels of her new mules, which have a tendency to slip off her feet if she walks too quickly. She watches the students file out before she leaves. Charlotte, a PhD candidate hoping to join the team for next year's excavation, meets her in the hall doorway.

"Would it be possible to pick your brain at the pub this evening?"

"Sorry," she smiles, keeping a slow, shoe-preserving pace. "I'm meeting a friend."

"Oh, great weather for it! Make the most of the sun while it lasts."

"Mm," Nell says, "I'm going this way, need to get my nails done first." She gives a small wave and crosses the foyer.

It has been a month since they came to Bristol, and in almost all ways it is exactly what Nell expected it to be. Bristol is showing up to the lab at the same time each day, but not knowing when the day will end. Bristol is late-night walks back to a flat where she was allocated the double bed, and Gunner agreed to sleep on the pull-out sofa, which is actually very comfortable. It is pacing, with purpose, between two sterile places. She keeps the flat clean. The lab is, of course, spotless. Nell buys fresh razor blades at Boots then stops for

Tender

half an hour at the salon Mia mentioned, to have her latest in-fills done in matching lilac. The technician shapes her tips to neaten them, and she watches glittering dust gather on the table beneath their hands. This is her second appointment since she arrived in the city.

She and Gunner need to submit their draft for peer review soon. She has no doubt it will pass. She ensured with a quick control-F that the words *violent* and *ritual* do not appear. The report includes a reference to the carbon dating for Unum's skin and Duo's bones (though they will be further explored in Ingrid and Bill's forthcoming paper), followed by various peat samples at different depths of the trench, the thistles, and scraps of pottery discovered after Nell and Gunner had left. The AMS results confirmed Ingrid's predictions: four thousand years old, plus or minus around a hundred years, depending on the object. They're some of the oldest and best-preserved remains in England, coming from the cusp between the Neolithic and Early Bronze Ages. This was a time of transition from stone to metal, the end of hunter-gatherer life. And with the strange allure of the floral burial chambers, they have the right balance of what the community knows and doesn't know to create buzz.

That's why they're lecturing now, taking turns between Nell and Gunner. Four sessions each, one for each seminar group. The lectures are forty-five minutes long and consist mainly of displaying photos and speaking vaguely about the experience on the dig. Ingrid in particular was hesitant about allowing Nell to lecture, but after seeing the sheer blandness she and Gunner stripped their work down to, she approved the schedule.

Lauren Du Plessis

The nail technician shows Nell out. Her nails are restored to soft ovals that won't catch on things. She books her next appointment in advance and sends a photo of them to Mia, who responds, *Perfection!*

Nell steps into the sun outside. A breeze caresses her cotton wrap-dress and she allows it to guide her down the street. To any onlooker, she has achieved her goal. Exceeded it, even. She is punctual, sweet-smelling, and almost always wears an agreeable smile. Her life looks intentional, happy, and normal. She is once more a well-behaved ornamental flower in the human garden.

It is a lie.

Today's Thursday, which means she must beat him home, and just like last week she feels excited and sick.

Gunner's black sport socks are strewn on the bedroom floor, so she scoops them into the laundry basket. The autumn sun glares through the windows, so she closes the blinds. She takes a photo of her new nails gripped around her pink trowel in the soft light. Angled so her wrist is at the bottom left of the image and the trowel tip at the top right, it will create balance on her feed, where the last few images have had points of focus in the top left.

There's a new load in the dishwasher. The ficus and cheese plant are watered. All the windows and vents are closed – nowhere for sound to escape. She ticks everything on her list, then opens the kitchen drawer to take out the meat scissors, sanitises them in boiled water, and heads to the bathroom.

Old clothes on one peg, mauve silk dress and sheer tights on the other. The water warms until steam pools

Tender

in the bath. She places the makeup mirror on the edge of the porcelain and then steps in with the scissors and the razor. The running water helps to keep things moving, but she can't possibly stand. She needs space to rock and convulse.

She splatters some of Beth's homemade remedy over the thistles, although it doesn't seem to work as well in Bristol. However much Nell slathered and massaged it into herself throughout the first week, the thistles didn't wilt or fall away. They are smaller, less painful, but seem intent on regrowth. New furling runners, fresh blooms, any time she feels anything too strongly. Her father was right. She just can't help herself.

She sighs. The thistles must be maintained, but there is no way she could walk out into the fields and bury herself again. So she has developed a more thorough and clinical procedure.

The top is the worst. Leaning close to the mirror, she prepares her breath.

"Pain is just a signal in the brain, it's not real," she reminds herself, and begins to prune the thistles along her hairline. The blood forms shining beads on her reflection, dyeing her scalp. Her hand travels in an inverted U-shape, outlining the frame of her forehead. The meat scissors, with their serrated portion in the middle, are ideal for stripping the largest flowers away. She moves in patient lines, squashing the pain into a ball in her mind and breathing it out. As usual, when she approaches her eyebrows her eyes stream. Blood trickles in too, replacing white with red. She pauses to duck further under the shower and rub away the worst of it. The thistle florets cling to her wet skin, matting around her collar bone, under her breasts, and in her hip crease. She kneels up to wash them off. They clump in the drain until she clears them with her fingers, and drops them into a soap dish on the side.

Now she must do the same again. Her neck, her arms and torso, her hips and legs, her hands and feet. Some blissful areas remain untouched by the growths, and she washes them as usual with soap, grateful for the precious seconds of nothingness.

The scissors gum up with flesh-like gunge, a paste mixture of her and the flowers. She slides it off between her thumb and fingers, cleans the blades the best she can, and rests the scissors on the lip of the bath.

She snaps a new blade into her razor. It has to be sharp. The more ruthless, the better – she's tried a blunt one before, which snagged on every prickle until she felt faint and had to lie in the lukewarm water until the pain dulled.

She moves the razor over her body in lawn-mower lines, up and down, back and forth. It cleaves the calyxes clean off, leaving open sores. She pauses to rinse, shaves, rinses, cries. And all the time the roots in her brain nudge her thoughts, firing off the reminder that she will need to do this next week, and the week after, as long as she continues to do what she does on Thursdays.

So far, her maintenance has sufficed. Nobody has commented on her skin, and she has heard nothing terrible from the dig or from Liz's patient care team. In public, she watches Gunner closely, and listens in to any talk about him from the students. By all accounts, he has returned to his normal self. She uses this to assure herself that the pruning works and the pain is worth enduring. It also

Tender

proves that, in moderation, they can continue with the routine they have fallen into.

In retrospect it was inevitable, with Gunner around all the time. But the first Thursday it happened, she was shocked at herself. She cried in the bathroom. Was he really so much a sundew that he had digested all of her common sense? And could he be safe with her, with her barbed flesh?

It had been the second week in Bristol, at drinks with their new colleagues. Nell had felt herself glowing with alcohol and confidence. It was all going so well. And there was Gunner, across from her, singing her praises in front of the others, and raising his glass while meeting her eyes.

They got home late, and he asked her how she'd become even more beautiful since they came here. She explained how she wanted to be good, and prove she was worthy of her place here. He told her she was good. He told her she deserved to be happy, and to do what she really wanted. And her willpower, which had lasted ten days and three strawberry ciders, was overtaken by the thistles.

Now, living in their own place, they truly can hide everything from outside eyes. There's nobody to hear, nobody to pry, and every week Nell pares the evidence away.

When she's done in the bathroom, she drops the sludge of florets and leaves into a bag and hides it in a wooden bin under the sink. When it fills, she'll sneak downstairs to empty it in the big compost tub outside the building, at the edge of the communal green. She has done this several times already, but the little bin always seems to be full, chunked up with brown and green. She tries not to think about it.

Lauren Du Plessis

Gunner gets in at seven.

"You here, Nell?"

"In the bedroom!"

A close one today. Nell shifts the dress into position over her hips and sits down to pull the tights on. It's the way the rose-pink mesh covers any stray hairs or prickles sprouting from the backs of her knees, parcelling them away like they never existed. It's the firm grip of boots over her ankles that climb up her calf. She stands and assesses herself in the mirror. That levitation lights a warmth, blooming upwards through her legs and into her core. It's power. It is the princess slaying the dragon, the fairy casting a healing spell. She smiles at her reflection.

The first thing Nell notices when they walk into the restaurant is the man at the door staring at her. Then, when her eyes scan the illustrated labels of wine bottles displayed above the bar, they lock with the bartender's. She smiles politely, aware of the silk from her dress brushing her sensitive skin.

The restaurant is dark, moody, with orange lights hanging from the ceiling on each side, and the tables at the centre left in darkness. The room trembles with conversation, and Nell gets the distinct impression of a bubble, something real and illusory at once, that could decay into droplets at any moment.

"We'll take a table on the side, please," Gunner says. The waiter leads them to their table, in and out of the light. Her vision is golden, black, golden, black. Her dress shimmers. Eyes are on her, then away, then on her again.

Tender

Her feelings, wavering between delicate pride and shame, flicker too.

She takes her seat opposite Gunner under the spotlight. He opens a menu and passes it over the table, then pours them both a glass of water from the bottle. They clink glasses.

"How was your day?" he asks.

This is how their routine begins, updating each other on their new Bristol lives. While Nell spends her free time at the same seat in the lab, Gunner tends to a planter of opportunities – observing other lectures, meeting professors, assisting Ingrid and Bill. Next week the three of them will give the big London talk, a review of their work at a small conference that Bill had a hand in organising.

Nell hasn't booked her train ticket yet, and she isn't sure she will. Wouldn't it be nicer that day to sit at her station and swirl water through the flotation sieves, write labels on sheet after sheet? As Bill suggested when he first showed them round, she spends hours opening and closing the drawers of specimens from the collection, comparing artefacts from the dig with the thousands that have come before, from excavations all over the world. Every ecofact from the dig reveals something new, the patterns like kaleidoscopes of cells under the microscope. In the still air, time as suspended as their specimens, she can experience nothing – which is ideal, because it keeps the thistles from growing any faster than they do naturally. She's trying to keep the shaves down to once a week.

"So, what will it be?" The waiter gives her a small wave, and she realises Gunner is holding his hand out for her to order first.

"I'm going to be a bit of trouble," she says. "I'd like the duck, but could you please hold the sauce? And for my main I'll go for the fish. Can I have the roe on the side? And the sauce on the side in a little pot if it's not too much trouble?" Now the waiter is eyeing her cautiously, waiting for the next instruction. "That's everything," she adds, self-conscious.

Gunner begins his own order, checking each dish for hints of animal. The waiter reads their order back to them in an unimpressed tone, before leaving them to talk.

They have kept their weekly evening out on Thursdays, to avoid crowds and minimise the chance of bumping into colleagues. There are at least two more weeks until their part in the process is complete, which leaves two more of these easy, tempting moments. In truth, Nell hopes she'll be able to stay far longer, even if she is now well into her overdraft.

When their last course arrives, Nell spoons a few bites of the dessert into her mouth then fixes her lipstick and lets Gunner eat the rest.

"Have you spoken to Erica?" Nell asks on the walk back. Another tradition: checking in on the state of a WhatsApp chat Gunner is unwilling to relinquish. She would never take his phone, but Nell has crept around the flat, observing messages over his shoulder.

Wet dreams about Nell? Erica would ask in the morning.

Stop it, Gunner would reply.

Do you miss me?

I'll see you soon!

Nell dreads to think when exactly 'soon' refers to. At one time she might have judged this sort of behaviour, but

Tender

now she has sympathy for Erica. She would never have known how easy it is to slip into unreasonable behaviour if she hadn't done it herself this summer. Erica does not know how to conceal, how to keep feelings inside.

Rather than giving Nell a straight answer (which he rarely does), Gunner holds the front door open for her and says, "I love that you don't have a filter with me, Nellie – you always say what's on your mind. That's so much better for me, and I know it. I don't need people paying lip service. You're straight with me."

This is not a lie, but it also isn't quite the truth. Slotting into her old self again sometimes feels too much like a game, and an exhausting one. Should she nod sweetly like this, make a fuss over his chivalry? Should she hover in the hallway, taking off her shoes one at a time and bending slightly, so he can appreciate her ass? What is old her, and what is the thing that woke up on the fen, trying to claw its way back through her body?

Their final Thursday tradition is the contained and predictable madness that settles over them both. But because she knows it's coming, she can monitor her body and temper the growth.

The walls between their personhoods have all but crumbled. Gunner is vulnerable under her touch. The truth is he's a little turned-on by fear. He likes to be wide-eyed and guessing. Their safe word is *pickles*, so he is free to say *stop* and *no*, and grin when she continues with whatever she is doing.

Lying there with his head buried in the scoop of her neck, she remembers thinking that the rest stop would be the last time the two of them had sex. She was so sure that the thistles would vanish on reaching the city, along with all signs of what she has started calling *The Other-Nell* in her mind.

She closes her hands around his arms, holding him in place so he won't look at her. She doesn't want to think about whether they are each doing what they really want. It makes the roots writhe in her gut.

The Other-Nell was never her, but is it fair to herself to keep it alive these nights? It should be gone by now.

Her libido retreats, like a waning flower at the end of the day. Phototropic movement, it's called: the way plants move to optimise their exposure to sunlight, closing up when it fades. Now she's acutely aware of their bodies, pressing against each other, sweating and oozing. She's left hollow, which of course the thistles love even more, squeezing through her pores like the worst five o'clock shadow until Gunner rolls off her and she goes to the bathroom.

A couple of extra petals are showing. She clips them, and sneaks to the kitchen to add them into the wooden bin.

XIV

They submit their paper together, fingers on the left mouse button, over mugs of ice water. After several days of intermittent rain and scalding heat, the air is thick enough to take a bite out of. Nell can feel Ingrid's shallow breaths fanning the top of her head. She and Bill stand over them, supervising the submission. They have barely spoken to Nell since they arrived, but insisted on inviting the botanists to their lab to submit the paper. Ingrid raps her fingers on the table. Up close white marks speckle her nails, presumably from years of drumming the beds into oblivion.

Her name may be on the cover page, but Nell's main job was pruning Gunner's prose. If the goal now is to put as much distance as possible between herself and the Other-Nell, which it is, then she cannot write her own experience into it. Besides, it turns out Gunner's way with words extends to writing. All she had to do was fix some grammar and find clarity in his occasionally excessive use of adjectives.

Nell spins on her chair when the confirmation page loads. Tria is displayed on a table in the centre of the room. Under lab conditions they better resemble an alien, a sinew-stretched organic mass of once-human parts that is now something else entirely. With no soil to cushion them, their skull wears a forlorn expression. As the others congratulate each other, Nell circles the body to find the hole in their skull, one hand knitting under her hair to find the same spot and massage it absent-mindedly.

"Have you got everything before we go tonight?" Gunner asks.

Nell starts. She never told him that she planned not to attend the conference. In her mind she prepares a smiling excuse (period pain, perhaps, or that she wants to extend the twice-weekly visit to her sister). But Gunner sweeps four orange tickets from his pocket.

"I'm treating. You've got to be on the front row, so I can pretend I'm just giving the lecture to you."

"How special," Ingrid says. "To all be back together tonight."

Nell's teeth grit. She stares down at Tria's body.

"Is Mia coming? She's in London," Gunner says.

"Of course she is," Ingrid says.

"Would anyone like more water?" Nell asks. She gives them all a smile, one that informs them she is good, she is coming tonight and it will be wonderful.

She stops at home to neaten the thistle growths. Another fistful of gunge goes into the wooden bin under the sink. She really must empty it soon. It will start to smell.

Long gobs of rain smack the pavement as Nell hails a taxi and rides to the centre. It does not feel like a hospital. It isn't, technically. At the A&E ward, Nell was taken aside to discuss

Tender

how she felt about her sister's state, and she gave as little detail as possible, terrified that Liz would be sectioned and wheeled away somewhere for months. She ended up staying a few nights at one of the acute mental health wards for observation, which Nell couldn't help noticing are all named after plants when she checked the website. Poppy, Sycamore, Cherry, Oak Tree. Then their mother found a small, private inpatient centre where she could recover.

It's garish. A purple, swirling casino carpet clashes with large, modern paintings of abstract shapes on the walls (she can imagine the psychiatrists asking *what does this look like to you*). One line of the strip lights overhead has blown its bulbs, so Nell's shadow has a ghost walking alongside it. Even after shaving so close this week, and touching it up an hour ago, she can almost see a fuzzy outer edge to her form. If she squints, she can force it back into a human shape.

The bedrooms, on the other hand, could form part of any household, deliberately bland in their layout. Liz's room is in the corner of the building, and contains a bed, a wardrobe, and a desk with a stool tucked under it. There is a clear plastic vase on the windowsill, where summer flowers inject the space with powder blue and obnoxiously sunny yellow. Hydrangea, rose and yarrow, all of them coming to the end of their flowering season. The petals are symmetrical, as if they were drawn and rendered rather than grown.

Nell pulls her attention to Liz, asleep on the bed. Her left sleeve is caught on the blanket, pulled up to reveal the white strip bandage where she has been jabbed with needles. Nell traces the skin, seeking out a revelatory bump or crack.

"You won't find anything," Liz says. Her eyes don't open, but she draws her arm back under the covers. "They cleaned out my stomach. You were there. Just like when we were kids."

Nell sits. "How do you feel today?"

"Like a matter of time." Liz blinks and shifts her gaze out the window. "I'm scared to come out again. Here, it's someone's job to make sure that nothing gets you. The thing you gave me, it can't get me."

"Have you told your therapist anything?" Nell asks, awkwardly patting the lump of blanket where Liz's arm is.

"Yeah, I gave in last session, and told her all of it. You never know, it might have been an obscure disease – a floral flavour of schizophrenia or something."

"All of it," Nell repeats. "And what did she say?"

"Well, have you ever tried telling someone you hear the flowers talking, or you think you're changing into something else? What do you think they said? She put me on such heavy stuff I barely remember who I am from one moment to the next, regardless of whether I'm in a state of metamorphosis." She frowns.

"How long until you leave?"

"I'm probably going to check out today or tomorrow."

"Really? So you can go and get the girls? Move on from it?" *Like me,* she thinks, *why can't you be like me,* even though it's such a selfish thing to think.

Liz's arm reemerges to grab her wrist. "Can we move on? Given what we are?"

She can't avoid it any longer. Nell threads her fingers between Liz's. "You said you were transforming. Does that mean what I think it does?"

Tender

"I saw the way you moved at Charlie's party, how you were scared to expose any skin. I knew you had flowers too."

"But you never said anything."

"Said anything? When... when would you like me to have said something? Hasn't the silence been enough? I have watched you putting on a performance for other people's benefit. Exactly what I've done. We've been telling each other the whole time. Don't you get it?"

For a moment, just a precious, awful moment, their skins seem to slither against each other, knotting their hands tighter.

"I'm savouring the time that I have here. Because I'm scared that the second I go back out there, back to the girls, this thing will somehow come back. And I'll start the cycle all over again."

"No, Liz! Listen to me. You don't have to be afraid. I have it under control now, and I'll show you how you can do it, too." Nell leans in, pressing Liz's arm into the bed. "Think about what you just said, about performance. It works, I'm telling you. I just let it slip, and everything got fucked up. It's my fault and I'm sorry. But I've got it under control now. Why don't you come and stay with me for a while, see for yourself? We have a sofa bed, or you could share with me. You don't have to suffer anymore, neither of us do."

Liz sits up straight. "No, I want to be alone. When I get back, I'm going to landscape the garden. It'd give me something to do, something to be in control of. My therapist thought it was a good idea."

"But the garden is just grass, isn't it?"

"Not that shitty lawn. The field."

Lauren Du Plessis

"The field?"

"I own it. It was supposed to be our garden. I guess Mum and Dad never wanted to go to the trouble of looking after it. But when we bought the house, the field was on the deed. David messaged me the other day, and you know what he said? He said he was sorry I tried to kill myself, and I could keep the house if it helped."

Liz laughs. Nell feels her mouth opening and closing around non-existent words.

She rarely went back into the field. After the 'incident', as her parents liked to call it, their dad hired someone to build a new, grey fence along the back of the lawn, cutting them off completely. She was told not to speak of it. Nell learned to hold her tongue in the therapist's office. She held it so well she tied a knot in it, a gnarly one like the root of an old tree. And she grew over the top.

The taxi swings around London streets, from King's Cross to Fitzrovia. Buildings pack tight together, their insides pulsing with activity like busy vacuoles. Gunner sits opposite Nell, rehearsing lines, as she festers in a well of motion sickness. His speech will be the third of the evening, following Ingrid and Bill's, and another archaeobotanist's lecture on UK soil conditions, and the subsequent disappearance of anything it preserves. Dried-out peat bogs, and acidification of previously alkaline soil, all leads to the same result: erasure.

Aren't we humans hell-bent on erasing ourselves, Nell thinks passively. Now Liz has told the doctors all of their esoteric sisterly secrets, how long before they come after her, too?

Tender

The taxi pulls up to a high-rise, all blue glass and golden light, and attendants show them through the foyer to a table lined with name tags. The pin would ruin Nell's silk top, and her woven bolero wouldn't fare better. As she tries to find an appropriate gap in the fabric, the attendants fuss them up the stairs to a corridor on the first floor. No sooner has she fixed it into place on her lapel than Gunner is gone; swept towards the conference room at the far end. He looks back over his shoulder.

"Front row, remember! I'll see you after."

His hands tremble at his sides. Nell watches after him, as he caresses the doorway on his way through.

She takes a deep breath. The warm air from an overhead fan scratches her throat, but it's better than the streets, bloated with pollutants. The sign outside the conference room is printed in an attractive serif font, with a large swirling A at the fore of *Archaeobotany*. She aligns it in a square shot and adds it to her profile and story and considers a trite tag. #Grateful. But she isn't grateful. She is too busy thinking of Liz, and herself, and disappearing.

Inside, a pianist plays jazz on a small stage at the far end, with a projector behind him, listing the order of events. Most people are already taking their seats, eating the last of their entrées from fir-green napkins. She weaves through to the front, allowing people to notice her without having to make conversation. There are faces from Bristol, tutors she remembers from university, a few journalist-types testing camera shots. Predictably, the sole acceptable pattern of the night is floral. Dresses, shirts, pocket squares, and even full suits feature explosive dinnerplate dahlias, ruffled linen roses and embroidered lavender.

She finds the back of Ingrid's head on the front row, and makes her way over. But before she can say anything, there is a hand on her shoulder.

She prays to turn and see Mia's wide smile, to dive into the gap between her teeth and go wild-swimming in her conversation.

It is not Mia.

"You're Elinor, aren't you? Gunner said I wouldn't be able to miss you."

Erica has an asymmetric fringe to her reddish hair, so that only one eyebrow is visible above her severe grey eyes. This eyebrow raises when Nell chokes on her "Hello." She's wearing a red suit with a white ditsy floral pattern which feels decadent – weighty but soft – as she threads her hand through the crook of Nell's arm and leads her towards two empty chairs at the front.

"Is the coast clear?"

"Sorry, what?"

"*Gunner's not here, right?*" Erica whispers as they sit.

"I think he's backstage. What are you doing here?"

"Fantastique. I have to rescue you before you get too far down the rabbit hole."

Nell's body seems caught, unsure whether to tug her arm free or lean in. She wonders, briefly – and rudely – what colour bra Erica is wearing beneath her blazer this evening. "What do you mean?"

She tuts. "You know full well what I mean. I have to extricate you from the emotional black hole that is this man-child."

"Did Gunner put you up to this?"

"What? You think he'd get me to get you to break up

with him? The man's smitten. No, I'm doing this for me and you and all of womankind."

Erica pulls Nell tighter to her, so they are sitting like the girls Nell used to sit behind in school, permanently joined at the hip. The faint murmur of thistle movement in her becomes a snarl, the movement impossible to ignore. She's terrified that Erica can somehow feel it too. All of her muscles turn stony.

"So… do you really want him back?" Nell asks, her voice low. This isn't a conversation she wants anyone she knows to overhear. Anyone at all, actually. How did she end up in a personal drama, on a night where her work ought to be in the spotlight? Why is this still happening?

"I mean, I'll take him. Don't get me wrong."

Nell finds herself pressing her elbow into Erica's waist, not enough to hurt but enough to cause some discomfort. "Who do you think you are? Trying to take him back when he's told you to stop?"

"He never told me to stop. Not with his eyes." Erica jabs back, and Nell bares her teeth. The thistles ignite.

"Leave us alone," she hisses.

Erica lets go. "Okay, fine. That's really what you want?"

The lights turn off, and a polite applause buoys the room. The first lecturer walks onto the stage, and from a small curtain at the side Nell can see Gunner waiting, his head bobbing from side to side as he mouths words, as if his speech is a song that's stuck in his head.

Thirty minutes weep by like a wound. She can't prod at it. She must hold her head high, smile pleasantly, and behave.

In the break between talks, after the applause dies away and people begin to chatter, Erica lowers her voice.

"Babe, I've got no doubt he will shower you with love. That's what he does. But you'll never be enough. Never enough. The man's a pit. *I* love him, but still. A chronic mess. Trust me, it takes one to know one."

But he's a chronic mess who wants to take care of her, Nell thinks, a chronic mess who tells her what she wants to hear. And nothing that she doesn't.

"Elinor, listen to me. You don't have to like me. All I'm saying is you have to be sure about this guy. If you really want to, waltz down the aisle of madness. But just know that's what it'll be. Or you're going to be another tool in his arsenal of self-pleasure."

"He takes care of me."

"Bet he does. He's the sweetest man who'll ever break you in two."

Gunner was right; everything she says is a drama, a theatrical, unnecessary metaphor. Layers on layers of artifice. "Why do you even like him? You talk about him like you hate the ground he walks on."

"I can say this stuff about him because I'm the same. This is honestly self-deprecation. I've lived with Gunner. I *love* Gunner, he's one of my best friends. You just have to know what you're in for."

Nell stands. "You don't know anything about me. I might be what he needs."

"So you *are* a couple then?"

"Yes." Nell moves a few chairs down and sits. She fixes her hair, checks her nails, messages Mia.

Where are you?

The response comes almost immediately. *So sorry, thought Ingrid told you. I can't come anymore, the twins have*

Tender

scarlet fever! Babysitting duty all week. She sends a picture. The girl and boy are curled up, red across their noses and eyes, snuggled in a blanket on a leather sofa. Mia's thigh is just in frame. *Still so cute,* she adds. *Have a lovely time tonight, remember you're a star!*

Ingrid and Bill walk onto the stage and begin their talk. Nell reels in silence, plummeting down a deep well of other people's feelings. Other people seem so truly themselves. Whether they're being honest or lying at any given moment. Erica's audacity seems a part of her, something she isn't ashamed of. Mia's unbridled caring is sweet enough to make her molars ache. Her head begins to thunder. She wishes she could be something honest. Or, if not, she wishes she could lie without it hurting so much. Be what she needs to be without this feeling of rotting inside. To be able to examine herself without wanting to destroy herself. It's all so fucking hard. To be a human in animal flesh. *Why not a flower,* she thinks. *Why not a thistle.*

Ingrid says the word *wildflower* as she switches slides on the projector, and Nell wants to cry.

They put them in the ground where it gets soft, at the very edge of the village. The deep beds took weeks to dig out, out of sight of the three who would one day inhabit them. Now they are here, and they lower the three bodies in. Faces down, so the earth knows they have heard, that they have been listening, watching and revering.

Other offerings are eased into the bog with the bodies, pushing through the bad milk, afterbirth texture. Hands sink, up to the elbows in the sucking ooze. It receives their sacrifice through popping bubbles. Then they pat the ground flat, like nothing ever happened there.

And so they think the earth has eaten all that it needs – wandering back to their homes, waiting for the good harvest and the end of the sickness that leaches along the tracks from village to village. They sleep on their backs, faces among the stars. Someone has been sacrificed, so the others can be happy.

But the earth is not full.

Next year it will want more, and then again, and again.

The earth cannot change what it is.

Nell blinks and Gunner is halfway through his speech. She's mouthing the words along with him. Where did her mind go for half an hour?

She shifts in her chair and glances down the aisle. Erica is playing a game on her phone. Gunner paces the stage with notes in hand, avoiding the front row and instead meeting the eyes of every other person in the room.

She is jealous of him. How nice it must be, for the world to feel simple and natural. She wants to feel straightforward. She wants to tell Gunner that she loves him.

Is it love if she has known him for two months, if she barely knows him at all? If he is obnoxious, if he has hurt her, if he would stand in the limelight ahead of her? If he is what Erica says?

But when Gunner reaches the end of his speech, he gestures for her to stand, and the audience applauds. His smile cleaves her down the middle.

"This work would not have been possible without Elinor's incredible eye for detail and a passion for plants

Tender

that I've never seen in anyone else. She sees things I can only dream of." He invites her onto the stage, and she looks out over people who until now have been followers on an Instagram page, or names dropped in email chains. These are the people who think she matters. The sound rises. It's the sound of love. They love her and she loves them, all connected like a system of fungi.

The clapping grows even louder. She loves it here. And she loves Gunner, and wants him to love her.

Nell's hearing goes out in one ear. Snap, like someone flipped a switch. The applause turns to an echoing clatter like wind through treetops, and she expects to hear a high tone, as sometimes happens when she goes through a tunnel in a train. But there's another sound instead: the twisting, wrenching sound of plant roots growing over each other. Gunner whispers something into this ear and she cannot hear it. She smiles and nods, and as the audience trickles towards the doors for the drinks reception, she tells him she's going to the bathroom.

The finger in her ear won't clear it out, however sharply she sticks her acrylics into the wax she finds there, however much she rolls into little orange balls and drops in the toilet bowl. She cannot hear the world. She can only hear what's inside her.

It creaks. Low and then louder, like tightening rope, like a nature programme sped up a thousand times. She holds her breath, tries to hold her body still. Give it no sustenance, nothing to cling to.

No use. She leaves the cubicle, thumps her hands either side of the sink and stares into her reflection, looking for it behind her eyes. She turns her head, where a lock of her hair frames her ear. Stares into the hole. Can she see her insides twisting? A cochlear contorting?

"Elinor."

"Shit!" She turns to Ingrid. "Sorry, I was lost in thought. That was all pretty overwhelming."

Ingrid's eyebrows crinkle in pity. "Oh, I know. I *hate* having all those eyes on me." She says *hate* like she means *love*. "You know that used to happen to me. First time I worked on a body in Sweden, people loved it. It became a national news story."

She visibly judges herself in the mirror, cleans the lipstick at the corner of her mouth. Bold, dark pink against the rosaceous white of her face. There remain flecks of peeling skin on her neck, her suncream is clearly not a high enough SPF.

"Do you know why people care so much about dead bodies thousands of years old?"

"Why?"

"Because we're vain. That's it. I fundamentally believe that about people. We want to know that things will matter long after we are gone ourselves."

She looks at Nell in the mirror.

"Your mascara is running. Let me help you."

She reaches into a black clutch and removes a cotton pad, which she wets under the tap.

"Close your eyes. There. Now, we'd better get to the reception, hadn't we? I'm sure there are lots of people who want to talk with you."

She continues to dab the cold cotton. "It was a good paper. You didn't say too much – interesting but uncontroversial. Very wise. You know, at the beginning of my career I had a lot of ideas like you. In Sweden, on that dig… I posited that the body had been prepared. Mummified, if you will." She clicks her tongue. "I had convinced myself. And do you want to know what happened when I shared this? They used my ideas as an excuse to belittle me."

Nell keeps quiet, even though cold water is seeping into her eye.

"Of course, six months later we have our lab results and guess what? I was wrong. Of course I was wrong, I was a little upstart who thought she knew better. I'm lucky anyone listened to me after that. Professional damage control ever since. All this time I've been trying to prevent you from doing the same. Even though it's Bill and I working on the bodies, you and Gunner are the stars of this project. I knew it from the moment I saw you working together."

She gets misty-eyed but blinks and removes another cotton pad to dab at her face. "I'm sorry. I'm so sorry. I don't know why I'm getting emotional now. Maybe it's the relief of getting the talk over with."

"No, no," Nell says, "I'm sorry. You and Bill should be the more important ones: you're the ones they should be paying attention to. It is your dig after all."

The words feel dirty as they leave her mouth, but it's definitely what Ingrid wants to hear right now because her face lights up.

"Thank you, Nell. Let's go get a drink, shall we?"

And she takes Nell's wrist as if she were a child and leads her out of the bathroom, into the room adjoining the conference hall, where they have cleared tables to the side and laid out a buffet of canapés and glittering champagne-filled glasses. Gunner waves, takes two glasses, and brings them over.

"There they are!"

There's another short round of applause, although Nell makes sure to stand behind Ingrid.

Hour one. Nell and Gunner tour the room, linked arm in arm under blooming chandeliers. People follow them to the buffet table where they pick up champagne flutes and hold them by the stems.

"You're Elinor?" asks a reporter for a student newspaper.

"That's me." It is her, the woman in the pink dress with the cut-out back, whom everyone now has their eyes on. Gunner tucks his first and middle finger behind the silk and touches her spine. Through the lightness of recognition and the fizz in her head, she doesn't register the itch in her feet.

Then Erica comes over. She hugs Gunner.

"I'm not going to congratulate you. You know you were amazing. Mr – and Mrs – bigshot botanist."

He begins to pull her away. "Not here. Nell, can you give us a minute? I'll catch up with you."

So Nell wallflowers around Ingrid and Bill for a while. She finds a good lighting angle for someone to take a picture of her under. Then she goes in search of Gunner once more.

He's nearby, mid-conversation. Erica has vanished.

"It reminded me of something from my childhood, actually," he tells the man standing next to him. "My dad

Tender

used to take us all around the world on tour, and this one time we were in Spain. I found the skull of a cat on the dig. It was probably the highlight of my childhood, which sounds strange, but I couldn't believe that I was touching something that died hundreds of years ago. And now, being on the first team to lay eyes on the bodies..."

"You found the third body? The one with the flowers in the eye sockets?"

"That's the one. Holding that thing in my hands..."

His lips keep moving. Nell knows that kind of lie well. Your conversational partner asks a leading question, and rather than correcting them you just let it be true. Gunner has let this be true. For this person, Gunner is Tria's discoverer. Nell scans the man head to toe, reads his name label. *Thomas Bridges, Curator, British Museum.* Will he be the one to write the label when the bodies go on display, and who will he write on there, she wonders.

Gunner continues the Spain thread. He has never told her the story of the cat skull. She positions herself in vantage points to preside over his conversations for a while. He tells the museum curators Latin names for the plants they've found, and reporters about the wording they might use in articles. *Historic. Groundbreaking!* They chuckle at his pun.

Hour two. The chandelier lights are dimmed, bringing the space in, shrinking it around swaying bodies. The sound system, which began playing classy jazz, now plays the kind of chart ballads where each individual track sounds like part of a larger whole and everyone knows every word, although nobody thinks much about what they mean. Nell half-dances with Gunner.

She folds her hands into his pockets, anchoring on to him. He plays his fingers across her spine like piano keys. Closer. The lights darken even further, so that the sconces on the distant walls are like glowing eyes in the night, another set to watch them. She shivers with pleasure. It's hard to believe that just a couple of months ago she was alone in her flat feeling so sorry for herself, in her pyjamas, feeling far from beautiful.

Now she is expansive. She feels all the things about herself that she loves. Spilling out like water over rock falls. The world is pollen gold and she has everything she wants right here.

Hour three. Bill and Ingrid shrug on their coats in a doorway. And Gunner, whose stomach was pressed up against hers just a moment ago, pulls back.

"Are you working in the morning?" Nell shouts over the chatter, her voice booming in the cavern of her chest. She loses balance a moment, then rights herself.

"Actually, I'm meeting Erica and the other London crew for a late dinner."

Anything that had grown down through their feet into the ground and looped together is sliced. She steps away.

"But I thought Erica left?"

"She did." His smile doesn't fade. He has prepared for this conversation. "But I said I'd spend some time with them. They already found a bar round the corner. You know I don't come down that often."

"So I have to go on the train back by myself?" What a stupid, childish question. But it's the only thing she can ask that doesn't sound too accusatory.

"You could go with those two." He points over to Ingrid's receding figure.

Tender

"But that means I have to go now. Don't make me go back with them. Can I come and meet your friends? This is our night."

The closer to his body she gets, the hotter her face is. The sharper the tears. People are looking, and she doesn't care.

"I don't want you to see Erica again. I want you to stay with me."

"Where's this coming from?" He puts his hands on her shoulders. "You've got nothing to worry about. Nothing's going to change. I'll be home by tomorrow afternoon."

"She said horrible things about you, you know."

He squeezes gently but it burns her skin. "What things?"

"That you're not good at being in love. That nothing's ever enough for you."

He exhales heavily, but the left corner of his mouth still plays upwards. "Man, she's a troublemaker. But she's not told you anything you don't already know about me. I'm a bit messy, aren't I? You know that. But that doesn't change how I feel about you."

Is love supposed to feel like disgust? Is it supposed to feel so overbearing, like it could wring you in two, does everything always turn overexposed and fulgid, the world so dazzling and full of detail, and not only do you want to never let this person go, you never want to let anything go?

"I love you, Gunner," she says.

Gunner steps back, glancing at a small but growing audience of peers, who anxiously pull on their coats. "Oh. *Oh.* Nell, you know I love you, too." He steps back towards her, takes her hands. "I do love you. But... do you want a proper relationship? Like an exclusive, proper thing?"

"It doesn't have to be exclusive. It just has to be real. You do love me?"

"Of course. Of course I do."

She notices the itch at last. It has travelled over the last three hours from the balls of her feet through artery and tendon, up to the backs of her legs into her thighs. Through her pelvis and now it punctures her heart. Her eyes fill and she buries her head into him, wanting to force so deep that she blends into him, like compost bedding down together. Hands gripping his jacket, so tight she could tear holes.

"Nell," he whispers, "you're drunk, sweetheart. Come on, let's try and get you on a train home. I'm going to see you to the station. I want to make sure you're okay."

"But you're not coming home with me!" She is a void, dragging the eyes of all remaining guests to them now.

"Nell, please."

"Don't do what she did to you! You can't just be here when you feel like it, I need you here."

The thistles wrangle for air, and she sees tiny blood specks seep into her dress.

"Nell, people are looking."

His words cut her silent. Suddenly the old her is back where she belongs, and the eyes of others matter. She pulls her bolero tighter around herself, hugs her elbows, and leaves the room.

Gunner walks ten steps behind her, all the way to the train station. But when she boards, and twists in her seat to search the rest of the carriage, he is not sitting ten seats back.

XV

Nell staggers through the front door and the smell drapes around her – a bubbling waft of decomposition. So she goes first to the can of air freshener, clumsily finding the pump and misting the kitchen and lounge. But this is worse, candied rose so sickly she tastes alcohol in her throat again.

She turns the dimmer of the kitchen light, smearing beads of condensation around the casing. Why is the flat wet?

The fruit bowl on the island is browning. Her hand reaches for a speckled apple to throw it out, but opening the cupboard under the sink only releases more of the unsettling smell. It must be the cuttings. The smell is so wretched she has to slam the door quickly and clamber back to standing to throw up into the sink. She turns on the stream to wash it away, eyes squeezed shut. No reminder needed of how fucked she is.

She will empty the compost tomorrow, when she feels less like she's falling apart at the seams. She limps to the television and switches it on for company, then crosses back through swirling motes caught in rays of broadcast light towards the bedroom.

Lauren Du Plessis

"What the fuck?" she asks, then goes quiet as the sound of wind brushes through her. Wind, or breath. Did Gunner change his mind, sneak onto the train, and somehow get in ahead of her? Nell stumbles towards the bed. There's nobody there. She pulls the duvet back to climb in, then remembers she needs the toilet.

The showgirl-style mirror lights illuminate her swimming, drunken form. She's never seen the thistles drunk before. Even shaved close, her skin is like the surface of an oil spill, shifting in eddies of pink, purple, brown, red, green.

She sucks in breath and holds it. Then, she grabs the meat scissors and plunges a blade into one cluster, digging it under until it meets resistance. It levers upwards, popping out a green calyx. Cold creeps up to her shoulders, but there is surprisingly little blood.

There is no pain, but the smell is overwhelming. It leaks into the room, a combination of metallic twang and honey sweetness that makes her think of bodies and grass. She bandages it quickly, too dizzy to tweeze anything else out.

Two hours have passed. She must have fallen asleep because she wakes up on a towel on the bathroom floor. Her head is a little clearer, so she sets about tidying away any sign of her mess. She wipes the sink down and soaks the towel in the bath before hanging it up. Gunner still isn't back.

The kitchen stinks as badly as it did when she got in, perhaps worse. With the fug lifting she is sure this is what a corpse smells like. She holds her nose to open the sink cupboard and finally pulls out the compost bin.

Tender

The bag is a wet, heavy mass that slaps against her back as she slings it over her shoulder. She carries it slowly down the cold stairs and out to the communal compost.

As she wrenches the lid up, a rat runs out from behind the store and dashes between her legs. Her scream is the first sound she's heard in hours and lights pain in her head and all throughout her hidden root system. She drops in the gunge and, finding she left her key back in the flat, sits on the outside step and curls her head into her lap.

Since arriving in Bristol, she hasn't let Beth enter her mind. That creeping sphagnum, the lure of her comfort, shouldn't have held onto her like this.

"Beth," she whispers. "Mia. Lizzie. I need you."

What are you doing out here, Nell! That's what she expected to wake up to. Gunner would carry her upstairs, hold her hair back if necessary, get her an early morning slice of toast, take her to bed and fold into her. But this time she wakes up alone on the grass patch, her bones throbbing from hours of sleeping in the cold.

She wakes up in parts, as if the wrinkles of her brain have been unwound, twisted into sections like sausage meat. She lifts a hand to swat something from her face. Its black head gets caught between her acrylic and the skin of her fingertip. Some kind of beetle. She rolls it away.

Her back itches. She slaps her hand against it. The itches travel in a hundred directions, up to her shoulder blades, into her armpits, across to her stomach. They settle in the pockmarks where she has shaved and dug out thistles.

Lauren Du Plessis

Finally, the message reaches the part of her brain that tells her something is all over her.

Her body shudders with life. Droves of ants circle her heels in lines. She kicks instinctively, screaming. Beetles shuffle along the wrinkles in her silk dress. Her hair itches with the wriggle of larvae.

Nell shrieks and snarls, shaking her whole body.

And the earthworms. She wears earthworms around her neck like wet chains, sees them turn their eyeless heads towards her from her chest. Her hands reach for them but stop short, the wetness already too much.

Burrowers, decomposers. They want to drag her into the ground. She is all-touched, all-invaded. They want to get under her skin, into it, through it.

Her hands swat a body that no longer belongs to her. She scrambles to her feet, writhing, swiping her nails anywhere she can reach.

The eaters peel away and fall, their bodies hitting the grass soundlessly. She beds her fingers into her hair, shaking it violently. There are insects in her ears, in her nose, her mouth. She covers and shuts herself as best she can, panicking so badly she is foaming at the edges. Where are her edges? What is Nell and what is not?

When most of them are finally scattered or dead around her feet, she stops to absorb her surroundings. It is dawn. The front door is closed and the corridor dark. One upstairs light is on, a woman standing at the window and staring at her in shock. She dashes back towards the compost bin and the wall of the building, out of the woman's sight.

On the concrete, the creatures receding from her body are forming lines towards the compost bin. That's when she smells it again. The body smell. She's never had a compost bin before, and she knows it's supposed to help their well-kept flower beds grow nicely, but is it supposed to smell this much? She's never heard any of the neighbours complaining. Perhaps it's normal.

No, this is not normal. The way it snakes through the air and into her, drawing her in. *Open the lid. See for yourself.* She knows this pull, so strong it is almost a voice inside her. In the trenches, in the field, in the flowers, it spoke to her. As a child she called it the fairy witch magic. Morgan le Fay. She has come across other names – Gaia, Ceres, so many goddesses of the ground – but to her it has always been an old thing, disembodied, more like a force than a being. The earth mama.

She raises her arm, still peppered with retreating ants. The wood of the lid is worn and splintered. She tucks an acrylic underneath it to lift. The thistles inside her burst into movement. They grow faster than she's ever felt them, as if clamouring after whatever lies inside. She pushes the lid up to expose the contents to the air, and leans over the lip to look inside.

The next thing she remembers is someone letting her into the building, shouting at her to get a grip, leading the way to her open door, muttering under their breath as they walk off.

Nell turns the lock and melts to the floor in the dark.

"I can't," she sobs, "I can't."

She crawls over the vinyl to find her phone, scrolls through her contacts, and makes a call.

"Liz! You have your phone!"

"Elinor, what on earth's going on?"

"Where are you?"

"I'm home, of course. I told you I'd be leaving. What's happening?"

"I— I had a bad night. I don't think I'm as in control of this as I thought. I need… make sure you don't go into the field, okay?"

"Why? What are you talking about now?"

"Just look after yourself. And the girls. Don't come here."

Liz stammers, "You are safe, aren't you?"

But Nell is already rushing to the bathroom, throwing up whatever was left of the canapés and champagne. She sits back and wipes her mouth, then speaks into the phone.

"I am. And I need to keep it that way."

Nell spritzes the air with a new bottle of jasmine and rose. Its lightness finally covers the stench of throw-up, sweat, and soil.

She climbs into bed. Something tickles her, and she scrambles. But it's a strand of hair, one of Gunner's.

She doesn't even question herself. She spins the hair between her finger and thumb, then puts it between her lips. This makes her want to vomit again, for a moment, but she holds her tongue and the hair against the roof of her mouth, and at least Gunner is with her now.

She was eleven when she discovered the calming power of perfume. It was her first week at secondary school, and already the deputy head had taken a dislike to her. He presided over the lunch queue each day, marching up and down it checking for poorly-tied ties and other bad behaviour.

Tender

Nell wasn't hungry that day; in fact, she had an enormous knot in her tummy and wanted to go home. She hadn't made any friends yet. The only kid she knew, from down the road, knew all about her hospitalisation and how weird her family got after it, so he wanted nothing to do with her.

The knot grew and grew, sucking up her guts into a tight wad. She tried everything her therapist was teaching her, about breathing calmly and imagining the scary feelings floating by. But the louder she breathed, the more other kids began staring at her and backing away, forming a bubble of emptiness around her in the line.

Eventually the deputy head came over and told her to grow up, it was lunchtime and what could possibly be so frightening about that. She burst into tears. He pulled her out of the line and to the doorway where they went into the lunch hall.

"Stand there until you calm down," he said.

So she did. She stood in petrified, bleary silence while all the other children walked past her, staring at her with horror or grinning fascination. She waited until everyone was in the hall, and the deputy head wasn't looking. Then she ran.

She knew the way home, following her bus route. It must have taken almost an hour on foot, but she made it. Both her parents were at work and Lizzie was at primary school just up the road. But there was a spare key in a secret spot under a loose paving stone, so she could get inside.

Once she was in, she wiped her feet and took off her shoes. The plan was to go to her bedroom and barricade

263

the door before going to bed and sleeping for as long as she could. The stillness of the house, the world on pause, was just what she needed.

But on her way, she passed the bookcase on the landing, where her mother had left a stray bottle of perfume. *Penhaligon's Orange Blossom*, the label read in intricate, oldy-worldy letters. Having nothing better to do, Nell unscrewed the glass stopper and cautiously held it up to her nose. It was expensive, she knew, because Dad bought it for Mum as a special birthday present and she was very happy with it. It smelled like oranges, for sure, and a bit of wood and then something sweet, like vanilla ice cream. Actually, the more she sniffed it, the more it seemed to smell like everything at once. She'd always thought perfumes were boring things her mum used, but it was really nice.

She went into her parents' bedroom, where she was definitely not allowed, and sat at Mum's dressing table, which was even worse. She lined up each of the perfumes – there were maybe seven or eight – and tried them all out. Each had a label of ingredients. *Heart note of lavender, bases of cedar wood and fern.* In each one there seemed to be a tree extract, and one from a green plant, and a flowery plant or a fruit. She liked working out what each plant must smell like in real life, when separated out from the mixture. She sat there for a long time, and for the first time in a long time she felt calm and happy.

Nell wakes up knowing she needs to put a few things right. She cleans the flat first. Finally puts the compost out, only cracking the lid slightly, so she doesn't have to see inside again. Sprays and polishes everything with a lemon

Tender

detergent, even rinses out the little sink bin while holding her breath. She clouds herself with perfume and takes a moment to breathe. Then she messages Gunner.

Hey, I'm really sorry about last night. I know I got possessive and needy, but I really care about you and wanted to spend the night with you. And I was pretty drunk! I hope we can just forget all about it and go back to normal. Love you.

Then she opens her wardrobe and rearranges the shoeboxes at the bottom, to find the skull fragment.

She enters the university building and goes straight past her lab, climbing the stairs to Bill's office. Nobody is visible through the window in the door, so she proceeds to the lab where Tria is.

Ingrid is showing some students around the body. Nell knocks, waits for her to notice. She holds up her hand. *Five minutes.* So she waits in the corridor, holding this terrible thing the Other-Nell – the one that grew from the trenches – did.

The students file out.

"Come in, Elinor!" Ingrid's voice sounds around the corner.

She can't find words for what she's done, or what this means, so she paces the length of the table to Tria's head, and takes the fragment from its tissue wrapping.

"What have you got there?" Ingrid asks.

She lays it carefully at the top of Tria's skull, convex side up, so the blow is clearly visible. Ingrid walks slowly towards it. Then she stops, and runs her hand through her roots until they catch in the tangles of her curls.

"Elinor, explain."

But she doesn't have to. Ingrid leans over the head, her face right up close to the fracture.

"Where did you find this?"

"The day we started clearing out the brambles, after the trench got overgrown. It was lying in the soil. The roots must have brought it up."

Ingrid straightens suddenly, and her eyes turn so fierce Nell flinches in anticipation of a slap. But then her brow softens, tired-looking. How many times has she stared at Nell in this way, as if trying to figure out what she's dealing with?

"Why on *earth* did you keep this from us? Who are you to make decisions about this? I thought you'd finally come around to our way of thinking, Elinor. And now, right after we present our work, you decide *now's* the time to undermine us?" She pauses to wave her hand in a beckoning gesture. "Well, speak then."

"Don't you see what it means?" Nell reaches gingerly towards the fragment. "You understand, right?"

Ingrid exhales heavily. "Of course I understand. It's a trauma injury."

She doesn't even seem surprised to be proven wrong.

"I don't understand you, Elinor. All this time – for a *month* – you've had evidence that strengthens your theory, and you didn't tell us."

"You didn't want to hear it."

She tuts. "But you kept this to yourself! This potentially huge discovery! What have I told you about us being scientists, about us listening to evidence? You found the evidence and you didn't hand it in. You didn't fight for more inclusion in the paper. What is it? Don't you want success? Don't you want people to listen to you?"

"So, you *do* believe me then?"

"It's not a question of belief. You have the evidence right there. We'll have to look at the other two bodies now, see if we can find something else. And we'll be going back next year with fresh eyes on the whole thing. I assume you'll be there? So long as you've learned your lesson?"

"I—" Nell's eyes reach for the window. A gust of wind blows through the trees outside, leaves spattering against the glass. She can't go back, not to the ground that whispers. The spirit of the earth, that invasive mother, which almost reclaimed her last night. Not when she needs more than anything to shut her ears. "I'll have to see."

Ingrid sighs. "I suppose I should say thank you, although I really, really don't understand you. Is there anything else I should know about? Do you have another body hidden at the flat?"

"No, that's it." Nell pulls up a stool and sits. "You've studied this kind of thing before. What do you think it means, if these people really were killed?"

Ingrid sits back too. "You already know my answer to that. I'm not going to form any more opinions until we get back there. Or until something reveals itself in this body. This is clearly a far deeper case than we could have imagined. No point raising conjecture about it."

"Will you tell anyone?"

"Of course I will! Bill and I are writing our own paper. I will invite you and Gunner to review it, of course. This is certainly an important point to include. I'm sure it will cause plenty of excitement."

Lauren Du Plessis

"Of course," Nell says, "I wouldn't miss it."

Ingrid doesn't seem to notice the curl of lip and bare-toothed smile.

In the downstairs bathroom, she fills the air with perfume once more. Deep breaths in for four and out for eight. Empty her stomach and chest completely. She coughs at the bottom, her insides feeling dried out, but she hasn't done a full exhale in a while, so maybe that's normal.

Despite the calming scent, a feeling of discomfort builds inside her. How dare Ingrid blame everything on her? Everything she did, it was to help others feel comfortable. Except, she supposes, losing her shit after the Bristol trip. But that wasn't really her, was it? That was the Other-Nell.

She shakes herself. It's over. Her whole, true self has been revealed and there are no more secrets. Maybe now the pull will ease, the voices will disappear.

At lunchtime she walks through to the market square and buys Gunner's favourite filled crêpe, wrapped tight so she can get it home in one piece. There's just enough time in her hour break to drop it back at the flat so it doesn't stink up her bag. On the walk home she passes groups of students billowing out of lectures. There is one boy in particular, not a student she recognises from her groups but someone who seemingly knows her. He stops on the edge of his group and stares directly at Nell. Lanky, wearing a blazer that seems too warm for the weather, which bunches in odd places on his arms. His eyes are wide as if he's shocked to see her. He's not looking into her eyes though, but at her body. She can't

Tender

decide whether to be flattered or horrified, and so gives him a polite smile and walks away.

She drops her keys at the door and bends to pick them up. It's still there, the rotting smell. She tries to blot out the memory of a half-drunk hallucination. *Don't think about the compost bin*, she tells herself, *nothing good can come from what's in there.*

She puts the crêpe in the fridge and decides to wait around a while, in case he shows up to drop off his bags. The glass of water she pours does little to quench her thirst. She starts to walk to the bathroom, but realises she doesn't need to go. It's like there's nothing in there. However much she drinks today, she doesn't need to pee.

Fifteen minutes pass in silence and Gunner doesn't come, so she heads back to the lab.

Her afternoon similarly feels like a checklist, one item after another checked off in neat little boxes while she waits for any sign of him. Did she say too much last night – should she not have told him how she felt? The water bottle at her side fills and empties throughout the afternoon, as she stops her work behind the microscope to sip every so often. She waits for hunger, for tiredness, for her bladder to tell her brain it's full. But her insides are quiet, waiting. All that exists in her mind are the questions, what she should or shouldn't have done.

Clouds hang low over the sunset, the sky like a slowly crushing ceiling. She eats dinner at the flat because she supposes she has to, even if her body isn't remotely interested. In the bathroom she assesses the thistles. They're swollen like barely contained anger. Nell rubs scented lotion over the abrasions, and goes back to the sofa to wait in a half-sleeping state.

The door clicks open at eight in the evening. No how-are-you, no sorry-I-didn't-call. Gunner nods and walks straight into the bedroom, his mouth opening for a silent *hey*. Nell stays on the sofa, touching the back of her head where Tria's skull fracture was.

He uses the bathroom, shuffles around the bedroom for a few minutes, then reappears.

"Hi," Nell says.

Gunner opens the fridge. "How was your day?"

Nell struggles with how to position her legs while he's not looking. "Pretty dull. I got you one of those crêpe-things from the market."

"Oh wow, thank you." He takes it out and turns on the microwave. "So you got home okay after last night?"

"I got locked out. But one of the upstairs neighbours let me in. At least, I think it was."

"Oh shit. Hope you weren't out in the cold for too long."

"I think it was a couple of hours." She isn't sure if she's telling him this to test him in some way, or because it's the truth.

His face crumples, and he waits for the microwave ding without speaking. Grabbing the crêpe and tearing the top open, he comes over to the sofa. Normally she might tell him to keep it in the kitchen, but the sink still smells a little like corpse and she'd much rather he didn't notice.

"So what did you get up to last night?" she asks.

"We had a couple of drinks and walked all the way to Primrose Hill, stared at the lights for a while."

Tender

"You and?"

"Georgie, Markus, Arjun and Erica."

It shouldn't bother her. She said so in her message to him – she wants to go back to normal. But her eyebrows inch up without her permission, and he sighs.

"Nell, let's not do this. I need to talk to you."

She draws her legs up closer to her chest. "About what? I'm fine. Let's forget all that and just have a relaxed evening. A movie, maybe."

"Nell." He says her name with heavy emphasis. "Something has changed between us." Suddenly he stands, runs his fingers through his hair. "God, I knew this was a bad idea. I knew it and I did it anyway. You're like a goddamn siren."

"What are you talking about?"

He doesn't look at her. "Meeting you has been very intense, like… hypnosis, almost. That sounds so weird. But I don't know if it's good. But then you keep calling me back…"

"When? You make it sound like I've forced you into a relationship. You're the one who was all over me when it started."

"Nell, you bit me!" He turns on her, quick. Not his usual self. Then he recoils and walks towards the bedroom. "I think I need to leave."

"Leave?" Nell follows him. "You mean move out?"

"Well, does this seem like a healthy relationship to you? I need to go before one of us gets hurt. Hurt any more than this, anyway."

"But… you… don't you want to talk things out?" She's doing that thing she always does, smiling in blinking disbelief. Trying to appear and feel innocent. She reaches out to touch his arm, asks with every fibre of her being for him to stay and tell her kind things. "I told you I love you and you're moving out?"

He keeps his eyes down on his packing.

"Do you love Erica? Are you going to her?"

"No! I mean, I don't know. I need to get my own place here for a couple of weeks. Get a hotel or something. Then I'll head back to London, start preparing for the next excavation. Just keep my mind off all of this for a while."

"So 'this' was just while it suited you." She steps back from the bed. "You know, I did everything I thought you'd like. Everything I thought would make you happy. Last night you said you loved me back."

"Last night was humiliating." He covers his face with his hands. "You know someone took a photo of you shouting at me? You're probably tagged in it online."

"So the minute I'm not the perfect girlfriend you dump me?"

"At the start of the evening, we had everything. Now we're the butt of a joke. If we can't even get by one night in public, then we've got issues."

"Issues you won't stay and try to fix."

"There's nothing to fix! We were broken from the start, Nell. I'm sorry but I've been doing this for the wrong reason. And so have you."

The anger is so fierce it stretches beyond her body like vines, like she could shoot one towards him and tighten like a boa constrictor, watching him squirm until he doesn't anymore. Nell grabs his bag from him and throws it on the floor, kicking his clothes into a mess. He watches.

Tender

When she's calm enough to speak, she says, "Go, then. Get out. But I hope this leaves scars."

"Why? Why can't you let go of things that happen to you?"

"Because I'm a *human*! I hold onto things that hurt me and things that make me happy! Those things are written on me, they're a part of me. So I hope you remember this. I hope this becomes a part of you, and I hope it haunts you."

He gathers his things again, begins walking towards the door. "See, Nell, I can't. I can't with this."

She slams the door in his face and falls apart, sinks down the wood and hits vinyl, draws herself into the tightest ball possible.

She gave him the slopes of her body, all the beauty of her surface self. She even gave him her heart, decisions made on the spur of the moment. He saw her worst moments. She crawls to the living room floor and rolls onto her back. The pile of the rug depresses underneath her. She's two floors up, but there is the slightest sense of sinking, as if the world is giving in with her.

There are two things the human brain seems equipped to do. The first is to judge, and this seems to be how everything terrible happens. Nell has judged people, situations, decisions – sometimes well and sometimes poorly. She has judged her mother for buying Liz and her cheap polyester dresses while she bought herself Penhaligon's Eau de Parfum. She has judged her sister for taking every taunt of a classmate and for marrying a man who doesn't love her. She judged her relationship with Gunner, and somehow believed it was good.

Lauren Du Plessis

But more than anyone else, she has put herself on a slide beneath a microscope lens, and judged. Every breath; Instagram post; verruca; outfit; packet of crisps; fart; manicure; masturbation; essay; mucus; article; afternoon of fucking; self-immolation.

The other thing the human brain is built for is to imagine. Imagine better, or worse. Beauty, or horror. So Nell tries very hard not to think about all the things she has misjudged, and imagines the only people she knows who have gone back to the earth mama.

Sunshine arcs over her head, stab-bright until it fractures between tears as she closes her eyes. Her body shakes uncontrollably, her fingers grasping at tufts of grass for comfort, for something to touch.

Perhaps she was chosen by lot. Perhaps there is something wrong with her that her companions cannot yet understand. It doesn't matter. She has been chosen, and she sits on the edge of the bog, her ankles and knees already dropping into the earth.

She meets the eye of the man opposite. He is resigned. He understands his fate, whatever the cause. They are touched by the earth, and they will go back to it.

The elders conduct the ceremony around them. The people are gathered along the banks. The songs foretell their fate. Their liquid – their blood and saliva and water – will be given and rejoin whatever lies below.

When the ceremony is over, the thrum of the drums begins, mournfully slow. An elder holds the back of her head, not harsh but firm. By the hair. There is no escape

Tender

without unbearable pain. Which will hurt more, she wonders, suffocating in the ground or the ripped-out hair and inevitable arrow through the chest that a break for freedom would result in?

The blow is sudden and somehow unexpected. She experiences three panicked breaths of pitch darkness and the sensation of her bladder emptying, before her body gives out underneath her and she collapses forwards.

She doesn't feel the hand anymore, but it presses. Turns her face to the woven thistles. They seal her in, thinking she is gone.

XVI

Twenty-eight years ago, a thing without a name was torn atom by atom out of the earth and puttied in a womb. From the moment she started to split, like badly timed laughter, unstoppable and so delicious, the other one was there. A few years later, a grain of it got caught in her digestive tract. That was when a radicle sprouted and bedded down, an anchor in her nerves.

They had been friends for a day, but she wasn't ready then. There was no rush. The other one could wind through her curves and bends, stem upwards and further upwards until it twisted and folded into a calyx at the nape of her neck and hummed a quiet suggestion. She's coming back. Everyone does, in their own way and at the time that's right for them. There's just one final step. The hardest one.

It wakes up in the dark. No, not it. She. She wakes up in the dark. She is Nell, but not the Nell lying on the rug in the flat upstairs.

She slowly locates each part of her. Left foot above head. Right hand embedded in gut. Formed in parts, now coalescing into a whole. She eases her face from side to side to break the surface of the mulch, and gulps in thick air.

The breath gives her enough strength to break into phototropic movement, seeking light. She pulls her hand from her abdomen and beds it down on the foliage around her, pushing her body up to the cracks of sunlight around the edges of the lid. She has the instinct, the orientation of the world, embedded within her without thinking. She takes a moment to wonder at how clear she suddenly feels, how full of instinctive knowing, then pushes the lid open with her head.

The light is not from the sun, but a streetlamp. Overhead, cloudy orange puffs across the sky, no stars. She unfolds herself carefully out of her container, arms elongating, forming fingers. She scoops them over the lip and her feet hit the floor, sprouting toes. She crosses to the door and holds out her new fingers to grip the handle. It's locked.

She stands under the light, soaking it in while she thinks. It feels good on her face, a warm touch. The building is beautiful, too, shooting up into the sky and forming nests within it for so many individual lives. Each one different. She smiles. She can't believe she's here. Awake, and clear. It took all that to finally know what she has to do.

Around the side of the building, a hallway window is cracked open for ventilation. It's a muggy night, and she can already sense mould spores. Her body tells her to move, so she holds up a hand, exploring what this body can do. The thistles flourish around her fingers, stems reaching towards the gap.

What she could always have done. She had this in her all along and she pushed it away. What a waste!

Tender

She twists herself node by node through the window, knotting and bending to the floor where she restores her shape. She is naked, of course. Probably best not to let anyone see her who isn't supposed to. She crouches and hurries past locked doors.

When she reaches the right door, she breaks herself back down to climb through the letterbox.

Moonlight, periwinkle. Some sign of a struggle: a sock on the floor, kitchen towel strewn across the island, television still on at a low volume. Nell, Old-Nell, lies on the rug. Her head has lolled to the side, facing out towards the window.

She stands over this sleeping version of herself. Old-Nell looks so peaceful, but so tired. Eyes sunken, lips dry. Covered in scars from old thistle growths. It's sad. But this is also the version of her that opened the lid before, and chose not to help. That shaved parts of her off every week for the last month. Agonising, peeling and pressing away what should have been precious. So she can't help but feel a little anger.

But it was to be expected. Old-Nell is holding onto something with a grip like a newborn. It will take work to prise it out.

She walks into the bedroom, not worried about making noise. The sooner this is over, the better. At the bottom of the wardrobe, her dig backpack droops in an unloved pile. Inside are her trowel – now with a small crack in the handle – her brushes, and dental tools. The pocketknife. She may need all of them.

"Hello?" The voice coming from the living room is already shaking. "Gunner?"

She hasn't found her voice yet, and decides it's probably best not to reply. Old-Nell gets up and thuds about, first around the kitchen area and then into the bedroom. The intruder hides in the wardrobe.

"Is someone there?" Old-Nell's voice crackles. She makes her way to the bed and is about to fall onto it, when the wardrobe door creaks open.

They both freeze. Here is not the best place, it can't happen now – there would be nowhere for the burial.

"Who's there? Don't try anything, I can grab a weapon any second." Old-Nell already sounds defeated, though.

Old-Nell stares at the wardrobe door. Can she see her? It must look like meaningless darkness to those tired eyes.

But she doesn't need to see. She can smell.

"Get out," Old-Nell says. "Leave me alone."

She tries to retreat further into the wardrobe, keeping her face out of sight. But Old-Nell knows she's there. Now there can only be the chase.

Old-Nell snaps into action. She grabs the clothes she was wearing yesterday, and changes while shivering violently. Barely stopping to pack, she grabs a large handbag, checks her phone charge, and heads for the door.

"The next time I come back I'll be leaving for good!" she stammers. "So you need to get out of here and leave me alone, okay?"

Then she hurries out of the front door and slams it shut. Poor Old-Nell.

The wardrobe door falls open and she clambers out. Does the packing. Checks under every piece of furniture. Carries the bag with her as she follows. Neither of them will be coming back.

Tender

Old-Nell is still waking the car up when she reaches the parking bay. It's easy enough to sneak open the small boot and climb in with the bags, while she fiddles with her keys in the front.

The drive takes half an hour at night, roads empty. Old-Nell's breathing doesn't let up, heavy and brimming with panic. She sobs every so often, then seems to get a hold of herself.

Curled foetally in the boot, the bump and curve of the car's movements are soothing, like being carried by a mechanical mother. There's plenty of time to think.

It is so strange to be free. She's been tied up inside her old mask for so long that being out is like being born again. There have been so many new starts recently, but this one will be different because there is no other choice.

She is not just a person: she is the soil. Microbes that have not changed in millions of years. She is the roots that draw water, water that saturates and drowns. She is Nell, but entropic. She is herself, but free.

But of course, to Old-Nell, she is a monster.

The car turns sharply and pulls up. Her head thuds against the boot and she holds her breath. She hears the driver's door open and shut. The rear door opens, handbag lifted out, and there's another rocking slam. They have arrived.

She waits for the footsteps on gravel to quieten, then uses the trowel to prise open a gap in the boot door. It takes a while, and splinters crack off the trowel into her fingers, but she makes just enough space to fold herself through.

The farmhouse. She has never been here at night. Well, *she* has never been here at all, she supposes. Only the first sprouts of her, the ones that grew in Old-Nell. She lets out a sigh. There are stars everywhere, like a mesh over the sky. This is the kind of place you feel like you're touching the universe. It's no wonder Old-Nell was so drawn to it. It feels like home.

But there are no lights on. From a hiding place behind a tree, she watches Old-Nell pound the front door.

"Beth! Beth, are you there?"

No answer.

"Beth, I'm sorry but I need help!"

The house is utterly dark. She senses no movement within, other than the easing of wooden beams and gentle stir of woodlice in the eaves.

"I'm sorry, Beth! I should've listened to you, what you said about the real—"

Old-Nell's head whips around, as if she's heard something, the whites of her eyes all visible. She runs to the back of the house where the French doors are, pounding all the way like she could make the walls fall in.

"How can you not be home!"

Fear radiates off her. And anger – at Beth for leaving her, at Gunner for leaving her. Everyone leaves, however much they say they love her. And she must feel it. It's essential for her to burn herself from the inside out. And then it will be essential to extinguish it.

"Who's there?"

Old-Nell has seen her. It's obvious. Now they are two identical bodies standing opposed, a mirror staring at itself.

Tender

"Beth?" But the realisation dawns quickly. "Not Beth. Who are you?"

But she already knows.

Finally, a new voice rushes from Other-Nell's mouth. "It's okay." The scariest thing about that sound is that it is Old-Nell's voice, coming from the wrong mouth.

Old-Nell's scream echoes over the marsh, only dampened by the thickening mist on the horizon. She breaks away from the French doors and sprints for the trenches, wielding her handbag through the air. She searches frantically for a ladder, but by now the holes are almost completely filled in, keeping the ground covered for next year.

Other-Nell arrives at the edge and looks at her, squatting in the uneven ground as if it could envelop and hide her.

"We have to let go now," she says.

Old-Nell rocks. "No, you have to go away now! You're not real, you're not real!"

She staggers to her feet, rips off her shoes, and turns on mud-speckled heels to run.

The Other-Nell follows. Old-Nell is already a hundred metres out into the next field, trampling Beth's crops. Every exhale is an extended scream, interspersed with desperate coughs as she chokes on the fen air.

There is no choice but to follow. Other-Nell sets out over the field, stopping to right the cabbages before their harvest next week. They pass a scarecrow and the maw of a small harvester, and then the farm ends and it is all open fields.

Old-Nell's feet begin to sink as she runs, and her clothes soak through with moisture and dirt. She must be cold, exhausted, but every check over her shoulder seems to power her onwards.

Minutes pass, turn to an hour, and Other-Nell's breath catches. Wouldn't it be so easy to stop now, to allow this other her to just exist, with all her fear and poison and aching loneliness? Old-Nell is clinging to life, sticking to it.

But ahead, Old-Nell buckles and stops near a patch of forest. She hides poorly in the thicket.

It doesn't take long to catch up.

"You know this forest? It leads right up to Liz's." The Other-Nell sits beside Old-Nell, traps her. "Where you first learned I existed. You've run a long way."

Old-Nell sobs. "Don't hurt me, please!"

They're heartbreaking, the tears spilling down her cheeks. Just a girl, really. She doesn't want it to hurt anymore.

"It's not a question of hurting. I'm you, you just don't know it yet. You haven't wanted to know it. You've been burying me and cutting me off of you your whole life. It's not your fault, it's how you learned to be. But it's okay now."

She reaches out, holds Old-Nell by the collar, pulls her closer.

"No, no!"

Other-Nell feels her eyes brim with tears. "I'm so sorry. I really needed you. You protected me through everything, through our parents and school and everywhere we didn't fit."

"Why are you doing this! I'm not you!"

"You are, I promise you are. You've worked so hard to keep us safe. You can rest now."

"You're a monster! Why would I keep you safe!"

Tender

"Because you thought we could never be acceptable, right? We were never enough. So you had to be our mask. You had to keep everything right on the surface, so I could grow safely inside."

"No, no!"

"It's okay. You can be free now."

"I don't want to be free!"

"I know. Your cycles kept us safe. You did your best and I'm proud of you."

She kneels next to the old version of her. When she examines her neck, her wrists, the seams are already yawning open. Old-Nell has been coming apart for a while.

She snaps open the pocketknife. Old-Nell screams again.

"It's going to hurt, but not... not in a physical way. All you need to do is take deep breaths."

Old-Nell whimpers. Her chest rises and falls.

"I love you. But we've both got to let go now. Only one of us can go forward and I'm so sorry, Nell. It can't be you."

The knife handle is cold and plasticky, but feels solid. It will do the job.

It enters Old-Nell's skull between her nose and her left eye. It is like stabbing a sponge cake. Around the edges of the deepening cleft, the skin wrinkles back, exposing brown crust layers.

Old-Nell makes a sound like *uc-uc-uc*.

No blood. Old-Nell's eyes sink down, looking for it.

"See?" Other-Nell says. "It doesn't hurt, right?"

Silent tears run down Old-Nell's face as she shakes her head.

And so they continue. This should be easy enough,

Other-Nell thinks. As easy as hacking your old self apart can possibly be.

She makes the first large cut. The slit runs from the body's gut up to its collar bones, a thick browning line. Then, with gritted teeth, she inserts her thumbs at the two sides of the cut and flares her shoulders, pulling it open. Within a few seconds the cavernous torso is open like a double door.

They look down at it together.

There are no organs, just wads of plant matter, dense curled-up balls of burgundy, dark green and indigo. Growing around and through them is the original thistle growth, now woody and brambly with lack of nutrition. It ate away too much. There was no way this old her could have survived.

"Where…" Old-Nell stammers. "How…"

"I don't know. I don't how it happened, Nell, only that it did. But do you see now? Do you see why I have to do this?"

Old-Nell closes her eyes. "Because I'm tired."

"Because we can't live like this anymore."

"Okay." Her breathing grows thinner and thinner. "It was really hard living like this."

"Shh. I know." Other-Nell rests her forehead down, so they touch lightly.

Then she's gone. And Other-Nell is Nell.

The pocketknife is enough to cut the body into parts, some dried enough to simply snap off in her hand. She takes off the feet and hands, the limbs in halves, and divides the torso in six. At last, it doesn't look like a person anymore. Only a few handfuls of knotted weeds.

Tender

Nell places each of them into a careful pile. This is all her hurt and her anger, after all. She must be careful. She pulls the clothes it was wearing onto her own body as a shield against the settling chill, then sets out to return to the farm.

She finds a more substantial shovel in an unlocked shed and digs six holes over a wide area near the stream. With the skin quickly disintegrating, worn to holes like moth-eaten cotton, there is no way to distinguish it as human. Still, a proper burial is in order: as proper as she can manage, anyway.

The holes are small, cylindrical, a few feet deep. It takes many hours to dig them and her beautiful wool jumper is ruined, but it feels strangely calming. She drops each body fragment into its hole and covers it. The stream's water will soon penetrate the burial chambers and dissolve everything.

Those people, those distant Neolithic souls. They knew something. And maybe it wasn't the same thing. Maybe she could never imagine what they went through, just as they could never picture this moment of hers. But they all know something.

The final part she buries is a fragment of the torso. Where the gut was, she guesses. She finds a dense, dried-out knot. Perhaps this was where it began. She can't bury it – it wouldn't be fair to completely cut herself off from who she used to be. Old-Nell will always be a part of her. So she picks the knot up and walks back to the place across the farm, the tree roots where Beth planted her a month ago.

It's boggy now, the ground unstable. In the mosses grouped along the tree roots, she catches moonlit reflections bouncing off dewdrops. She sits, then lowers herself to her belly. There is a small cluster of leaves she knows instantly as roundleaf sundew, and their ridiculous, miraculous appearance here is enough to make her laugh, so her stomach pangs against the uneven ground.

"If you're looking for your next... victim, or protégé, or whatever," she says softly to the red sundew leaves, "be gentle with him."

She turns her head and rests against a root. She languishes a while in the dawn shadows, face turned up to the light, exploring the feeling of breath in her new lungs.

When the sun is up, she goes to slip the knot of Old-Nell into the left pocket of her slacks, but finds it's already filled with car keys. On the right side, she finds something smaller and lighter. She pulls it out. A hazelnut – the one Beth gave her for protection. She smiles sadly, and wonders if Beth was protecting the old her, or, as she suspects, her new form.

In the car she writes Beth a note. She redrafts it several times, unable to find the right words. She leaves it at, *I'll visit soon. Nell.* She posts it through the letterbox before driving away.

Her hand casts a long shadow etched in gold on Liz's door. Old-Nell would think carefully about how she would appear when the door opens. Now there is only the dawn around her.

"Elinor!" Liz is wearing an enormous dressing gown that exposes only her head, fingers and toes.

"You know what, I actually prefer Nell." It doesn't matter that she looks like a dug-up thing, crusted with

Tender

earth, dregs of herself ringing her nail beds. She pulls Liz into a tight embrace. "I'm so glad to see you."

Liz breathes heat into her jumper. "Have you been rolling around in mud? Please tell me it's dried." When they break, she adds, "Something's different."

She holds up a hand.

"Oh my god, you don't have your nails done. I don't think I've seen your actual nails since we were kids."

"Will you help me paint them?"

They sit in Liz's room as the air continues to brighten. Her hospital flowers line the windowsill, though some are now drooping and still others seem cut, or perhaps bitten, their heads missing.

Charlie shuffles in sleepily and gets into the double bed next to Genie's cot. The four of them, in one space.

"You picked up the girls," Nell says.

"Of course. All those drugs made me say stupid things. I wouldn't leave them at Mum and Dad's any longer than I had to. We should be here, together."

The girls sleep as Liz dots globules of pink varnish into perfect little ovals, and Nell tells her everything.

When she's done, Liz looks up at her. "Where is…"

"Buried in the fen."

She waits for panic, but Liz only raises her eyebrows, forehead wrinkling with concern. "Is this going to happen to me, too?"

"I don't know."

"If it does, will you…?"

"Of course."

Liz rolls up her dressing gown sleeves to work on the edges of Nell's nail varnish. Her arms are embroidered

289

with tiny, yellow-orange flowers with pinked petals. She murmurs as she continues painting. "I'm not sure what they are, maybe you can identify them later..."

Nell leans to touch their foreheads together. "I think they're Fox-and-cubs."

Liz smiles, just slightly. "Oh. I kind of like that."

"Are you scared?"

"Fucking. Terrified." She casts her eyes over the girls, to check they didn't hear her swear. "Please stay, Nell."

"I need to pick up my stuff from Milton Keynes, tell the landlord I'm moving out. But then I'll come back."

"How are we going to do this?" Liz says quietly. "I need to get a job. We'll have to sell the house and move somewhere smaller..."

Nell takes her sister's hand. "We'll make a plan in the morning."

Liz squeezes. "What if it isn't just us... what if this is the start—"

"Liz. It's okay. I mean, I know it isn't, but it is."

"Okay."

They turn to watch the girls. In her dreaming, Charlie has laid her hand through the bars of the cot. Blinking her eyes open and closed, Genie stretches to meet her.

ACKNOWLEDGEMENTS

First, a thank you and apology to botanists (and archaeologists). I hope this book is a small gesture to your amazing work, and that you're not too mad I used the word 'petal', where I meant 'floret'.

Now, the dream team. My deepest gratitude goes to Abi Fellows, my agent and champion, who followed me through a garden of genres and helped me find what I wanted to write. To Gary Budden, my publisher, thank you for taking a chance on my work and helping me chisel out the final details. To the wider Influx team: Dan Coxon, Laura Jones-Rivera, Fleur Tizard, thank you. And a huge thanks to Luke Bird for designing the cover that none of us could get out of our heads.

Early drafts of some chapters were workshopped by my talented cohort at City University's Writers' Workshop, and tutor Katy Darby. And to all early readers who offered comments, I appreciate you giving your time so generously.

Mum, Dad, and Jim: I think this book was quietly growing in every country walk, every time I lost a welly in the mud. I'm lucky to have you.

This book would be less unhinged without the encouragement and endless ideation from my husband, Darren. You are truly my partner in reckless creativity.

Finally, to C, little magic thing. I love you.

ABOUT THE AUTHOR

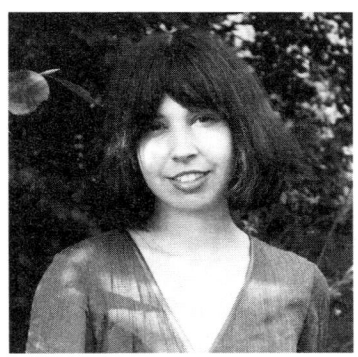

Lauren du Plessis is a British writer of speculative, folkloric, and weird fiction. Her short stories have appeared in *Litro* and *Mslexia* among others. She earned her Bachelor of Arts in Literature at Oxford Brookes University, and has worked across marketing and narrative writing, mostly for games. She lives in the bluebell-saturated chalk hills of the Chilterns with her family.

Tender is her first novel.

Influx Press is an independent publisher based in London, committed to publishing innovative and challenging literature from across the UK and beyond.

www.influxpress.com
@Influxpress